dandelion

Jamie Chai Yun Liew

dandelion

ARSENAL PULP PRESS
VANCOUVER

ARSENAL PULP PRESS
Suite 202 – 211 East Georgia St.
Vancouver, BC V6A 1Z6
Canada
arsenalpulp.com

The publisher gratefully acknowledges the support of the Canada Council for the Arts
and the British Columbia Arts Council for its publishing program, and the Government of
Canada, and the Government of British Columbia (through the Book Publishing Tax Credit
Program), for its publishing activities.

Arsenal Pulp Press acknowledges the xʷməθkʷəy̓əm (Musqueam), Sḵwx̱wú7mesh
(Squamish), and səl̓ilwətaʔɬ (Tsleil-Waututh) Nations, custodians of the traditional,
ancestral, and unceded territories where our office is located. We pay respect to their
histories, traditions, and continuous living cultures and commit to accountability, respectful
relations, and friendship.

This is a work of fiction. Any resemblance of characters to persons either living or
deceased is purely coincidental.

Cover and text design by Jazmin Welch
Cover and interior art by Ophelia Liew
Edited by Catharine Chen and Shirarose Wilensky
Proofread by Alison Strobel

Printed and bound in Canada

Library and Archives Canada Cataloguing in Publication:
Title: Dandelion / Jamie Chai Yun Liew.
Names: Liew, Jamie Chai Yun, author.
Identifiers: Canadiana (print) 20210390808 | Canadiana (ebook) 20210390816 |
   ISBN 9781551528816 (softcover) | ISBN 9781551528823 (HTML)
Classification: LCC PS8623.I37 D36 2022 | DDC C813/.6—dc23

For my mother and migrant mothers everywhere

小
Small

WHEN I WAS ELEVEN, my mother walked away from her family. She didn't say goodbye. She didn't leave a note. She didn't call. I never saw her again. I have no idea where she is or what happened to her.

Every Mother's Day, I have the same ritual. I stay at home to avoid seeing mothers and daughters brunching. I don't look at my phone, evading the pictures, the tributes, and the new memories.

It's been twenty years since my mother left. This Mother's Day, I am rubbing my ankles, swollen from bearing the weight of my pregnant belly, and thinking about how my mother used to rub her left ankle the same way when she was tired, stressed, or anxious. I look out the window and see a woman pushing a stroller, her mother walking beside her. I look down at my belly and worry about what kind of mother I will be. I am scared of doing this without my mother. Most of all, I am afraid of bringing a child into this world.

Part 1

之前
Before

氏
Clan

MY FATHER'S OLDER SISTER AUNTIE CHOO NEO placed chicken satay sticks on the backyard barbecue. She shot a dirty look at Mother. Auntie complained that Mother didn't cook the way Father liked and often referred to her as "Father's light-skinned child bride." She told Mother to stop playing and start cooking. Mother rolled her eyes behind Auntie's back. My little sister, Bea, and I laughed with her.

Auntie Choo Neo came over every weekend to cook dinner. It stung Auntie that we lived in the Heights. She and Uncle Stephen had bought a small bungalow near downtown Sparwood, a more modest house than ours given that there was just the two of them. She visited weekly, hoping her presence in Sparwood Heights would elevate her status, our Mother whispered to Bea and me. I asked Mother why Auntie needed more stature when she was already tall, with broad, sturdy shoulders. Mother replied that status was more than just physical, that Auntie wanted to appear rich, powerful, and all knowing. Whenever she came, Auntie Choo Neo proudly wore her kebaya Nyonya, a brightly coloured, fitted, embroidered blouse paired with a batik sarong.

I hopped off the swing and ran over to Auntie Choo Neo. Although she picked on Mother, she was my elder, and one of the few people I had known my entire life. The oldest of Father's siblings, she loved to lecture, correct, and order Mother around, but not me. Auntie would let me hover, but she kept a careful distance. If I inched too close, to rest my hand on her or hug her, she would pull away as if afraid she would catch something.

The turmeric in the marinade must have brought Auntie some warmth that spring day in 1987, as she taught me how to make satay. As she was preparing the sauce that accompanies the skewers, she told me, "The secret to this recipe is to allow the nutty spices to make space for one another." She permitted me to dip my fingers into the dark, rich sauce, to savour the flavours dancing in my mouth.

"Lily!" Mother bellowed. "Stop sticking your fingers in the bowl!" She was sitting at the picnic table, rubbing her ankle, tracing her fingers around the bones on both sides of her foot. She had told me she had injured it as a teenager in a bicycle accident, and it was never the same after that.

"Ayoo, Swee Hua," Auntie Choo Neo scolded. "No need to yell at Lily. She is learning how to make satay from the best."

Mother's eyebrows furrowed and her eyes narrowed, like a cat watching its prey. Then, as though retreating on soft paws, Mother dutifully set the table.

Auntie Choo Neo reminded Mother to set an extra space at the table for those who could not join us. My cousin, her son, Winston, was the only missing guest. The only person who defied Auntie Choo Neo, he chose not to come to Canada despite her efforts, and now she talked of Winston as if he were dead. I had heard Mother describe Auntie Choo Neo's "eulogies" as if she were kao peh kao bu, crying about dead parents.

Auntie talked about Winston as we ate dinner. "Aya, jin hao se, so young and yet a life already wasted."

Uncle Stephen sighed. "Gao liao, enough already."

"You give up on your only son so easily," Auntie growled back. "If you were a good father, he would be here. He would not be stateless. He would be Canadian."

"Aya, Choo Neo," Mother said. "He's got permanent residence in Brunei. He's not without status. You should be proud of him. He has started his own business. He's building his future. He's not living in a long house with the Iban."

Auntie Choo Neo scoffed, surprised that my mother would dare challenge her. "He might as well be with the orangutans in Temburong on the Brunei River! How can you think he has a future when he is nobody! His car dealership is like that plastic bag blowing in the wind. It's flying high now towards the clouds, but once it falls, it will be treated like the garbage it really is."

"Choo Neo, at least you know we're safe in Canada," Uncle Stephen reminded his wife. "Thanks to Ah Loy's foresight to sponsor all of us, we are not without status."

Auntie Choo Neo turned to Father. "Yes, Ah Loy is a dutiful brother. But what good is it for us to be here when my son is languishing back home?"

"It's never too late," Father said. "You should continue to talk to Winston, put some sense in him."

Mother laughed bitterly. "Time will tell if there is any sense in moving here. What would Winston do here? Work in the mine with you and Stephen, Ah Loy? He's running his own business back home, driving a nice car, and living in a nice house that is being cleaned by an amah. He's his own boss, and he has youth on his side. That is more than I can say for the two of you."

Father shifted in his seat, set down his satay, and pushed his plate towards the centre of the table. "You envy Winston, Swee Hua," he said, "but his life is a house of cards. He relies on a Malay to even have his business. His name is not on the ownership papers. Everything he has built could be taken away just like that. One day, a storm will come, and everything will tumble down. No amount of money could help him crawl out from under the rubble and rebuild. If I were Winston, I would ask, 'Why would I put my life and that of my children's at risk?'" Father wiped his mouth with his napkin and continued. "We are nothing to those in power. They don't recognize you. They don't look at you. They can discard you and kick you out. Winston, like all of us stateless people, is expendable, and I don't want to wait for the day when my life and the lives of my children come crashing down.

I'm sorry, Choo Neo, but you do have reason to worry. If I were his father, I would drag him out of that jungle and bring him here."

Bea grabbed the last satay stick and placed it on her plate, pausing to see if I would protest. I didn't. Everyone saw Winston so differently.

Mother chimed in again. "Here, yes, you have papers, but nothing else, Ah Loy. We live in a valley far away from the city, and you work underground. Our children are separated from so much family. They are not learning their language or their culture. The other day, I heard Beatrice tell someone that she doesn't know Chinese because she doesn't need it. The air here can freeze you to death, and the food is flavourless. Think about the asam fish head soup back home, with fresh galangal and lemongrass. The green everywhere and the mangoes growing in our backyard. Think about the pungent smell of durian."

Even Auntie Choo Neo nodded slightly and murmured in agreement.

"I can see why Winston chose to stay where he is," Mother said. "Let me ask all of you: What's holding us back? We have citizenship now. We can go back home."

"Home?" Father harrumphed. "How can you call that place home? Why would I leave a place that has welcomed me and my children to go to a place where people look at us like we're the shit floating downriver from the stilt houses of Kampong Ayer? You can't even have a beer without the state taking that away from you, too. Who wants to live in a dry state?"

"We can drink all the teh tarik and eat all the cendol in the world," Auntie added, "but Ah Loy is right. We would always hunger for more. The joy the food brings to our lives would be a distraction from the worry that we would be kicked out or denied something one day. Even the heat is tiring there."

"Then we can come back to Canada," said Mother.

"I don't want the yo-yo life," retorted Auntie.

"It's not right. We can't go back," Father said. "We chose this place, and it chose us. We have to give back the way it has given to us."

"There is no betrayal in wanting to go back to where we came from," Mother argued.

"That's all that place is now, Swee Hua. A place where I came from, and that's it," Father maintained. "We barely existed there. What future did I have, working under the table, wondering if I would still have a job one day? I could eat like a king, but my children would be learning Malay or denied schooling? What for?"

"You're fooling yourself, Ah Loy," Mother insisted. "Only a certain kind of person can truly feel secure in this cold country."

"Ayoo! You're both wrong." Auntie Choo Neo threw up her hands. "It's not as if we've forgotten where we came from, Swee Hua. But Ah Loy is right. We did not belong back home. As long as we are together, we can remember and pass down our traditions, even here in Canada. We will always find home, wherever we find family. We cannot forget who we are."

In bed that night, I was hypnotized by the sound of the train travelling through the valley, rumbling over the tracks that had been laid there decades earlier by other hopeful migrants. I wondered how Father, like those migrants, could leave the land of his birth and turn his back on it forever. How could Mother be so devoted to returning to her homeland? My parents were two sides of a magnet; the same place repelled one and pulled the other.

山
Mountain

WHENEVER MOTHER REGALED US WITH FANTASTICAL TALES of her exotic birthplace, bursting with the sultry equatorial heat, the mangroves' briny clutch, the sweetness of the rambutan, the sharp spiciness of fresh galangal, and the salty shrimp paste, Father brought my mind back to the Rockies, reminding me that I had never been to the beaches and rainforests of Brunei. Draped with shawls of coniferous trees, strewn with silver rocks, and capped with snowy barrettes, the mountains surrounded us in Sparwood. We worked in them, played on them, and lived among them. We could never escape them.

My father told me that the mountains reminded him only of work. He gazed sadly at the belly of the mountain—where the coal mine was—squinting, drawing on a cigarette. The mine's smokestacks—four of them crowning the mountain—resembled the cigarette perched between his lips, its ashes building like the coal waste pushed from the mountain's burning innards. Father spoke with such sullenness about working in the mine that I imagined the mountain casting a shadow on his face, like a ghost clinging to his stubble.

To my mother, the mountains were the walls of a prison. They contracted like an accordion, teasing her by giving her space, and then rapidly closing. She grumbled that Father had promised her excitement and adventure in a modern city, that he hadn't thought of her when he brought her to this secluded town. It didn't help when I pointed out the sound of the trains echoing in the valley. "Nobody knows we are here. I can't die here," she would vow. "Nobody knew you lived in the sultanate of Brunei before either," Father would remind her. "It's better to die here than rot in the heat back home." It was as if they were pollen that was lifted by the wind and landed in this place when the air quieted, unplanned, unprepared, planting themselves in soil they did not choose.

Bea and I saw the mountains as our playgrounds. We biked on their paths, hid among the pine, spruce, and fir trees, walked along the creeks, and played with the bugs and frogs. We sought refuge within the greenness of the mountains.

Sparwood was a modest town, with just 5,000 inhabitants, most of whom were employed by the mine. Those who did not work for the mine worked for the people in the mine. The library, post office, grocery store, mall, and recreation centre were all built in part by the mine and for the benefit of those working in the mine.

Although the mine and its economic health were of mutual interest and concern to everyone in the small town, sometimes the mine was the only thing the townsfolk had in common. Sparwood was divided in multiple ways. Most of the town was situated downtown, where there were amenities like the school, grocery store, and post office. Sparwood Heights was a newer suburb, located in the higher elevated lands along the Elk Valley Highway, across the Elk River from Sparwood proper. A golf course and a Christian church were built within this mini-community. The townspeople often took to the neighbouring Cypress Hills on their motorbikes and ATVs. No matter where you were in Sparwood, though, you could always see the mine in the distance, perched on the mountain.

Aside from the geography, the town was divided in other ways. Greenstar Mining, the company that owned the main mine in Sparwood, was a large corporation with employees all over the world. A few of the people managing the mine came from big cities in Canada and the United States. They lived in large houses in one cul-de-sac in Sparwood Heights called Sycamore Road. This was where the nicest cars, the largest boats, and the biggest mansions could be found. All the houses faced the golf course. People in town, including my parents, would gossip about all the material possessions the residents owned on Sycamore Road. Nobody ventured there unless invited, including kids.

Father routinely bragged that he had scrounged together all of his overtime pay to put a down payment on our modest three-bedroom home in the Heights. He was proud to live in a new house, something he never imagined to be possible. Father showed me the photos of the house being built, many of which had my pregnant mother and a toddler version of me posing in front of the lot, with the chaotic construction zone behind us. Week after week, he drove us along the Elk Valley Highway until we reached the suburb to watch the house slowly rise from the ground. He had an entire photo album dedicated to the house and proudly showed it off like an athlete would display a gold medal. Bea sulked whenever Father and I flipped through the photos because she wasn't born yet.

Our house was on the main thoroughfare, Ponderosa Drive, where many of my father's workmates also lived. Over the years, Father identified our neighbours to us by their occupations: truck drivers, lift operators, machinists, electricians, dozer operators, welders, and mechanics.

Intersecting with the end of our street, noticeably more upscale than Ponderosa Drive, was Hickory Crescent. This was where many of the townsfolk who worked in what my father called "management" lived. Their houses were bigger, with larger yards and nicer cars. Those who worked in management for Greenstar Mining were not the executives from the corporate office but rather middle managers, as Father put it. Some were foremen, working in the mine alongside my father but bossing him around. Others worked in the office buildings for the "bigwigs on Sycamore Road," as Father called them. I caught Father giving the management who lived on Hickory distrustful glances. The same look I would give the bullies on the playground.

During that summer of 1987, a new neighbour moved in across the street, at the intersection of Hickory Crescent and Ponderosa Drive.

The expansive house had slowly been erected upon a large hill over the previous months. For months, the loud double smack of shingles being stapled accompanied the constant hum of lawn mowers.

The new build was a mansion compared to the modest two-storey, three-bedroom houses planted on Ponderosa Drive. We heard from the workers that the house was to have six bedrooms and a large walkout basement. One day the construction stopped, and suddenly, there were moving and delivery trucks flanking the street. Several men were bringing in new appliances, furniture, and boxes. I was sitting on the front steps of our house when I saw a short, plump, bald Chinese man wearing glasses surveying the scene, his posture erect and firm. He was dressed in a suit. None of the men who lived on our street wore suits to work. He noticed my parents outside doing yardwork and crossed the street towards them. He walked with purpose, almost strutting.

Mother was weeding the garden, dressed in a rainbow tube top, high-waisted shorts, and a pair of clogs. She stood when she noticed the man approaching and took off her gardening gloves. Father was mowing the lawn, wearing a free T-shirt he got from last year's Coal Miner Days celebration. It was white with a picture of a large dump truck. He looked up and turned off the lawn mower.

Mother was taller than the newcomer, who started speaking to her in in a language I didn't recognize. I moved from the front step and hugged Mother's side while she had a friendly conversation with the man. I looked up in amazement at the unfamiliar words flowing out of her. She seemed so foreign to me in that moment. Father walked up awkwardly with the lawn mower, his knees grass-stained, and introduced himself haltingly in the same language. I watched, fascinated, as he let Mother take the lead.

Switching abruptly to English, Mother turned to introduce me. "Lily, this is Mr Lau. He is moving in across the street with his family."

The man looked at me and said, "Call me Uncle Sam."

A woman emerged from the large house across the street, and a girl ran after her. Mrs Lau was Uncle Sam's opposite. Taller than her husband, she was also so skinny that I imagined I could hear her protruding collarbone rattle as she spoke in her raspy but high-pitched voice. She was wearing a linen dress, green and sleeveless, betraying her slightly hunched back. The couple smelled like a new car, fresh, with lemon and vinegar.

After Mrs Lau said some words in the other language to my mother, she looked down at me and gave me a wide smile. Her teeth were large for her tiny mouth. They protruded slightly but were not unattractive. Like Uncle Sam, Mrs Lau had a refined air, her hair tightly and neatly bound atop her head. She switched to British English to introduce herself as Auntie Elizabeth and her daughter as Hilary. I was enamoured with her accent. She resembled an Asian actress from *Coronation Street*, glamorous and proper.

I held Mother's hand and looked at Hilary. Her hair was long like mine but cut just below her shoulders. It was jet black, slightly darker than mine. We were the same height, our foreheads and eyes meeting perfectly. She was wearing a purple T-shirt that read *Coconut Joe* and a pair of jean shorts with Keds sneakers. I was wearing a white T-shirt that said *Mountain View* and khaki shorts with flip-flops. She eyed me the same way I looked at her, with awe. It was like looking into a mirror. I had never felt this way before. There were a few other Asian girls in town, but most of them were younger than me. I didn't have any friends at school.

I once had a friend named Caroline Anderson, from grade one until grade three. The other girls teased her, calling her "old man" because her hair was short and so blond it looked white. Caroline didn't care what people thought of her. That was what I liked about her the most. And she didn't care that I was Chinese. I wished I could have been more like Caroline, but the things people said and did stuck to me like glue. I could still feel the stickiness, like unwanted tree sap that I couldn't get off my skin or clothes.

Caroline lived next door to us in Sparwood Heights. She taught me how to skip rope and play hopscotch, and she had so many board games that we never grew bored. Caroline only had a dad and never once mentioned her mother. There was one picture of her in Caroline's house. She was in a swimsuit, sitting on a large rock at the edge of a river, holding baby Caroline in her arms. The picture was in a frame on the mantel.

Because Mr Anderson had to work different shifts, some days there was a teenage babysitter named Wendy at the house. On those days, Wendy would drive us to the rec centre and get us in for free because she was a lifeguard there. She always winked at the boys at the front counter. When her babysitter wasn't available, Caroline ended up at our place. Her father would buy us a few groceries on his day off to say thank you. My parents thought he was a kind man, even though he brought strange things we didn't eat, like Pop-Tarts and Eggo waffles. Mother started eating Eggos a lot after Mr Anderson brought them for us.

Caroline was one of the few non-Asian people to eat dinner with us. She loved our food, which pleased my mother. Sometimes Caroline would bring leftovers for her dad, but he never ate them, and she never told Mother. Caroline said it was better this way because she got to eat all the leftovers herself.

One day, Caroline told me that her father got a new job in Penticton, where her aunt lived. She was moving. She explained that her father wanted to live closer to his sister, who offered to help out with Caroline. We promised to write to one another, and our families pledged to make trips to Penticton and Sparwood. We wrote a few letters back and forth, and Caroline sent me a friendship bracelet she'd made with glass seed beads. I treasured that bracelet, wore it often, and kept it in my ballerina jewellery box. Over time, the letters started coming less frequently.

When Caroline left, I had no friends. Looking at Hilary, though, I started to loosen my grip on my mother's hand. I was about to ask her if she wanted to play when Bea ran up and stood next to Father. Hilary eyed her, too. My sister was slightly taller and bigger than I was. She was often mistaken for the older one. But her pigtails and her fidgeting betrayed her nine years, and Hilary quickly turned her attention back to me.

Auntie Elizabeth turned to me and said, "Hilary is eleven, like you. She'll be joining you in the fall for grade six at Mountain View Elementary."

"Beatrice, fetch the Bundt cake I baked earlier," Mother said, and then started telling Auntie Elizabeth about our school. When Bea returned, Mother gave her the cake and said, "Welcome to Sparwood."

"Thank you," Auntie Elizabeth said and walked back across the street, holding Hilary's hand.

Mother released my hand and began to turn the jade bracelet on her wrist, winding it around continuously. She continued to fiddle as she watched Father shake hands with our new neighbour. Father's hand was large, cracked from doing manual labour in the dry mountain air. Uncle Sam's hands were soft, pudgy, and smooth, like the river rocks at the bottom of a mountain stream. Father towered over him, but Uncle Sam held his head high, meeting my father's eyes through his spectacles. Father's broad shoulders seemed to curl inwards, like an intimidated bull retreating to its pasture. Uncle Sam turned around and marched back to his new home.

"Why'd you give away our cake?" Bea asked.

"We are welcoming new neighbours. It's always good to give something sweet to bring sweetness to their new lives," Mother explained.

"What language were you speaking with Uncle Sam and Auntie Elizabeth?" I asked.

"Cantonese, a Chinese dialect. They're from Hong Kong, where most people speak this dialect."

"How do you know how to speak it? How come I don't speak it?"

"A lot of my friends in school when I was younger spoke Cantonese. I learned from them. Your father doesn't know Cantonese as well, since he went to English school. Our common dialect is Hokkien, the language you understand."

Mother looked again at Father. He wasn't smiling, the vein in his temple pulsing in time with the smoke that emerged from his cigarette. She placed her hand on his arm, but he brushed her away. Mother told Bea and me to go to the backyard to play, but I dragged my feet long enough to hear Father ask, "Why did you have to be so friendly?"

"They're our neighbours. Don't you want to have good relations?" Mother said.

"He's management, Swee Hua. Did you see how they looked at us? They're looking down on us."

"From that house on the hill, yes, but that is all. Give them a chance, Ah Loy."

"I don't need to give them a chance. I know his kind."

"We're all Chinese. We need to stick together."

"It's not as simple as you think, Swee Hua," Father said, and roughly pulled the chain to restart the lawn mower.

⬜ Mouth

IN THE SUMMER, the doors to our houses opened to the feasts of childhood summer delights: laughing, swinging, running, and cycling.

After Hilary moved in, I started to spend a lot of time in the front yard. I helped Mother weed her garden, careful not to pull the long pointy iris petals or the poppy leaves, both of which were no longer blooming. The poppy leaves were tricky because they looked like prickly thistle. Sometimes they looked like dandelion leaves, and Mother told me to pull them out. I worked alongside Mother until Bea called me out to the street to ride my bicycle. To keep our play out front, I crafted games on the street with chalk and enticed my sister to join me. We did some hopscotch, played some games with our skipping ropes, and then drew a maze. When Bea grew bored, she retreated to the backyard, but I didn't follow.

It was on one of these days, when Mother was inside preparing dinner, and Bea had gone to the backyard to play on the swing, that Hilary finally emerged from her house. I watched as the garage door rose noisily and she walked out with a toy that looked like a replica of Saturn made out of plastic. The planet was pink, and the plastic ring around it was black. She placed the toy on the driveway, stepped on its ring, and started bouncing. I had never seen a toy like that before.

Hilary saw me watching her from my bicycle. The wind was picking up and the orange, triangle-shaped flag at the rear of my bike was flapping noisily. It was like we were peering from two turrets in different castles on two separate mountains divided by a wide and deep valley.

Finally, she crossed the street with the toy in her hand and said, "Wanna try?"

I nodded and set my bicycle down on the sidewalk. Hilary placed the toy on the ground, but I didn't know what to do. She said, "Put one foot on one side, and then when you put the other foot on the other side, start jumping." It took a few tries, but I eventually started hopping around the sidewalk and laughing.

I paused to catch my breath. "What is this?" I asked.

"It's called a pogo ball." Hilary crouched down and started fingering the colourful beads on my bicycle spokes. "What are these?" she asked.

"Just for decoration. And they make a cool sound. My mom thought they would make my bike look nicer."

"I love these. I've never seen them before," Hilary said.

"Do you want some? My mom bought so many."

"Really? I'd love some. I'll go get my bike." As Hilary ran back across the street, I ran into the house to grab a package of beads. We sat on the sidewalk clipping them onto her spokes.

"We should go for a ride," I suggested.

"Yes! I can't wait to try out my new bike jewellery."

At that moment, Bea appeared and eyed Hilary's pogo ball like it was a lollipop.

"Do you want to try it?" Hilary asked.

Bea eagerly jumped onto the pogo ball and wobbled back and forth until she was bouncing down the sidewalk like Tigger chasing Rabbit. Hilary laughed as my sister bounded away.

Then Hilary invited us inside her house for the first time.

"This is my brother, Phillip," she said when we entered. "He just got a new computer."

The computer was placed prominently between the Laus' living and dining rooms on a desk, facing a long window. A couch sat next to the desk, still wrapped in plastic, as was the top of the coffee table and the remote control for the television.

Phillip was lanky and tall, his hair combed very neatly to the side. Hilary stood as close to Phillip as she could and talked rapidly about everything he could do, showing him off like he was her prized pet. *Is this what it's like to have an older sibling?* I wondered.

"It's a Commodore Amiga," Phillip announced.

Bea sidled up next to him. "What are you playing?"

Phillip elbowed Bea and Hilary out of the way, reclaiming his space in front of the keyboard. "*Simon's Quest.*"

Bea and I had never seen a computer in anyone's home. The screen pulled us into a trance.

"How do you play? Can we play?" I asked.

"No," Phillip said.

The role-playing game was like a story unfolding, controlled by Phillip. We watched him type requests to make Simon buy and sell items, find clues through conversations with other characters, and fight enemies, all in a mountainous landscape. Phillip reached a summit, but he was unable to pass that level. Hours went by before we got bored and returned to the outside world, the game's soundtrack ringing in our ears.

"Does your sister have to come with us?" Hilary asked when we were back outside.

Before I could answer, Bea said, "Mom says I have to go anywhere Lily goes. Right, Lily?"

I glared at my sister. "Shut up, Bea."

"I'm coming whether you like it or not, Jie Jie," Bea replied.

I looked at Hilary and shrugged. Bea was stubborn, and she knew she would win. My parents had no tolerance for my attempts to exclude my sister. My objections were always met with "You're the jie jie." I hated those words, even when my parents explained that it was an honoured title. The only other time I heard it was when father would bellow, "Jie!" to summon Auntie Choo Neo. Bea knew she could get my attention by calling me Jie. It was these times when I wished I were the younger sister.

Hilary understood that we had no choice. So the three of us rode our bead-speckled bikes through the neighbourhood. On most of the roads and playgrounds, we were not welcome. When we ran into two boys who lived down the street from us, they pulled the outer edges of their eyes with their fingers and asked if we could see. Hilary replied, "Our eyes are bigger than yours!" but the boys laughed and threw rocks at us. When we ventured to the park, two notorious bullies, May Donahue and Ann Cooper, flung sand into our eyes and screamed, "The monsters have arrived!"

I thought that these moments would become easier with Hilary beside me, but they didn't. Instead, they were seared into my memory like a scar.

Once, May Donahue ordered her dog to attack us. Although we knew that her cocker spaniel had a mean bark, we didn't think he could harm us. Still, we didn't want to find out. We ran from that dog like she was a wolf protecting pups, jumping onto our bikes to escape. We found solace in the woods at the edge of the Elk River, off Cypress Trail, where the trees spoke to us softly, the wind caressed our hair, and the water provided a refreshing place to play.

The trail wasn't groomed, which meant we had to help each other over the large boulders and tree trunks. Despite this, it looked as if the forest had laid out a red carpet for us, with the fallen pine needles drying in the heat, the padded bed below our feet cushioning our falls. We found a peaceful part of the river and descended towards the cool water. We took off our socks and shoes and waded in the water, watching the striders and the minnows rippling the surface. The silt from the mine flowed between our toes. When our feet got too cold, we rested our backs against the trunks of trees, tracing the paths of caterpillars as they artfully ascended into the canopy. We watched cocoons swaying in the wind and hoped to see a butterfly emerge. The sun dried our feet and warmed them like a wool blanket in winter. We picked daisies and wove them into our hair to make crowns, fashioned delicate bracelets from the blooming forget-me-nots.

Sometimes the forest wasn't welcoming, but we always came prepared. The mosquitoes, especially after rain, invaded our sanctuary, but we applied Tiger Balm to our bites. Occasionally, the bites on my legs swelled to resemble large red-hot eggs, soothed only by the coolness of the river water and menthol. Sometimes kids would smell the herbal ointment, pinch their noses, and tell us that we stank like skunks. We didn't care. We knew the balm was magic.

Often, we shared our provisions with the forest's other inhabitants. We would scatter Father's stash of sunflower seeds and watch birds come down for a meal, distinguishing the different species not by their common names but with names of the characters from our favourite TV show, *Jem and the Holograms*. Bea would peel the bark off white birch trees to make plates for the birds. "Eating off the ground is uncivilized," she said. And we brought snacks, mostly penny purchases from Woo's Confectionery. Hilary loved the sour candies, and Bea was partial to Swedish Berries. Bea and I were able to bring Haw Flakes and White Rabbit candy after we returned from trips to Chinatown in Lethbridge or Calgary. Hilary sometimes brought dried seaweed. Most of the time, we held tea parties with the queen as our imaginary honoured guest.

Auntie Choo Neo was obsessed with Princess Diana and the British royal family, and Bea and I would pore over the magazines that she left at our home. After Father once scolded his sister for squandering money on magazines, she reminded him that he was of English breeding in Brunei, that he was a British subject, and that he should take pride in that and maintain an interest in the monarchy, since the Crown was our head of government in Canada. Father had, for a short time, attended St. Peter's, an English school in a former British colony, and spoke the Queen's English. I heard people express surprise at his proficiency. To them, the way he spoke did not match his face.

My aunt's pride in her spoken English justified her interest in the British royal family. She was also interested in the royal family in Brunei, but not in the same way.

"Why does Auntie Choo Neo wish bad things on the sultan's family?" I once asked Mother.

"Auntie, like your father, doesn't like the royal family in Brunei. They blame them for their statelessness back home," Mother replied.

"Are they to blame?" I asked.

"It's complicated, Lily. Yes and no. They run the country, so yes, they decide who gets citizenship there."

"So why didn't they want to give citizenship to Dad and Auntie?"

"When it comes down to it, it's because they're Chinese."

"They don't like Chinese people?"

"No, it's not like that. They want to make sure the country stays Malay. Chinese people are not from there. They migrated there."

"But Dad was born there."

"Yes, but to them, he will always be a foreigner."

"So why are Chinese people there? Why was Dad there?"

"Our ancestors left China when things were not good there. People were starving, fighting, dying. They left to save themselves. Some went to Brunei. Others went to other places in Asia and around the world."

"And they didn't go back?"

"It was many years before people thought about going back, but by then, they had built lives elsewhere, and their children didn't know China. You know, your father and I have never been to China."

"Why?"

"It's not that easy. We weren't born there. We can't just go there and stay."

"Do you want to go there?"

"Of course. One day. We may be a different kind of Chinese, but we are all Chinese, and China is our ancestral home." At that moment, the sizzling wok beckoned Mother to take up her spatula and toss the garlic and pink amaranth she had grown in her garden.

Father once contemplated hanging a portrait of the sultan of Brunei and his favoured second wife in our house, to the horror of Auntie Choo Neo.

"Aya, old habits die hard!" Auntie Choo Neo laughed, poking fun at her brother for lugging the portrait all the way from Brunei. "We are not in Brunei anymore, Ah Loy. There is no need to appease Bolkiah. You need not prove your loyalty anymore."

Embarrassed, Father threw the portrait in the garbage. He started wearing a Dunhill belt buckle and made us watch British TV shows and movies like James Bond, *The Bridge on the River Kwai*, *Lawrence of Arabia*, and *Coronation Street*.

One day, my sister brought a few of Auntie Choo Neo's magazines to the forest. A *Fortune* magazine had news on the sultan of Brunei, the richest man in the world. There were pictures of his parking garage filled with luxury cars and his 1,788-room palace, all acquired through oil wealth.

Hilary flipped through the magazine, gawking at the pictures like she was viewing exotic animals. "Where is this again?" she asked.

"Brunei. It's where our parents are from," Bea said.

"I've never heard of it," Hilary said.

"Well, you wouldn't have. It's a small country," I said, trying to take the magazine away from Hilary.

"I'm not done looking at it!" Hilary protested.

"It's really boring stuff. Don't you think Princess Diana is more interesting?" I could feel heat rush to my cheeks. I still didn't understand why my family was from Brunei. Any link to the sultan felt like a stain on my body, an unsightly birthmark that I could not get rid of, reminding me and everyone around me that we weren't like other Chinese people in Canada.

"It's not boring." Hilary wrapped her windbreaker over her head and said, "Why do they wear a scarf over their heads like that?"

"My mom says it's because they're Muslim," Bea said.

"They wear it all the time?" Hilary asked.

"Yeah," Bea said.

"Look at all the jewels on her. They must be so rich," Hilary said, admiring a picture of the sultan's wife.

"Well, look at how many cars they have," Bea pointed out.

"Wow!" Hilary said.

"I know," said Bea. "My dad hates them."

"Why?" asked Hilary.

"It's really complicated," I said. "Look, Princess Diana has amazing jewels on her crown too."

"It's because they didn't give him citizenship," Bea chimed in. "That's why we came to Canada. He tells us all the time we're lucky we were born here because otherwise we'd be stateless."

"Well, my parents came to Canada for school, and now we're all here. I was born here, too," Hilary said.

"It's not the same. At least your parents didn't come from Brunei," Bea said.

"No, we came from Hong Kong. It's British there, too," Hilary said.

"Guys! Let's go get a Slurpee," I said, desperate to change the topic.

"Yes!" Hilary said. She pretended to be the queen of England, giving us orders in a dramatic British accent. Bea was on the ground holding her stomach, laughing with tears in her eyes. I quickly stowed the magazine in my backpack, relieved we didn't have to talk about any of this anymore.

日
Sun

IT WAS THAT POINT IN A SLOW SUMMER DAY when the sun had reached its zenith and Father had turned on the sprinkler to relieve my sister and me and the grass on the front lawn. The heat turned us slothlike, and the sunlight refracting from the water droplets made the backyard look like it was adorned with gems. Bea and I lounged on our lawn chairs next to our parents, snacking on the snap peas Mother had harvested from the garden.

"Why does Hilary's family have all the fun? Why can't we go on vacation, too?" demanded Bea.

"Disneyland is too far away and expensive," Father said.

"You're not a typical Hakka," Mother teased him.

My sister looked curiously at Mother. "Hakka?"

"Your father is from the Hakka tribe. I thought marrying him meant I would live a nomadic lifestyle, but instead, your father brought me here, halfway across the world," Mother lamented with a playful smile.

"Nomad?" I asked.

"Hakka means 'guest people' in Chinese. They're like roaming foreigners in China who speak the Hakka dialect," Mother explained. "Historically, they were forced to leave their villages by enemy tribes."

Father interjected, "Your mother may look down on us Hakka, but you should know that we're descendants of one of the greatest emperors of China. We're from the cradle of Chinese civilization. Even though we've been forced over many generations to leave our home, wherever we go, we are able to thrive. We made barren lands into fertile farms where our Cantonese landlords could not. We are all over the world."

Mother looked at Father, her eyes filled with amusement but also affection. She laughed and got up from her lawn chair to hug him from behind, wrapping her arms around his broad shoulders, nestling her head into the crook of his neck, her hair trailing down his chest. She lifted her face and kissed his temple. Father kissed Mother's arm, and then motioned for Bea and me to come to him.

"Do you see this?" he asked, plucking a tall dandelion from the grass.

I nodded, admiring the petals reflecting a golden finish.

"It's a weed!" announced Bea.

"No, Beatrice." Father shook his head. "To some, this is a weed. But it's really a flower. Like a dandelion, the Hakka can land anywhere, take root in the poorest soil, flourish, and flower. Look at this one. It's growing in the crack of the asphalt." Father pointed to the driveway next to the lawn.

"But does that mean the Hakka are homeless?" Bea asked.

"Sometimes, Beatrice, sometimes," Father replied. "But home is where family is. So no matter where we are, if we're together, we're home."

"Okay, Dad," Bea said. "Then you should be a real Hakka and take us on vacation somewhere."

Father chuckled. "Okay, let's take the van on a camping trip!"

Mother jumped up. "I can't wait to leave this town. I'll get the maps and plan the route!" Mother looked the happiest I had seen her all summer.

We set out on our road trip in our brown and orange striped 1980 Chevrolet/GMC van. When we reached Highway 3, Bea started to count the striking signs with an image of a black crow on them. Bea and I sat on the flattened seats in the rear of the van, peering out of three sides of the rectangular vehicle, surrounded by windows.

"Look at all those purple flowers! There are so many!" Bea exclaimed.

"They're called purple knapweed," Mother said. An avid gardener, she taught us each plant's correct name.

"It's beautiful. It's making the ground all purple," I said.

Moving quickly, we were hypnotized by its deep colour, blurred through the windows. I recalled my teacher last year, Mrs Henry, telling us knapweed was a noxious and non-native species that was invading the valley. It may have been unwanted, but it was vibrant and strong.

The van wound through the valley, and moments later, we looked up and saw Crowsnest Mountain, guarding the north side of the pass. We were leaving British Columbia. I marvelled at how uneventful it was to cross the provincial border into Alberta. All around us I still saw Ktunaxa territory.

I learned at school that we were in Ktunaxa territory when Mrs Henry was sick and we had a substitute teacher. With Mrs Teneese, we spent a lot of time outdoors, where she explained that we were on the traditional territory of the Tobacco Plains First Nation, part of the Ktunaxa Nation. We looked at a map and I was amazed to see how Ktunaxa territory spread through large parts of BC and Alberta, and even the United States. Mrs Teneese said that the provincial and international borders did not mean that Ktunaxa territory stopped as well. Mrs Teneese did a blanket dance and showed us the artwork on some of the blankets. She also taught us how to weave and bead. We spent a lot of our class time walking through the forest behind the school, talking about nature. Mrs Teneese was supposed to spend the week with us, but she didn't come back on Thursday. Instead, Principal Waller stepped in until Mrs Henry returned. We didn't even get to say goodbye.

Our van passed Blairmore, where a large, treelike post with a carving of a mother crow sat in a nest with her little one. Bea and I admired the plummeting cliffside views at the edge of the highway as we careened around the mountain.

Mother urged Father, "Ka kin. Hurry up! I hate this part of the highway. I can't look. We're too high, and the crows are too many."

"What's wrong with the crows, Mom?" Bea asked.

"The crow is an omen of death. In Hokkien, the word for crow—'oh ah'—sounds just like the crow's cry." Mother demonstrated, "Oh ah, oh ah, oh ah."

"Mom! That's scary," I said, as shivers ran up my spine. "Oh ah means 'to bite' in Hokkien. When you see a crow, it means something bad is about to happen."

"Pfft, Swee Hua," Father scoffed. "Stop with that! It's all just stories! They don't need to hear these things."

"I am not joking, Ah Loy. My friend Che Eng, remember her? Her father lost a lot of money buying a tea plantation because he made the deal inside the mah-jong hall where a crow had been dwelling in the open rafters. Che Eng told me that her father was warned by the patrons that the hall had been cursed, but he brushed it off. As soon as Che Eng's father signed the deed to the tea plantation, he heard the crow cry out. Fate left him with a money-losing business, and he was forced to abandon the plantation when the crops dried out and died from disease."

"Is this a true story, Mom?" Bea asked.

"Yes, of course! Che Eng was my best friend. Why would she make this up? After five years of replanting, nothing could be done and the family fortune was gone."

Father tsked and said, "His problem was that he was buying the plantation in a mah-jong hall not at the plantation itself. It has nothing to do with a silly bird."

"Laugh all you want, Ah Loy. It's true!" Mother insisted. "Those who sign a deal while a crow is near never succeed."

Mother asked to stop at Frank Slide, where a roadside plaque read: *Here lie the remains of those who lost their lives in the tragic Frank Slide on the morning of April 29, 1903.* I shuddered, looking around at boulders three times the size of our house dotting the landscape like grains of sand. I had never seen the innards of a mountain vomited over the land this way, fossilized, standing still as monuments.

At the interpretive centre we learned that the limestone face of Turtle Mountain came hurtling towards the sleeping town of Frank at around four a.m. The slide may have been caused by mining. It only took 100 seconds to cover the town with 110 million tonnes of rock, killing 110 of the 600 residents who lived in the path of the slide. The bodies of the townsfolk remain under the rubble. Some people survived only to learn that their homes and entire families had perished. An entire mining town gone in minutes.

Father turned from the information panel, reach in his pocket for his lighter, and put a cigarette between his lips.

I tugged Father's arm and said, "When you work in the mine, are you scared?"

Once, on a school field trip, our yellow bus climbed the mountain towards Elkhills Mine, where Father worked. I saw the entrails of the mountain exposed by the open-pit mining. The mine that fed our town was alive, ripping the mountain apart from the inside out, stripping it down to the coal seams.

Father hugged me. "Things are different today than they were in 1903."

"Will Elkhills Mine fall on us, too?" I asked.

"I don't think so." He laughed and tousled my hair. "Lily, there is nothing to worry about. We're being told how to work safely every day in the mine. Why do you think I wear steel-toed boots and a hard hat? Why do you think we have foremen? To keep us in line. We don't like them because they take all the fun out of it, right? Things today are much safer than they were in the past."

"I wish you didn't have to work in the mine," I said.

"Lily, wo bo bang huat, I have no choice. It's the only thing I can do with the education I have. I was stateless and I couldn't finish school, not like you. In Brunei, I could not get a good job. Who wants to hire someone who doesn't have citizenship? It's a risk when the government can throw you out anytime. Do well in school, and you can work somewhere that's not underground."

Father pulled me and the rest of our family from the interpretive centre back to the van and sped down Highway 3. We made another stop, in the town of Hillcrest. We approached a parched cemetery. The gravestones were stark white against the yellow-green grass, like pieces of chalk sticking out of the ground. Mother read the informational panels, telling us that the mine at Hillcrest was the site of Canada's worst coal-mining disaster when a gas and dust explosion killed nearly 200 men. All that remained was this gravesite and the white fence enclosing it.

"Is this a tour of the mines, Swee Hua?" Father asked. "Not much of a vacation."

"Ah Loy, you said you wanted to get to know the country better. These are the tourist attractions near us. There is a lot of mining history here. There is no shame in the girls learning this. Haven't you always said this is our life now?" Mother said.

Father said no more, and we moved on to Lundbreck Falls, an impressive cascade of water falling from the Crowsnest River. The area was crowded with families cooling off from the hot summer day. After a lunch of my mother's version of coleslaw with rice wine vinegar and fried dace in a can, Bea and I put on our swimsuits and jumped into the cold mountain water, a welcome reprieve from the heat. My parents sat on the bank, Mother in sunglasses with a magazine in hand, Father with a cigarette.

Only after Mother had read all of Auntie Choo Neo's old magazines did she call us to come out of the water. As she towelled us off, I noticed a woman suntanning nearby. She peered at us first through her sunglasses, and then rested them on her blond, curly hair. She looked at us like we had just walked into a party uninvited.

The woman spoke very slowly. "Hello. Where are you from?"

"We're from Sparwood," Bea replied.

"Oh my! Your English is quite good. Where is your mom from?"

"My mom is from Sparwood, too." Bea seemed confused by the question.

The woman laughed. "But you're Oriental!"

Before the conversation could continue, Mother dragged us to the parking lot and into the van, forcing us to finish changing into our clothes there.

Father returned from the washroom and said, "What's the hurry?"

"Some woman kept asking where we were from," Bea said.

Father looked back and saw a lot of people collected on the riverbank. "What did you say?" he asked.

"Sparwood," Bea replied.

Father turned to Mother, waiting for an explanation.

"Be eio kin, lah. Don't worry about it," Mother said and kept packing up our things.

Father looked annoyed and sucked on his cigarette, as if to soothe himself. We set off on the next leg of the trip, and he played a cassette tape to fill the silence. No words were spoken between my parents about this incident, but our vacation had soured, like a soup with too many pieces of bitter melon left out to spoil.

走
Walk

WE DIDN'T STOP AGAIN UNTIL PINCHER CREEK. Along the way, I gawked at the dozens of colossal stalks protruding from yellow fields like massive steel flowers. The windmills made the mountains behind them seem small. They looked like an army that had invaded the prairie, ready to move together into battle. Some of the pointy petals were moving, the sharp blades rotating, winding around with the loud and forceful wind. We were tiny insects, racing to get out of the way.

The wind swirled around us as we got out of the van at Veterans Memorial Park in Pincher Creek. Mother wrapped a scarf around herself and commented, "We have met all four winds."

"What does that mean, Mom?" I asked.

"The hong come from four directions: north, south, east, and west. They don't come empty handed. Sometimes they bring sickness, or bad luck," she explained.

"Can they bring good luck?"

"Sometimes, but never let your guard down. It's better to prepare for the worst."

"How do you know when they will bring good luck?"

"You don't."

My hair blew rapidly around my face, and the pages of the book in my hand flapped back and forth. Bea's skirt danced wildly while her legs tried to stay firmly planted to the ground.

Father came around from his side of the van. He also couldn't resist talking about the wind. "The Chinook winds like to flow off the mountains and land here, in the Oldman River and Castle River valleys. That's why there are windmills here."

Mother shivered. "Why does the cold have to come back to us? Winter has just left, but its tail is clutching the land, not wanting to let go yet. Maybe it's an omen."

"Enough with your superstitions!" Father said.

Father had a kite he'd bought in Chinatown the previous winter. He said this would show Mother how beautiful the mountain winds were. But its delicate tissue was torn, so he spent the better part of the late afternoon repairing the kite instead of flying it.

The next morning, we were awoken by the cool mountain air and the cawing of crows. After breakfast, Father drove onto Highway 6 towards Waterton Lakes National Park. Father had decided we would do a day hike on Rowe Lakes Trail.

The trail cut through a dense wilderness along the banks of Rowe Creek before connecting to two different lakes along the path. We climbed uphill, Mount Lineham and Mount Rowe guiding us. The stillness of the lakes below made me feel both tiny and large at the same time. Tiny because of the vastness of the valley, the calm lake framed by mountains. Large because I had conquered the trail with my two legs.

We took in the view, awestruck. Despite it being the height of summer, snow-capped peaks rose from the rolling grasslands. Red flowers of Indian paintbrush dotted the foothills. In the distance, along the rocky edges of the mountain base, Arctic poppies drank in the sun, their pale-yellow petals framing their black and gold faces. Beyond them, bear grass bloomed. It looked like a field of white ghosts made of shining diamonds, welcoming the royal poppies to the mountains, inviting them to be plucked.

I was afraid that if I blinked, the flowers would be blown away by the wind. I watched my parents pause to look around. I had never seen them so stunned.

"I didn't think anything grew around here other than grass and pine trees," Father marvelled.

"It doesn't look real," Mother commented.

"It's beautiful." Father said.

"No, look at the water. It looks unnatural. The flowers, they look fragile, like they'll break, fly away. The flowers back home are bigger and last longer. All kinds of lotuses, frangipani, hibiscus. They are heartier and brighter!"

"It's different," allowed Father.

Mother looked away from the calm, quiet landscape and fiddled with her scarf.

The beauty of the valley charmed me. I wanted Mother to share my delight in the grass dancing beside me. "Don't you like it here?" I asked.

She swivelled her jade bracelet, encircling the cuff of her sleeve, and muttered, "It doesn't matter." Mother wrapped her cream-coloured cardigan firmly around her shoulders, buttoning it up. After her sweater, she fidgeted with her socks, rubbing her ankle briskly before pulling them up higher. Perhaps she really was just adjusting to the cool breeze, but I saw a person who didn't want to admit the scene was beautiful, that it was worthy of her attention.

"Doesn't the water look like a mirror, Mom?" I tried again.

"Jin ge, fake. Don't let it fool you. Things probably can't survive there. Back home, the ocean is where we harvest things, where the most delicious food is."

"What about the grass, Mom? Doesn't it look so soft, like you could sleep in it?"

"Don't be silly, Lily. It's too cold to sleep here. Back home, you could sleep outside. It's warm enough."

I felt like I couldn't enjoy the scene before me without betraying Mother's love for the nature in her homeland. She made me feel as if I was doing something treasonous.

"Let's go," she said. "We don't have all day, and it will be dinnertime soon."

Father pulled out his camera and asked Mother to pose in front of the lake. I wanted her to tilt her head like I saw her do in the pictures of her youth, but she said, "I don't feel like having my picture taken." Father snapped a photo of her anyway, settling for the frown on her face. To make Father feel better, I asked him to take a picture of me. He obliged, and then Bea joined me.

Seeing the scene, a young couple approached and asked if we all wanted a picture together. Father reluctantly gave his camera to the young man, and Mother then knelt beside me for the picture. We played the dutiful tourists to Father's satisfaction.

The young man handed the camera back to my father and asked him something in Mandarin.

Father was surprised to see a white man speaking Chinese. His eyebrows lifted, but he did not smile. He tried to ignore the man, but he was persistent, asking again. Father finally said in English, "Sparwood."

The man tried to continue the conversation, but Father moved away. Mother spoke to them in Mandarin to make up for Father's rudeness, and the couple moved along on the trail.

"What did they say?" I asked her.

"They're on their honeymoon. They're from Kamloops."

"They speak Chinese?" I asked.

"Mandarin. Everyone knows some Mandarin back home. The man said he studied Mandarin in university, and they're moving to China next year to continue their studies."

"What were they asking you?"

"They were asking us where we were from. I just said Malaysia."

"Why didn't you say Brunei?"

"Most people don't know where that is."

"Why?" I asked.

"It's a small country and when people learn we're from there, I have to explain where it is. Sometimes it's easier to just tell people Malaysia." I was surprised by how easy it was for Mother to lie.

"Why did Dad ignore them?"

"I don't know. Maybe he wants people to know he can speak English like everyone else."

When we returned to our van from the five-hour hike we were exhausted and hungry. Mother pulled out the hibachi and made some ikan bakar from provisions she had picked up in Pincher Creek. She dropped the tilapia she bought live onto her wooden cutting board and struck its head with a mallet. The fish's flapping body went limp. She quickly scaled and gutted it. She made it look so easy, yet I couldn't help but blurt out, "Ew, gross!"

"Where do you think your food comes from?" she said. "It's fresh and extra delicious this way."

Bea and I watched as Mother smothered the fish with a sambal of shallots, shrimp paste, chilis, and lemongrass, and then placed it in some banana leaves inside a grill basket. Waiting for dinner to be ready, my sister and I lay on a picnic blanket. Bea grabbed the book I had been reading.

"Hey!" I exclaimed. "I'm in the middle of that."

"Well, I have it now. You can read another one."

I tried to yank the book from Bea, but her grip was strong.

Father spotted this tug-of-war and yelled, "Lily, what are you doing? Share with your sister!"

"I was reading that book. My bookmark is right there!" I protested.

"You're the oldest. Just let your sister read it for now. She will give it back to you when she's finished."

"That's so unfair!"

"Lily, you only have one sister."

I knew I had lost this fight and resigned myself to looking through the pile of books strewn on the picnic blanket. I turned my back to Bea, wanting to forget I had a sister.

"I love this book. It's one of my favourites," Bea gloated.

Father discovered some watercress in the creek nearby, and Mother happily decided to make a soup to accompany our dinner. Since Bea had taken my book, I joined Mother in her makeshift kitchen and helped her cut ginger and place it in the pot of water.

Father was looking at a map of Waterton and suggesting other hikes we could do the next day, but Mother said, "Ayoo, we just did a hike today. Do we have to do another?"

"Swee Hua, each one is different. Don't you want to see more of what we saw today?" Father asked.

"That was enough for me," Mother replied.

"How about a shorter one," Father offered.

"You can go with the girls if you want. I'll stay here."

"But, Mom," I interjected, "this is supposed to be a family vacation. You can't stay here. Besides, there's nothing fun to do here. Come on the hike with us."

"It's just going to be more of the same," Mother said.

I thought about Mother's superstitious ways. Maybe she felt there was some hong out there that wasn't right for her. After dinner, I could see Mother and Father in the distance. Mother was moving her arms wildly, and Father was looking at his feet. He raised his head, trying to interrupt. I felt my back clench. I hated seeing Mother unhappy. The argument ended abruptly when she stormed off into the dusk.

It was dark before she returned. She looked like E gui, the hungry ghost who roams the streets like a shadow, her long black hair resting over her shoulders and back, searching for sustenance but finding only what is rotten. When the light revealed it was Mother, she was still sullen. We acted as if nothing had happened and crawled into the van. As Father snored, Mother sat upright, stroking her ankle as if she had tested it too much during the day's hike. I fell asleep watching her knead her foot with a steady force.

金
Gold

WHEN WE ARRIVED IN CALGARY, the first place my parents drove to was Chinatown. It was like crossing a border into a secret place guarded by the lions on the Centre Street Bridge. I imagined the lions nodding their heads at me, letting us pass the threshold without inspection. How did these stores and restaurants full of Chinese people get to exist together in one place? It was unlike anything in Sparwood. There was the reek of garbage but also the aromas of roasting meat, baos fresh out of the oven, and sweet tapioca drinks. I could hear the popular Chinese music my parents played, making me realize my father was not atypical. The sights, sounds, and smells were like a warm hug from my mother.

Our first stop was Dragon City Mall. We went to Rainbow Bakery, where Mother picked up some baos, bought some Hello Kitty souvenirs in the neighbouring shop, and then climbed the stairs to the Regency Restaurant, for dim sum. Once we were seated at a round table, Father sat back and Mother took centre stage. She assumed the role of conductor, setting the tempo, pacing out the delivery of our decadent meal, motioning for different players to fill out the spread. She was pleased with the ensemble she put together, urging us to eat more, placing different morsels in our bowls and on our plates, telling us what they were called. The background chatter of other diners, the clanking of chopsticks, the loud calls of the servers to the kitchen staff accompanied Mother in her virtuoso performance.

Servers wearing aprons brought carts of food in bamboo steamers to our table. Bea and I pretended we were royalty being presented with the kingdom's best gourmet meals on silver-domed serving platters. We sampled the food and chose which should be served in the palace. My favourite was cheong fan. I savoured the smoky-sweet barbecue pork. Bea loved the tender shrimp and pork shiu mai, while Mother relished the chicken feet. Father ordered the nuo mi fan and slowly peeled the lotus leaves open, revealing a ball of rice studded with surprises of pork, peanuts, and other tasty morsels.

After lunch, Father bought us ice cream for dessert. The day was hot and he wanted to walk by the Bow River, so we went towards Sien Lok Park. Father and Bea were ahead, walking quickly. After passing the two lions guarding the entrance to the park, Mother and I gravitated towards the large cone in the centre. The sculpture was called *In Search of Gold Mountain*.

"Where is Gold Mountain, Mom?" I asked.

"That is what Chinese people called Canada in the past," she said.

"Why? Was there a lot of gold here?"

"It was called Gold Mountain because many people thought there were good opportunities to work and make money here. Many Chinese men who came sent money home, and those in China were able to build houses and survive."

"Do Chinese people still call it Gold Mountain?"

"I don't know. Maybe some feel it is still the land of opportunity."

"Did you?"

"I didn't think about coming here before I met your father. It was his dream."

I held Mother's hand tighter. She let it go and stopped walking to hug me instead. She looked into my eyes and kissed me on the forehead.

As we ate our ice cream, I watched the old Chinese men sitting around the sculpture playing Chinese checkers and other games I had never seen before.

"Mom, why are they out here playing games? Are only men allowed to play?" I asked.

"They're the old men who first came to Canada. When they came, they weren't allowed to bring women or their families, and now they have no one but themselves, growing old with no wives or children."

Mother watched them like she was peering into the mirror and trying to smooth the wrinkles on her face. "Let's go," she said abruptly. "Your Father wanted to walk by the river."

足
Foot

IT WAS MIDSUMMER, and the buzz from our road trip had long dissipated. I peered out the open back door to see Bea sitting on the steps in her T-shirt and shorts reading a book, her hair was in two braids down her back. The door was wide open, and I was waiting for Mother to yell at her to shut it. Instead, she was transfixed by the view. The green trees climbing out of the ground in the backyard looked like a jungle, as if my sister were sitting at the precipice of another world. The grey, white, and blue of the kitchen framing the doorway looked sterile, antiseptic, and empty, while the world beyond looked alive, vibrant, and wild. I loved seeing Mother at peace.

I was jarred back into the present by the violent sound of a spoon banging around in a coffee cup. Mother was knocking the spoon about in her cup of instant coffee so rapidly that it had created a whirlpool. I had never seen anyone else stir coffee like that.

"Why do you stir your coffee so quickly?" I asked.

"I like to make sure everything is mixed," she said.

"Mrs Castelli stirs her coffee slowly," I remarked.

"People do things differently everywhere. There is no right or wrong way."

I eyed Mother and wondered if I would stir my coffee her way or Mrs Castelli's way when I grew up. Would it be a slow, gentle tapping, or this rapid, frenetic vortex in a cup?

Mother sighed. "The days are so long here! Back home, the sky darkens around five every day, no matter what."

"But summer solstice has passed. The days are getting shorter," I insisted.

"It's like the day is stretched out here. Back home, the darkening of the sky meant that it was time to cook, and the fasting would end. Here, people have to wait and suffer longer."

"We don't fast?!"

"No, but my Malay friends did." Mother told me about the tantalizing smells of spices, curries, and long-simmering soups that would waft from the houses.

Bea turned and invited Mother to come play with us outside.

"You know, I used to love playing tennis when I was your age," she replied. "I loved the Brunei Tennis Club. I spent so much time there that I felt like I lived there."

"It sounds posh, Mom. Was it expensive to be part of a club like that?" I asked.

"Well, yes, but my father was a successful businessman, so he could afford to be a member."

"Really? But weren't you stateless, too?"

"I was born in Malaysia, so I had citizenship there. But I didn't have citizenship in Brunei."

"I don't understand. They let you stay in Brunei?"

"Yes, we were permanent residents there. My father worked with a lot of important Malay people. It was easier for me than your father because of that."

"Okay, are we going to play tennis now or what?" Bea said.

Mother hated wearing socks. She loved to feel the floor beneath her feet and said it was unnatural to keep our feet bound away, festering in what she called a mitten. Father said it was because she grew up in the jungle. Even in winter, she refused to wear socks. She wore them only if absolutely necessary, and then ripped them off as soon as she could, as if they were shackles. However, the suggestion of tennis prompted Mother to put on some socks and running shoes.

We decided to bike down to the tennis court next to Woo's Confectionery. Mother agreed it would be nice to visit with her friend Auntie Miriam. She was one of the few other Chinese women in town, but she was very different from Mother. Auntie Miriam was born in Canada and did not speak Chinese. Her grandfather was among the first waves of Chinese people to come to Canada, those who helped build the railway in British Columbia and settled in the Interior. He paid the head tax for his son to come to Canada. Auntie Miriam married a Chinese man, Ed Woo, whose family also came before the head tax was imposed. They owned the only convenience store in downtown Sparwood.

The summer heat rose from the pavement, the ride on our bicycles giving us some relief from the stuffy air. "The hot weather always reminds me of home!" Mother called over her shoulder. Her hair flowed across her face, and she kept looking behind her to check we were following. Her pale legs whipped her pedals faster and faster, and Bea and I laughed with glee. Mother's red and white striped shirt flapped in the wind ahead of us like a flag as we pedalled harder to keep up.

The centre of Sparwood was eerily quiet. The summer spurred an exodus from the town, and when we rode by the post office and the library, no one could be seen. I saw the Canadian flag floating atop the buildings and a few cars—white, green, red, grey—but those were the only signs of life. Everything was geometric. Square windows, rectangular buildings, a straight line of parked cars. Orderly, clean, still. But lifeless. What a contrast to the stories Mother told Bea and me about the energy and chaos of the Asian markets, where she would push her way through crowds of shoppers over the sticky, wet floors to get to the vendor to discuss which daily produce was fresh and what she wanted to cook that day.

"The heat brings life back home," she said. "Not like here. Here, the heat leaves the town lifeless."

We leaned our bikes against the fence at the tennis court, where the heat was bouncing off the surface in waves. Bea and I brought out the balls in our pockets, and Mother untethered herself from the racquet bag, unzipping it and taking out the racquets inside. As Bea and I were bouncing the balls, we saw three teenagers walking towards the court, racquets and balls in hand. Mother didn't notice and started bouncing a ball with her racquet.

"Hey lady, we're going to start a game in five," one of the boys said. "Our friend is just running late, so you may want to find someplace else to go."

"We were here first," Mother said firmly. "You can hit some balls on the wall until we're done."

"Listen, lady, we play here at the same time every day. As soon as our friend gets here, you gotta go."

Mother turned her back and volleyed. I was amazed and scared. I didn't know what would happen next. I looked their way but tried not to stare.

"Way to go, Mom. You tell them," Bea said, grinning.

"Never mind them. Lily, pay attention!" Mother ordered.

Bea and I worked hard to keep up with her, even though she was hitting the ball gently into our corners. Ten minutes passed and the teenagers approached. They gathered mid-court by the net and started murmuring and pointing at Mother. "We gotta get that Chink lady off the court," the leader said.

Mother turned around. "There are only three of you. How are you going to play doubles with just three people?"

"Come on, lady. We play here all the time. We can switch to singles."

"This Chink lady can be your partner, Theo," one guy joked. Two of them laughed and Theo looked horrified.

"I'm willing if you are," Mother said.

The teenagers were astounded and started laughing, thumping each other on the back. Theo shook his head. "No offence, lady, but we just want to play with each other."

"Hold up, Theo. This may actually be kind of fun. Let's make a wager. We each put in five bucks, and if whoever plays with Chink lady wins, he gets the whole pot. If Chink lady loses, we all just take our money back, but Chink lady has to buy us all Slurpees at Woo's."

"That is not fair," Mother said. "I get half the pot if my team wins."

"All right, Chink lady."

"Stop calling me that! First rule. And how do I know you aren't setting me up?"

"You get to choose your partner," Theo piped up.

Bea looked worried. I was in awe that this negotiation was even happening. It was like someone had changed the channel on the television and I was watching an entirely different show.

"Listen, uh, Chinese lady—your sisters will have to sit this one out. Okay?"

Mother laughed. "You hear that, girls? You have to watch, okay? My name is Swee. Use it."

Mother made the boys volley and demonstrate their serves before she chose her partner. It was an amusing show where the young men were suddenly trying to impress her. She decided on a guy named Bryan, and it seemed to be a point of pride for him to be chosen. The rules of the game were established and some strategy was discussed in their tiny huddles. Bea and I ran into Woo's to grab Slurpees and told Auntie Miriam about the upcoming match. She sat on the bleachers with us, retreating to the store whenever a customer came.

The game started out slow. The players danced around, leaning forward on their toes, gingerly dropping the balls within the white lines. Mother broke the stalemate. At five foot six, she was much shorter than any of the boys, but she was swift. She darted back and forth and hovered like a hummingbird. In response to the soft lobs sent her way, she brought her arm up and then down ruthlessly like a diving falcon. Mother's team racked up four straight points from her wicked smashes. Her opponents tried to avoid passing to her, but Bryan was more than pleased to give her the lead, and it soon looked as if Mother was playing singles. Her slices left her opponents spinning. The other team sent a long, shallow pass over the net as Bryan ran off the side of the court to leave space for Mother, who was hovering at the back line. She backhanded the ball along the sideline to the edge of the back end. In! Bryan and Mother high-fived. The other team got serious and tried to trip Mother up with short volleys, but she hit them back so quickly that it was as if she had two racquets, one in each hand, winning a few points. The other team started to send some cross-court shots, but Mother was small and fast. She ducked and let Bryan take some shots.

This went on for an hour, and the game was tight. Beads of sweat formed on the teenagers' foreheads, and the sheen on their arms and legs made them look oiled. Mother, a bit out of breath, didn't sweat much. She adjusted her tennis cap and occasionally wiped her sweaty palms on her shorts, but she did not look worn.

In the last set, Mother's team was up 5–4. Theo called her the Asian curse, and her opponents surged with energy. The rally turned aggressive.

"You losers gonna let a little Chinese lady whip your asses?" Bryan taunted.

While Mother's partner made valiant efforts to protect her, the balls kept coming directly at her. I saw her pivot. As she was turning around, Bryan was able to get to the ball, but it hit the net. Mother's body, however, did not recover from that last play. One part of her body was going in one direction, and the other part went in another direction. She landed hard on the pavement. Bea, Auntie Miriam, and I stood up in the bleachers and the game stopped. As the yellow tennis ball rolled out of the court, everyone stood like statues. Mother was on the ground clutching her ankle. Bea and I ran over with

Auntie Miriam. Mother tried to get up but shouted in pain with each attempt. She pushed her sock down to reveal the large swelling.

"That does not look good," Bryan commented.

"I think this means we won." The other team gave each other high-fives.

Auntie Miriam took control. "Swee, I'm going to help you to my car," she said, handing me her keys and instructing me to put our bicycles inside her store and then lock it up. Mother did not argue, and by the time we reached the car, there was no sign of the teenagers. They had fled with their racquets, our balls, and the money. It was as if the game had never happened.

Auntie Miriam drove us to the health centre. "I hope it's nothing serious," she murmured. There was no hospital in Sparwood.

"I'm sorry you had to close your shop," Mother said, embarrassed.

"Nonsense! I'm happy to help," Auntie Miriam insisted.

Mother only had a sprain, and the doctor said that icing and stretching it would improve it in a few weeks. Mother nodded silently, eyeing our tennis bags empty of the balls that had run away with her teenage opponents.

When we finally got home, Father was upset we were so late, but Auntie Miriam had brought some takeout from Oriental Palace, the one Chinese restaurant in Sparwood. She calmed Father by explaining that Mother had tripped outside of Woo's Confectionery. Bea and I looked at each another in silent complicity.

That night, while I was sitting at the top of the stairs, unable to sleep, I watched Mother through the wooden banister as she soaked her foot in a bucket of ice and massaged it with a Chinese ointment from her medicine cabinet. She rubbed her aching ankle, and then wrapped her foot tightly. The bandage made Mother's foot look more slender, her arch much higher.

Father didn't treat Mother any differently as a result of her injury, expecting life to continue as usual. She accepted a gift of Chinese slippers from Uncle Sam, using them as an excuse to hide her foot in bondage. For weeks, I would catch her glancing at her ankle or fiddling with the bandage, wrapping and rewrapping it. She didn't return to the tennis court ever again.

角

Horn

THE FALL CAME IN FULL FORCE. Mother hated it when summer ended. She talked about how things were dying, how we were forced to witness death all around us. She pointed out the yellowing leaves, the brown, rigid stems of long-gone flowers poking from the dry ground, and the flocks of fleeing birds. Mother said we should migrate as well. When Bea and I revelled in the beautiful array of coloured leaves, carting them inside to press them between sheets of waxed paper, Mother acted like we were undertakers and shunned us like we were bringing unsavoury ghosts into her home. Bea reminded her that things didn't die, they just went to sleep.

My sister and I loved the crunch of the fallen leaves under our feet. We spent hours in the front yard helping Father gather the leaves into a pile, and then we jumped into them.

As Father indulged us and raked the leaves again, Uncle Sam pulled up across the street after a day of work. A frown crested towards Father's chin as he waved hello, and then he quickly returned his attention to the pile of leaves. Father's cold shoulder didn't work, and Uncle Sam walked towards us. Father was forced to take off his work gloves and shake Uncle Sam's hand. Uncle Sam loosened his tie and greeted Bea and me.

"Some yardwork?" he observed.

"Yes. This year it feels like the leaves keep coming," Father said.

"Well, Elizabeth found this great company that hires high school students to do the yardwork. I can pass along their number if you're interested," Uncle Sam offered.

"Sure," Father replied curtly.

"Hilary speaks so fondly of her visits to your house. We should really get our families together more often."

At that moment, Mother emerged from the house and said, "That's a good idea. In fact, you should come to a celebration this weekend at the Oriental Palace. You can meet all the other families here in Sparwood. I'm sure Carrie and Ming wouldn't mind you joining their son's red egg and ginger party."

Uncle Sam accepted the invitation in Cantonese, but only after some cajoling and reassurances from Mother that she would secure a proper invite for his family.

"Swee Hua, why did you do that?" Father exploded after Uncle Sam went home. "It's not your place to invite others to Carrie and Ming's party."

"What's wrong with that?" Mother asked. "Carrie is a close friend, and I know she's been meaning to invite them. We Chinese are so few here, we need to stick together."

"He just humiliated me in front of the girls and our neighbours, and you go and invite him to a party?"

"What are you talking about?"

"He drives home from work every day and not once has he come by to say hello, but the one day he sees me working in my yard, he can't help but come and spit in my face."

"You're being dramatic."

"He offered to give me a number for a company he hires to clean up his yard, knowing full well we can't afford to do that. He is not stupid, Swee Hua. He is management and knows exactly how much money we make. He came here to rub it in my face that I have to do my own work in my own yard, while he sits in his house reading the newspaper as someone else cleans his."

"Not everything is about you, Ah Loy. He was just being friendly. Our girls are friends, after all."

Father said nothing else and finished putting the leaves in a garbage bag. I didn't know whether Father was being too sensitive, but the salt had been spilled, and his offended feelings were like millions of tiny grains spread on the ground. It was impossible to pick them all up again.

The celebration Mother was looking forward to was taking place because Auntie Carrie Kwan had given birth to baby Billy, and he had survived his first 100 days. Since it was now considered safe, a red egg and ginger party was planned to introduce him to the world. Mother explained to me that a woman had to be in confinement for the first 100 days of a baby's life to stay hidden from ghosts who would snatch the life out of the baby or bring bad hong into the mother's body, causing her to get sick.

Some women would have visitors during the period of confinement, thereby making the months of nesting and healing more tolerable, but Auntie Carrie's husband, Uncle Ming Kwan, forbade it. The baby was his first-born son, so he didn't want to risk anything happening to the boy. Uncle Ming was so strict that he also insisted on minimal contact over the telephone. I overheard Mother explaining to Auntie Miriam one day that Auntie Carrie did not require a lot of convincing, as she also believed that the feng, as Uncle Ming called it in Mandarin, or hong, as Mother called it, could come through the receiver and grab her or Billy. She did not want to go through the pain of confinement only to have a tricky wind make her suffer for the rest of her life. Mother told Auntie Miriam that she knew of women back home who suffered lifelong severe migraines, or worse, because they did not respect the power of the hong during their period of confinement.

This meant that Mother relied on me to carry messages and gossip via Auntie Carrie's daughter Holly, who was always waiting by the school bus to hand me a note in exchange for Mother's note. Holly was in grade three, a grade lower than Bea. My sister and I felt bad for Holly for being the only Chinese girl in her class, but she was very loud and could not be trusted to keep a secret, so we tried to avoid her. On the playground, I pretended not to hear her call my name, and I implored her not to call me Jie Jie. I hoped this strategy would help me make friends with the girls in my class, but inevitably, they would notice Holly calling me and run off.

There were times I could not ignore her. When Holly was getting teased, I had to step in, only to run away when things cleared up. This push and pull in the schoolyard made me feel sick. I hated the burden of being the jie jie of the playground, and I knew I was not the jie jie my parents expected me to be.

Holly often gave Bea and me treats to try to win us over. During the Mid-Autumn Festival, she brought us a mooncake, an extremely coveted delicacy. Her parents or a visitor must have made a trip to a larger city with a Chinatown, bringing the burnished cakes stamped with creative designs.

Bea and I came home from school the day of the party excited that Holly revealed there would be egg tarts. Father, however, was not one for parties. "Why such a commotion? You girls should be studying, not gossiping! Let's just stay home."

"Ah Loy, don't forget that Carrie was the first one to come to our home and bring us meals after we arrived," Mother admonished. "She introduced us to everyone, found beds for the girls and brought them to our door. She's always there to watch the girls when I need to go to an appointment or run an errand. Ming found your first car for you. It would be an insult not to go."

Father was unmoved. "I'm happy to send them an ang bao, of course."

"Ah Loy, it's not just the gift. We should be among those with good fortune." Mother glanced at me, and then whispered, "Yes, we lost a son back home, but it should not prevent us from celebrating the good fortune of friends."

"This has nothing to do with that baby," Father whispered back.

"Then what is it?"

Father saw me listening and relented. "All right, let's go," he said.

Mother ushered us upstairs to change. Bea started to put on the dress I wanted to wear, but I didn't fight her. I felt like a fake: I was not the oldest child. As a second child, I imagined, my life would have been easier. I wouldn't have had to be responsible for Bea. My goh goh would have looked after both of us. I could have been like Hilary. What happened to my brother? Why did my parents pretend he didn't exist? I was afraid to ask.

The Oriental Palace was not just the only Chinese restaurant in town but also one of the largest, making it a popular location for the families of Sparwood to celebrate milestones or simply enjoy Sunday dinner. The restaurant was filled with large round tables with Lazy Susans to allow everyone to share the family-style dishes placed in the centre. And it was always open, even when the town shut down during the Canada Day long weekend or the Christmas holidays. The menu was extensive, offering Chinese Canadian fare, since the majority of the customers in Sparwood were not Chinese, as well as Chinese and Vietnamese food that my parents could find back home, because owner Uncle Joe Ng was both Chinese and Vietnamese. Father loved Uncle Joe's banh mi. Bea and I always wanted Mother to order the lemon chicken, ginger beef, and fried wontons, but she insisted on ordering the Cantonese dishes she loved and considered authentic that weren't on the menu, like gong chow ngau ho, bo zai fan, and ai gwa: fat noodles with beef, clay pot rice, and eggplant.

The restaurant was often featured in the local paper when large banquets were held, and Uncle Joe knew everyone in town. He and Auntie Joan knew the town's happenings before anyone else, including gossip that was not supposed to be shared. I overheard Mother telling Auntie Miriam that Auntie Joan knew that Terry Miller's wife was pregnant before Terry Miller knew. Terry was the chief operating officer at the mine. All the miners chipped in to buy a baby gift for the man who was considered the town's boss, which is how he found out about his wife's pregnancy.

Uncle Joe had closed the Oriental Palace to the public for Auntie Carrie's red egg and ginger party. He rearranged the dining room, setting out big tables for the adults and small tables for the children. On the other side of the large room were a few mah-jong tables. Father noticed them and whispered, "Mah-jong! Swee Hua, this is more than just dinner."

Mother slid away from Father to greet Auntie Choo Neo, Uncle Stephen, and all of the other aunties and uncles attending the event of the year. Mother's eyes sparkled as she anticipated an evening of fun.

Father gave a soup pot to Uncle Ming and told him it was for Auntie Carrie. The warm, savoury aroma of ginger and chicken was inescapable.

The night before, Mother, Bea, and I had found Father in the kitchen—cooking. He'd noticed us staring at him from the doorway like he was a ghost. "Jiu gai!" Father had proclaimed. Mother had explained it was a traditional dish for new mothers, to help them heal from childbirth and provide vital nutrients to the baby through the breast milk.

Bowls of red-dyed eggs were placed in the centre of each table, along with the traditional dishes meant to share the good fortune of fertility: noodles for long life, fish for prosperity, and many desserts for a sweet life. Chopsticks were clicking and lips were smacking. There was boisterous laughter, and baby Billy was crying, ensuring the ghosts would stay away. Uncle Joe had his hands on his round belly like a smiling Buddha, relishing the joyful sounds reverberating in his restaurant.

All the guests came by to fawn over Auntie Carrie and hand her red packets filled with money. She thanked everyone and placed them in her clutch, clasping it shut tightly each time. Auntie Carrie celebrated the end of her confinement with great fanfare. She wore gold earrings, jade rings, and an extravagant floor-length cheongsam. Golden sequins sewn in the shape of a dragon slithered up the side of the red silk gown, and her mandarin collar was brought together by golden Chinese knots. The dress was very tight and fitted. She looked like a glamorous mermaid plucked from the sea.

Mother leaned into Auntie Choo Neo and said, "Choo Neo, Carrie's father sent her this dress when she was going to marry Ming, but the shipping took too long and she never wore it. What better time than now?"

"She must have starved herself while in confinement," Auntie Choo Neo sniped.

Baby Billy started to wail then, and Mother picked him up and rocked him. She held him close, nuzzling the top of his head. Billy stopped crying but was restless, squirming and grunting. Mother swayed and bounced him gently, but Billy would not settle. She sang to him and called him Ah Dua.

Father put out his cigarette and gently steered Auntie Carrie by her elbow towards her son. "He sounds hungry, Carrie," he said.

Auntie Carrie took Billy and arranged herself so she could nurse him. That seemed to settle him. I walked towards Mother to give her a hug, but Father beat me to her. I lingered behind Mother, waiting for an opening.

Father put his arm around her waist and drew her towards him. I could hear him whisper in Hokkien, "What are you doing? Why are you calling him Ah Dua?"

"It's just a term of endearment, lah! Don't be so dramatic, Ah Loy."

"Ah Dua was our son's name."

"It also means big brother."

"Don't get too close to that baby."

"Or what, Ah Loy?"

"Our son is no longer part of this world. He is long gone and was never meant to be."

"We left him back home, and I can never go and see him."

"He is back home, yes, buried next to my mother. But he is in another world now. It's time to let him go."

"That is all you do, Ah Loy. Leave everything in the past and let go of everything from back home. It's so easy for you."

"No, it isn't. It's not my fault he's gone."

"No, but you'll remind me it's my fault, right? I should have stayed home that day. I should have stayed in confinement."

"That's not what I'm saying. I don't care about confinement. It was your choice. And you were right to take him to the hospital."

"He was sick, Ah Loy. He had a fever. I didn't know what to do. I thought taking him to the hospital was a good idea."

"It was a good idea."

"There's a reason why we practise confinement. I should have been more patient. I should have called you. I should have called someone. And now he is far away."

"We're not far away. Your family, your girls, are here. Let it go."

"Don't get me started about what I've had to let go. I don't want to talk about it here."

Mother wrenched herself out of Father's arms and joined the table of aunties. She lit a cigarette and puffed smoke into the air above her. I could see the tears she willed not to fall as she looked up at the ceiling. She sat there smoking silently until Father approached her again. "Don't get too comfortable, we're going home soon," he said. Mother ignored him, and he moved to the table of uncles.

I stood in the middle of the restaurant between the mah-jong tables, frozen. The room appeared to be spinning, like I was sitting on a Lazy Susan in the centre of one of the large round tables. I slowly made my way to the foot of Mother's chair.

Everyone found a place around one of the two mah-jong tables, one for the women, the other for the men. Uncle Joe coaxed Father towards the men's table, but he did not take a seat. Uncle Joe took the west side, Uncle Ming Kwan took the east side, Uncle Ed Woo took the north, and Uncle Paul Tang took the south. Uncle Stephen,

Uncle Roy Song, and Uncle Sam Lau decided to sit this one out with Father. Similarly, the women took their positions, with Auntie Carrie taking the north side, Auntie Miriam Woo the west, Mother the east, and Auntie Joan Ng the south. Auntie Elizabeth Lau, Auntie Choo Neo, and Auntie Betty Tang sat behind them.

Arms made big sweeping motions over the table to shuffle the mah-jong tiles as if everyone was doing the breaststroke. "Let's go swimming!" exclaimed Auntie Carrie. *Clackity-clack.* The banging of the tiles was so loud that some of us covered our ears. As the ladies started stacking the tiles, I could hear Uncle Joe slamming his tiles together aggressively, trying to wake them, he said.

"Joan ah!" Auntie Carrie called out.

Auntie Joan looked up from the tiles.

"Tell Betty what you heard the other day when you were working in the restaurant."

Auntie Joan glared at Auntie Carrie. "Why must you do this now? Such a happy occasion and you want to talk about that."

The women started moving the tiles towards the middle, making a rough rectangle. Auntie Choo Neo shouted, "If not now, then when? What are we talking about?"

The aunties shifted in their seats as they glanced between Mother and Auntie Elizabeth. Auntie Joan looked at Mother and said, "You brought her."

Mother was about to say something when Auntie Elizabeth broke in. "I have no idea what everyone is talking about. I was invited here."

"Well, Elizabeth, to be frank, it's about the mine," Auntie Joan explained. "We don't mean to gossip, but the men's jobs are our life. And, well, your husband's position in the mine ..."

"Oh, I see." Auntie Elizabeth nodded. "Listen, what is discussed here stays here. I don't work for the mine, and I hate talking shop with Sam. I really have no idea about anything he does at work."

Auntie Carrie gave Auntie Joan an encouraging look. "Ah ya," Joan began. "Okay, the other day some very important people came into the restaurant for lunch. They think we don't understand English, or they don't care if we do, so they talk freely."

The women started pulling tiles towards them and turned them over to reveal their faces.

"They ordered spring rolls," Joan added.

The women started throwing their mah-jong tiles into the middle of the rectangle as they rapidly took their turns.

"Joan ah! Get to the story," Auntie Carrie urged.

"Okay, okay. I overheard Terry Miller talking to some men who came from Vancouver. They were talking about layoffs at the mine."

The women at the table stopped playing at once.

"Joan, are you sure you understood them correctly?" Auntie Betty asked.

"Of course! I'm no dummy! We're speaking English right now, aren't we?"

"What else, what else?" Auntie Choo Neo demanded.

"They said they were thinking about closing Crowcreek Mine," Auntie Joan said.

The women breathed a collective sigh of relief. "You should have said that earlier!" Auntie Carrie complained. "The important one is Elkhills!"

"Elizabeth, has Sam said anything?" Mother asked.

"Like I said, Swee Hua, Sam doesn't talk shop with me. And I wouldn't pay attention anyway. Trust me, if something big was happening, though, Sam would be worried, too. If Elkhills closed, he would be out of a job, too. We're in the same boat as the rest of you."

Auntie Betty started to raise her hand to attract Uncle Paul's attention, until Mother grabbed her arm tightly, like a snake strangling its prey. "Wait ah," Mother said. "It will spoil the night." Auntie Betty nodded.

Just then, Mother noticed me hiding at the foot of her chair. "Lily! This table is not for kids. Go play with your friends."

I ran towards Hilary, who was watching her brother play a new boardgame he'd received from their uncle in Calgary. Phillip confidently held court with the clutch of boys gathered around him as he explained how *Risk* was played. Earlier in the evening, he'd showed off his calculator watch, proudly demonstrating all the tricks it could perform. No girls were allowed to play.

Sadly, I wondered if my own brother would have pushed the boys out of the way to make room for me. I shook the thought out of my head.

I tapped Hilary on the shoulder. "Let's do something else. This is boring."

"It's boring because you don't understand the game," she said.

"No, it's boring because we aren't playing the game," I retorted.

I looked over at Joy Woo, who was the oldest Chinese girl in Sparwood at fifteen. As a teenager, she had no interest in playing with us kids. I jealously watched her sitting in the corner, pushing her glasses up her nose as she turned the pages of a book she'd been reading since she'd arrived.

I was the second oldest, which might have made me a natural leader, but I was shy. Most of the girls had no interest in being my friend. We would silently acknowledge each other in the schoolyard but usually go our own way.

Nonetheless, I went to join the girls sitting in a circle playing with some toys. Luckily for us, Carmen and Micaela Ng had a lot of toys at the restaurant. It was their second home, since their parents worked evenings serving the diners of Sparwood. We dressed some Barbies, and when we got bored of that, we pulled out the Cabbage Patch Kids, and then discovered a stash of Lego. Still, we envied the boys and their new game.

Finally, Carmen announced, "This is my restaurant! They have to let us play with them." Although she was just nine years old, Carmen was the sassiest of the bunch of us. Auntie Joan had named her daughters after characters in her favourite opera. Carmen was not just loud, boastful, and energetic, but she was also blunt and sometimes mean about it. She bossed around her sister, Micaela, like her personal servant. But Micaela didn't mind because she admired her big sister. Micaela would act like an attack dog or a sweet playmate depending on Carmen's instructions.

Carmen marched up to her brother, Harry, and said, "When's it my turn?"

Maybe it was Carmen's name that made her feisty, or maybe it was because she had an older brother who pushed her around. I had no training for the bullying I received outside of my home. I wondered again what kind of person I might be if my brother had survived.

"You're too little," Harry said, and shoved his sister to the ground. "Go away."

"I'm not too little!" Carmen yelled. "I'm going to tell on you."

"Go ahead. It's not my game anyway. It's Phillip's."

Carmen looked at Phillip, who just stared at her, annoyed. Carmen turned to Hilary. "Your brother is being mean. Why won't he let us play?"

Hilary paused, stunned that this younger girl was bold enough to question her. "It's for older kids," she said. "We're too young to play."

"If it's only for older kids, then why is Adam playing? He's younger than us!" Carmen reasoned.

Hilary's cheeks flushed. Over the few months we'd known each other, Hilary had sheltered me with her friendship. Once, May Donahue had demanded that I give her my Twinkie from my lunch box. I was about to hand it over when Hilary said that I was only interested in trading my entire lunch. My new friend was brave beyond words. May turned her nose up and ran away at the sight of my container full of chicken curry with rice and yu choy. I'd never seen May retreat like that before. From that day forward, Hilary imitated May's face when she saw my curry. I laughed, but there were also tears in my eyes at the memory of the disgust I had seen on May's face when she sniffed my food. That was the last time she asked for anything out of my lunch.

And so, I moved in front of Hilary and said, "Carmen, back off. If Phillip's being a jerk, it doesn't mean Hilary can do anything about it. Let's play our own game." I grabbed Hilary's hand and we walked back to our corner.

Carmen stood there, dumbfounded. I had never spoken to her like that before. "Yeah!" she yelled right up in Harry's face. "Let's find a girls' only game."

Uncle Joe saw the discord brewing, so he rolled out a television on a cart and slipped *Back to the Future* into the VCR. This pacified Carmen, and all the girls gathered around, using her large stuffed animals as pillows. Dan Tang and the Woo brothers abandoned Phillip to watch the movie. Only Harry stayed loyal, probably to save face from his sister's outcry. Phillip tried to seem unfazed, but we saw him angle his body so that he could see the screen. Bea leaned against me as I fought off sleep, the VCR quietly whirring in a corner of the restaurant.

The cigarette smoke hung around the ceiling, even though Uncle Joe had turned the fans on. The women had started smoking, too, and now the aunties and uncles were playing mah-jong together. Uncle Joe poured some beer for Auntie Miriam and she laughed loudly. Father was in the corner, smoking. He bent over to look at his watch and cleared his throat. Mother looked up from her mah-jong tiles and indicated that she was winning, so he had to be patient. Auntie Carrie flicked a tile with her middle finger to the centre of the table. Mother grabbed it before it stopped moving and placed it face down before her. She collapsed the remaining tiles in front of her and exclaimed, "Sik!" She had won.

At that, Mother got up and walked onto the small stage with one hand on her hip and a microphone in the other. A spotlight came on and everyone turned and started clapping. Auntie Miriam said to

Auntie Elizabeth, "Swee Hua is quite the performer. She could have been the next Teresa Teng, but she came to Canada instead."

There was always a moment at such celebrations, after things had slowed down, when Mother blossomed. She would pick a moment when Father had gone to the washroom, to the kitchen, or outside for a walk or a cigarette. When he returned, the sound of her voice over the speakers would pull him under her spell. Mother would put on brighter lipstick, stick a fake flower in her hair, and wear a larger smile. It was as if a different person were onstage.

Her repertoire was impressive. The crowd threw song titles at her in Cantonese, Mandarin, Hokkien, and even Hakka, and she belted out her versions while the karaoke machine tried to keep up. Father's face glowed with pride when Mother sang, but he also hated sharing her. I watched as he stared bitterly at Uncle Stephen, who climbed clumsily onto the small stage and grabbed Mother's waist, trying drunkenly to sing with her. Mother tried to push him away, and everyone started booing Uncle Stephen's poor attempts at accompaniment. Auntie Choo Neo yelled at her husband in Hakka. He stumbled off the stage, and Auntie Choo Neo grabbed his collar and pulled him out of the restaurant. They were gone for the rest of the night.

Mother's voice electrified the room and the crowd roared for her. The vitality of her performance and the vibrancy of her stage presence contrasted with the docile, fragile woman she was at home. I wondered if both these extremes were false, and underneath them somewhere my real mother existed.

When all the songs were sung, Mother left the stage and walked into Father's embrace. I wanted to insert myself between them, to be part of their moment, but I also didn't want to break it up too soon.

As we got ready to leave, we heard Auntie Carrie mumbling in mixed Chinese and English that she should have won at mah-jong because it was the night her only son was welcomed into the living world. The cash poured out of people's pockets, the cigarettes were butted out, and the empty bottles were brought into the kitchen.

Uncle Joe reminded people to bring home their da bao, and fathers picked up their sleeping children to carry them to the cars.

At home, Mother took my shoes and coat off and led me to my bedroom. Father followed with Bea. They slipped us into our shared bed and closed the door, but I was aware of their voices humming on the other side of the closed door.

The next day, Father was working a day shift, so he had left the house before Bea and I woke up. Mother's face seemed paler and her eyes droopier than usual, as if the night had sucked the life out of her. Her dress was on the floor next to the bed. She looked at herself in the mirror and traced the lines by her eyes with her fingers as if she had never seen them before.

The only thing that remained the same from last night was the jade bracelet. Mother never took it off. I touched the cool stone and asked, "Where did you get this?"

"This was actually my mother's," Mother replied. "I had my own, but it broke when it saved my life."

My eyes widened. "What do you mean?"

"Back home, I went to a party with my friend Che Eng. During the evening, I lost her, and I was left on my own to get home. Luckily, the person hosting the party offered me her bicycle. She told me to just take it; it was an old bicycle. I decided to ride home alone in the dark. I was on the shoulder of the road when a car came up quickly behind me. The car was turning as the road curved, and it hit me. I don't remember anything after that."

"You don't remember anything? Were you hurt?" I asked.

Mother embraced me. "I woke up in the hospital with my mother cursing at me. She said the driver had taken me all the way to the hospital and told my mother that he didn't know how I could have survived the crash." Her solemn tone matched the dullness of her eyes and the shabbiness of her nightgown. "The bicycle was completely destroyed, but somehow, I just had a sprained ankle. My jade bracelet had broken in two. But for that bracelet, I would be a ghost. My mother gave me her own bracelet as a replacement so that I would always be protected."

Every day, the jade bracelet hung from mother's tiny wrist, swivelling with her daily movements while she washed the dishes or pushed the spatula as she fried vegetables in the wok. It dangled there, sometimes looking like a jewel catching the light, as it did at the party the night before. Other times, it looked like the pavement of a worn road, eroded and dull, like Mother's face the morning after.

凵
Open Box

IN THE MIDDLE OF FALL, Po Po sent us a package. It was wrapped in brown packing paper and looked worn, as if it had travelled all over the world before coming here. Mother told us it had come by ship, and then by train, to Sparwood. Inky postal stamps were scattered haphazardly all over the paper like block prints. Some of them were in Chinese.

Bea and I had only met our grandmother once, when she came to visit for two weeks when I was eight. Although she lived half a world away, we knew about her through Mother's stories. And there were sporadic phone calls and letters. She had permed short hair and smelled like the prawn crackers she cooked during her visit. She was tall for a Chinese woman but stocky and firm. When she held or carried us, it was with confident authority but also warmth. She did not like to show her teeth when she smiled, but when she did, Bea and I stared at the gold tooth peeking out beside her dimpled cheek. She had brown freckles that we knew she hated because she would point at them and point at our cheeks. Mother translated that she wanted us to stay out of the sun. She could not speak English, and we could not speak Hokkien very well, but she was full of affection, candies, gifts, and laughter. No translation was needed for some of our conversations.

Bea and I eagerly opened the package, digging into the box like dogs pushing dirt out of a hole, looking for the bone at the bottom.

"There are no toys in here!" Bea exclaimed, then threw a dress back into the box and looked at me. I tilted my head at our My Little

Ponies standing in the corner. Bea nodded and we ran towards the toy box.

Mother was not impressed. When Father came home, he saw the dresses strewn all over the living room and asked what was going on. Mother excitedly flashed dress upon dress in front of him, but he shielded his face with his hand like he was trying to avoid the piercing sun. "Aya, Swee Hua. Sayang lui, what a waste of money. You know the girls don't like wearing dresses."

"Yeah, I hate them," Bea said.

"Me too," I agreed.

"You are both so ungrateful!" Mother yelled.

We hated the restrictions that came with dresses. The fabric would get caught in the wheels and chains of our bicycles. We had to sit demurely so that our underwear wouldn't show. We couldn't crouch to watch the ants carry objects three times their size without the dress getting dirty. Worst of all, wearing dresses felt like dragging around heavy pieces of wet cloth. We refused to wear them, and this made Mother angry. All of our dresses came from Po Po.

"We didn't ask for these dresses. If Po Po knew us, she wouldn't have bought them for us," Bea said.

Mother gave Bea a look of outrage. "Your po po doesn't know you because she lives on the other side of the world. She wants to know you and sent these beautiful dresses. You can respect her by wearing them."

"Swee Hua, calm down," Father said. They're just clothes. If they don't want to wear them, why do you want to force them?"

"How dare you, Ah Loy? You brought me here, so far from my mother, and you dare tell me it's okay for my children to disrespect her? You have done enough to sever any relationship she can have with them."

"Swee Hua, it's not my fault the world is so large."

"No, it's not, but you do not make it smaller. I know you want to forget everything back home. I know you have nothing there anymore, but I do."

"What is your mother doing sending us boxes of clothing like I can't provide anything! It's not like I'm still stateless, working under the table, trying to stay out of sight of the authorities anymore. E siah suay wo, she's embarrassing me. We should be sending her things."

Bea and I continued to toss the clothes around, hoping that something better was hidden among them.

"They're a gift, Ah Loy. Why must you take the joy out of everything? It's not an insult to you but a gesture of love for her grandchildren. She is not some stranger. Nobody has said anything about you being stateless and unable to provide. Why does it always come back to that?"

"That's easy for you to say. You had everything handed to you."

"So that's what this is about? You resent my family because we never had to suffer like you? Yes, I'm lucky, but I don't feel lucky right now. This is not about you, Ah Loy! The problem with you is that you blame everyone back home for your problems. Yes, you were stateless, but my mother had nothing to do with that."

"Aya, Swee Hua, of course I know that. I tried to sponsor your mother to come to Canada. It's not my fault her application wasn't approved. She can come visit anytime."

"Not everything is about status, Ah Loy. Not everything is about citizenship."

"See, that's the problem, Swee Hua. You can say that because you've never lived without it. Everything *is* about that. You have no idea what it feels like. I would rather die than lose my citizenship again. You cannot be a whole person when you're stateless."

Mother stormed upstairs with a dress she had discovered for herself in Po Po's box. Father lit a cigarette and went for a walk. They left us in the room with the clutter. It was as if the contents of the box spilled out messily around us held more than the clothes Po Po had sent. Bea and I didn't want to touch the remnants strewn about and abandoned Po Po's gift.

Yellow leaves fell everywhere, reminding Mother of the snow to come, she said. The coming winter was impossible for her to avoid, and she searched for any excuse to leave the house and shelter in the warm company of others. A visit with Auntie Miriam at Woo's Confectionery, a delivery pickup at the Oriental Palace with Auntie Joan, a stop at the post office, a book to return at the library, a trip to the grocery store, a snuggle with baby Billy at Auntie Carrie's. I loved watching Mother come to life again when she was around my aunties. Her eyes opened wider, her smile reappeared, her cheeks coloured, and her hands flew while she talked.

Mother even tried to find community closer to home. Looking out the front window, coffee in hand, she saw two neighborhood women walk by, their skirts swaying and the heels of their leather boots hitting the pavement in synchronized rhythm. Arm in arm, the two women strolled forward, their heads turned towards each other, bodies intertwined like Siamese twins. Mother waved and called out, "Cecilia! Sally!" through the window. Their heads turned to look, and they waved brusquely, with wry smiles, but kept on marching. Mother clung to her coffee cup the way they hung onto each other. Taking slow sips, she let the steam reach her nose.

"Is that Mrs Donahue?" I asked, looking out the bay window with Mother, tiptoeing over her banana tree to get a better view.

"Yes." The look on Mother's face reminded me of when I tried to join May and Ann at the park and they rebuffed me.

We saw the women walk back our way, and I followed Mother outside. Their children were running endless figure eights around them. Mother tried to push me towards them to play, but I wouldn't leave her side. Cecilia and Sally were engrossed in conversation.

"May went to a wonderful camp this summer. It's run by the same Girl Guide leaders she's with right now. You should sign Ann up next year," Cecilia said.

"Yes, I saw the flyer. They were camping somewhere near Spokane?"

"Is this a Girl Guides' camp?" Mother piped up.

"Yes, it is," Cecilia answered curtly before turning back to her friend. "Sally, I also wanted to tell you about this beautiful room divider that Bob brought home from his business trip. It's quite ornate. Hand-painted and Oriental looking. It's quite fetching and provides a bit of a break between the dining room and living room. I just love how a little exotic touch can add so much to a plain room."

"Sounds fascinating!" said Sally. "David and I have a room divider in our master bedroom, but we've gotten into the terrible habit of throwing clothes over it. It's plain and functional—certainly not from overseas."

Mother shifted from foot to foot, swaying as if she had a baby on her hip. It was as if she was getting ready to jump into the conversation but was weighed down by ghosts.

"Dinner is simmering in the Crock-Pot," Sally said, ignoring Mother. "So it couldn't hurt to take a quick walk over with you to see this room divider."

The two women clomped away in their boots like horses who had just spotted a juicy apple. Mother was left standing on the sidewalk as if she herself was a ghost. It was only after I tugged at her pants that she looked down.

Mother tried for weeks to join the women's conversation as they strolled by, but sometimes she didn't know what Cecilia and Sally were talking about. They would discuss food Mother had never eaten or seen before, home decor, and the summer activities they planned, like water skiing. When we went to the library, I watched Mother look up cookbooks, interior decorating magazines, and the encyclopedia in order to understand the women of Sparwood. By the time

Mother finally got it, the women would have already moved onto a new mystery for her to decode.

Mother's curiosity about these women's lives led to the three of us embarking on some interesting culinary adventures. Bea and I would help her bake, make jam, and roast peppers. Her masterpiece was her braided bread with homemade raspberry jam. Mother made everything look easy. Even Father enjoyed some of the sweet treats, despite how unfamiliar they looked to him.

Mother's overtures, however, never garnered any warmth from Cecilia and Sally. The women looked for ways to shake her off like a buzzing fly swarming their well-coiffed hair. They would pre-empt Mother's entrance into their orbit, protecting themselves from any foreign bodies.

One day, when Mother went outside to offer them some of the treats she'd made, Cecilia said reluctantly, "Oh, hello Sue," insisting on calling Mother that instead of Swee. "Listen, Ann had a particularly rough day in school today, so we're just making sure she has some quality time with her best friend, May." Their children stuck their tongues out at Bea and me as they hid behind their mothers. The previous week, I'd heard Sally say, "Oh sorry, Sue, I'm just heading home with Cecilia to ask her advice about some colour swatches. We don't have time to chat." And a few weeks before that, the excuse had been "Oh no! The wind has picked up. I think we need to get my winter coat before I keep standing out here."

Each time the women picked up their conversation and left, dragging their rude children along with them, Mother slunk back into the house like a snail into its shell.

When she was sad, I felt the weight of her sorrow on my shoulders. I went to her room to comfort her, but she just looked at me and said, "Wo pua peh, I'm not feeling well. Go outside and play with your sister. I'll feel better soon." I watched as she unwrapped her ankle, massaged it, wrapped it once more.

I could see Mother closing up like a flower wilting in the last days of summer. I clung to her side, hoping the warmth of my body would console her, but as I left the room, I saw her lie down and pull the covers over her head.

比

Compare

AS WE OFTEN DID, Bea and I followed Hilary home one day after school. Homework was a distant memory when we were summoned to set the dinner table after watching an episode of *Jem and the Holograms*. Steaming rice was piled in small bowls at each place setting. Phillip appeared out of nowhere and sat down. Everyone waited until Hilary's father had picked up his chopsticks before eating. Auntie Elizabeth placed some vegetables and stir-fried beef in his bowl. He lifted a piece of meat and chewed it noisily. Auntie Elizabeth then made sure everyone else had some food in their bowls. After a few loud slurping mouthfuls, Uncle Sam observed, "Oh, you can use chopsticks?"

"Yes, Uncle" was all I could muster.

Auntie Elizabeth gave Uncle Sam a warning look, but he ignored her. "I thought you used forks at home."

"It depends on what we eat," Bea said. "Sometimes we use forks if we're eating spaghetti."

"So your mother doesn't cook Chinese food all the time?" Uncle Sam said, rice sticking to his lips.

"Most of the time she cooks Chinese food, and sometimes we use forks for that, too," Bea said.

I felt my cheeks getting red. I wanted to kick or pinch my sister, but Hilary was sitting between Bea and me. Then Phillip asked for more soup in Cantonese.

"Our guests don't speak Chinese, Phillip, so be polite and speak English while they're here," Uncle Sam said.

"Actually, Lily and Bea do speak Chinese, but it's a different dialect, right?" Hilary spoke up, glancing at me for confirmation. I nodded and smiled at Hilary.

Hilary's father shot Hilary a steely glance and said, "It's a village dialect, Hilary. Let's not be rude to our guests." He then asked Phillip about his day.

Uncle Sam's remark made me want to slide off my chair and hide under the dinner table until everyone had finished. I already knew that Hokkien was a language few people knew about. Even Chinese people would look perplexed when I mentioned it, like I was telling them about some alien civilization.

Throughout dinner, Hilary tried to engage me in conversation, but I was too afraid to say anything more. Instead, I ate my bowl of rice and told Auntie Elizabeth her cooking was excellent.

After dinner, Hilary walked Bea and me across the street. We saw Father in the driveway, a cigarette dangling from his mouth, shovelling snow onto the lawn. He looked up at our approach and gave each of us a hug.

"And how is my long-lost daughter, Hilary?" Father asked.

"I'm fine, Uncle," Hilary replied. .

This friendly greeting lifted my spirits. I hugged my father tight, grasping at his warmth.

The next day, when the recess bell rang, Mrs Castelli asked me to stay behind. She showed me my assignment and asked me what the picture meant. I just stood there, staring at my shoes.

"Did you do your homework with Hilary?" Mrs Castelli asked.

I didn't know what to say.

"Your assignment looks very similar to Hilary's. Did you copy her work?"

I nodded, tears filling my eyes.

"Did you understand the assignment?"

I nodded again.

"The assignment required you to write a profile about your father and what he did for a living. Do you know what your father does for work?"

"No," I said.

"I see. Well, it's not permitted to copy another student's work," she said. "You should have come to me if you had trouble with this assignment, Lily. I've called your mother, and I'll be meeting with both of you after school." Mrs Castelli handed me a tissue and ushered me to the door.

I went to the washroom and stayed there until recess ended. Hilary came in and asked me what was wrong. I told her I wasn't feeling well. She looked concerned but didn't say anything else.

Mother came to the school that afternoon. Bea played in the playground with Hilary while we met with Mrs Castelli. My teacher explained that she suspected that I had copied Hilary's work. Mother's face flushed. She turned to me and asked me in Hokkien if what Mrs Castelli said was true. I nodded and tears streamed down my face. I didn't know why Mother had to speak to me this way, with these words. There was no need to point out again that we were different. Mrs Castelli pushed a box of tissues towards me and reassured Mother that this was not a serious issue.

Mrs Castelli told Mother that I didn't know what my father did for a living. Mother explained that Father was a welder who worked in Elkhills Mine. Mrs Castelli turned to me, smiled, and said, "I would find it difficult to understand what a welder does, too." She suggested that perhaps the reason why I was so confused was because I didn't speak or understand English as well as the other students. She noted how well Mother spoke English and encouraged her to speak to me in English as much as possible. She told Mother that I rarely spoke in class and was extremely shy. I was beyond embarrassed.

Mrs Castelli said that I would have to redo the assignment. She explained that part of the assignment was to learn how to interview people, how to conduct research, and urged me to ask Father what welders do.

In the car on the way home, I felt like I was outside of my own body. Bea and Hilary kept themselves busy with their own fun. They knew I was in trouble.

Mother didn't tell Father about our meeting with Mrs Castelli and helped me complete my profile. When we were finished, she told me that we would never speak of this incident again.

Early the next morning, Father returned from his last night shift of four straight days of work, but he didn't take a shower and go to sleep like usual. When I came downstairs for breakfast, he was sitting at the kitchen table with a cigarette in his mouth, still in his work clothes. When he saw me, he took the cigarette out of his mouth and stamped it out in the crystal ashtray on the table. The morning light pierced the prism of the dish and flashed a sharp reflection on him. He handed me my new assignment, a picture of Father standing in front of the largest truck in the world pasted to the cover.

"Lily, what is this assignment you had to do for school?" He must have stumbled upon my work while we were sleeping.

Mother entered the kitchen, and I looked at her pleadingly. She stood behind Father, floating like a ghost.

Father slammed his hand on the table and yelled, "Don't look at your mother!"

"I-I had to write about what my father does for work," I stammered.

Father then pulled out my original assignment. I thought Mother had thrown it away. He pointed to the picture I had sketched of a man sitting at a desk with his tie drooping in front of him. "Who is this, Lily?"

"It was supposed to be you," I murmured.

"Is it me?" he asked.

"No," I whispered.

"Then who is it, and what is he doing?"

"It's Uncle Sam, and he's working in an office," I whimpered.

Father's face went grey. I wanted to tell him that I had wanted no part of the assignment, and that is why I had copied Hilary.

Father turned to Mother and shouted, "A family's misfortune should not be publicly aired! How did you let this happen?"

She took a deep breath and puffed her chest like a proud chicken. "There is nothing ugly. It is the truth."

"The truth? The truth that even here I'm just like a coolie in the pewter mines back in Malaysia. So low that my own daughter is ashamed to write about it in a simple school exercise."

"Nobody but you is calling yourself a coolie!" my mother shouted back.

"Tell me. What else did your teacher say?" Father asked me.

With tears flowing down my cheeks, I tried to think of something that would not be about Father. "She told me that I don't speak well enough, and that I need to practise my English."

Father's eyes widened, and he glowered at Mother. "I told you that we needed to speak more English! You and your Chinese school upbringing. You should be speaking to her in English! We live in Canada now."

Father left the kitchen. We could hear loud music bellowing from the belly of the basement. I imagined him looking up at all of us perched on the crater of the mountain, staring at him in the deep hole, watching the darkness from underground consume him.

I truly didn't understand what Father did at work. I knew he left with his metal lunch box, steel-toed boots, and hard hat and came back dirty. I knew he hated going to the mine. It was only after Mother pulled out the photo of Father standing in front of Titan, the largest truck in the world, that I began to understand. Mother explained the job of a welder, moulding together pieces of metal and steel. Father had helped build something that was in *The Guinness Book of World Records*, but he wasn't proud of it.

I felt like we were on a tightrope, carefully tiptoeing across, Father holding my hands behind him. He taught me to tread lightly, to walk slowly. But most of all, he taught me to never look back and to emulate those in front of us.

止

Stop

THE MOUNTAINS DIDN'T LOOK SO PEACEFUL TO ME ANYMORE. A light blanket of snow covered them, but it couldn't hide the distress of the town when a strike suddenly erupted at the mines. People would stop and talk in the grocery store, at the post office, and even in the schoolyard while picking up their kids to try to glean any news about how bargaining was going between management and the union. Although I didn't fully understand what the adults were talking about, I could feel the weight of the negotiations on everyone. My father started to resemble Bixi, the mythical dragon with a turtle shell. His shoulders seemed more hunched as he lumbered around slowly with no purpose. People clutched their wallets, stayed close to home, and cancelled vacations. When I asked Father what was going on, he told me not to worry and to concentrate on my homework.

The chimneys of the mine still disgorged smoke into the air, but to everyone in town, it was closed. Men were not working, but they were all over town, as if they were in purgatory, smoking, drinking, and grumbling.

One day, when Bea and I went to Hilary's house to watch *Jem and the Holograms* and to do our homework, Hilary's parents ushered her into the kitchen to talk privately. In the living room, Bea and I moved closer together, taking comfort in our shoulders touching.

After a couple of minutes, Hilary burst out of the kitchen, grabbed her coat, and yelled at us to run. We gathered our things quickly and followed her outside, running across the street. We were out of breath when we reached my house.

"What happened?" I asked.

"They can't tell me who my friends are. They're not making any sense. I don't understand why I can't be friends with you right now. They're being stupid," Hilary said.

We watched TV and did our homework until Mother called us for dinner. We were having steamed pork and preserved salted egg meat loaf, with some fried broccoli and rice. As we began our meal, the doorbell rang.

"We're just sitting down for dinner. Hilary is more than welcome to stay." Mother's welcoming voice carried to the kitchen.

"Swee Hua, thank you, but Hilary is needed back home," said Uncle Sam.

I ran to the front door as Uncle Sam and Auntie Elizabeth walked over the threshold. Auntie Elizabeth's face was cast downwards as she followed uncle.

"Elizabeth, it's really no problem at all," Mother reiterated. "We can send her home afterwards. She's already sitting down."

Auntie Elizabeth didn't reply. "We'd like Hilary to come home now," Uncle Sam said.

Father walked briskly into the foyer, with Bea following. Hilary stayed frozen at the table.

"What is going on?" Father said, his voice raised.

"We don't want to disturb you. We just came for Hilary," said Uncle Sam.

"I don't want to go!" Hilary yelled.

"Come here now!" Uncle Sam was suddenly furious.

"What's the urgency, Sam?" Father asked. "Hilary is welcome here. She's just like one of my own girls."

"Hilary is not your daughter," Uncle Sam said. "Ah Loy, I just don't think it's a good idea for our families to mix right now."

"And why is that?"

"With everything going on at work, it's best to keep ourselves away from conflict."

"Are you talking about the strike? Leave that at the mine, Sam. You're causing the conflict here. Let the children play. Let's not make this personal."

"Hilary is my child, and I want what is best for her."

"Best for her? Are you saying it's not in her best interest for her to play with my daughters?"

"No, it's not that. It's just not a good time."

"Is your loyalty to management so important that you can't mix with us who do your dirty work?"

"That is not what I said! Don't twist my words!"

"I don't need to twist your words. How dare you come into my house and remind me that all of you up in that building think that all of us inside the mine, risking our lives every day, are good for nothing! You know something, Sam? I really didn't care to be part of a union. I was happy working and minding my own business, but your attitude has really made me think that I should pay closer attention."

"You have no idea what you're talking about, Ah Loy. I was educated here in this country, at the University of Toronto. I don't blame you for not understanding everything."

"You don't know what *you're* talking about!" Bea piped up. "My father went to English school when he was allowed to and was the first in his class. He would have gone to university too, but he couldn't. Just because we're not rich like you doesn't mean my dad isn't smart."

Auntie Elizabeth pulled her husband's arm towards the door.

Father's face was red as he called Hilary. She came reluctantly, crying. Her family left in a hurry and Father slammed the door behind them. I watched through the window as Uncle Sam tugged Hilary all the way home. The salt from the preserved eggs lingered on my mouth, stinging my chapped lips.

While Bea and I were washing the dishes, we heard Mother say, "Ah Loy, the strike has been going on for a month now. Maybe we should see this as a good time to think about moving."

Father sat at the table picking his teeth with a toothpick. "Move? Why? The strike can't last for more than another week."

"How do you know? Miriam told me that management is not in a good place and that the union is asking for the impossible. Maybe it's time to make a change."

"I know what you want, Swee Hua. You want to go home."

"Is that so bad? To go back to where you're from?"

Father laughed bitterly. "Don't talk to me about going home. There is no such place."

"But going back as a Canadian would open so many doors for us. No longer would people look down on you. People would come to you for things."

"What things? What could I offer them, Swee Hua? Wo bo lui, I have no money! That's what everyone is looking for. And what about our daughters? I want them to be raised in Canada. Why would we go back to a place that didn't want us?"

She looked at father like he was a stranger. "Our daughters will never know our family as well as we knew ours. We are alone here. They barely know where they're from."

"How can you say that? My sister is here, and you and I are here. That's all they need. This is their home. They are Canadian."

"We can have a good life there, too."

"No, Swee Hua."

Mother sighed and brought the rest of the dishes to the sink. The frown lines around her mouth were deep. "Why isn't the Canadian passport enough?" she whispered. "Why does he want to live in this cold land? Where's the Hakka in him?"

I think the Hakka in Father left him as soon as he held his Canadian passport for the first time. He was like the Burmis Tree on Highway 3. It had lived 750 years. In its old age, the tree was toppled by wind but propped up with stainless-steel rods by the Crowsnest Heritage community. Father would rather stay in a broken state than leave the place that gave him a home.

The strike was entering its fourth month when a massive snowfall descended on Sparwood. Our school bus fishtailed up Ponderosa Drive and we could hear the driver swearing at the tires spinning on the road. Everywhere was white; only the tire tracks in front of the bus showed us the way.

When Bea and I got home, we saw Father out front shovelling snow, the exhaust from his car billowing heavily.

"Where are you going?" I asked.

Father gave each of us a hug and announced, "I'm taking you skiing!"

"Yay!" Bea and I cried in unison.

Father's enthusiasm was buoyed by the 1988 Olympics being hosted in Calgary. We were mere hours away from the excitement and had seen the Olympic flame come through our town. My classmate Jason had boasted that he'd touched the torch and swore never to wash his ski mitten ever again.

Mother watched us pile into the car. "My ankle's not doing so well. I think I better stay home," she said.

The snow sparkled beneath the street lights. Once we hit the highway, the headlamps highlighted the dancing white specks before us. As we passed the Heights exit, I realized we weren't going to Sparwood Ski Hill, where Father taught himself how to ski and where he brought us down the hill between his legs when we were preschoolers. It was only once a year that he took us to the big mountains in Fernie.

While we waited for the chairlift, I marvelled at the strength of the tree branches around me. A foot of snow had collected upon each branch, yet they were bravely carrying these wet, heavy loads, sagging from the weight, as if they were wearing beautiful, full gowns of lustrous silk, lace, and tulle. Each was unique, with some donning short, stiff tutus and others draped in more elaborate robes. Sequined white confetti gave flair to the fashion show.

As the chair climbed into the air, I saw people below gracefully shifting from side to side with their poles guiding them forward. My breath was taken away by how high up we were, how small the skiers looked. A boy took a jump and fist-pumped in the air when he landed. Father swatted his thigh, pointed down at the hill, and exclaimed, "Did you see that?" Bea and I both nodded and said, "Wow!"

"Let's find that jump on the way down," Father said.

As we hopped off the chairlift, Father slid down the hill backwards. I laughed watching him swing around effortlessly, beckoning us to chase him. Bea whizzed by, and I pushed my skis from side to side, propelling my poles in front of me to grab the snow, gaining momentum. The cold air kissed my cheeks as we zoomed by other skiers. I tucked into a racer position, bending my knees to try to catch up to Father. Bea, to my left, copied me, and we raced down, determined to reach him.

When we arrived at the base of the hill, Father was waiting. "Again?" he asked.

While Father embraced the snow, Mother was afraid of it. She cocooned in the house, wrapping herself with wool blankets and scarves, peering outside with suspicion. She found temporary solace from the cold in hockey, especially in cheering avidly for the Edmonton Oilers. Hockey carried her through the long, dark days, pulling her forward through the winter season.

During a game between the Edmonton Oilers and the Calgary Flames, the battle of Alberta, Bea and I giggled next to mother on the couch as she yelled at the television. Father came home from the picket line to find her clutching a pillow, shouting and gesticulating.

"Aya, why are you so worked up over a stupid game?" he asked.

"This is not stupid. They are professionals. What's stupid is you freezing your butt off to slide down a hill on chopsticks," Mother replied, shooing Father away.

Father laughed. "Why are you cheering for Edmonton?" he asked. "We're closer to Calgary."

Mother looked at Father like he was a monster. "How can you say that? Wayne Gretzky, of course. He knows where the puck is going to be." Father's questions were distractions taking her away from the action, so she resorted to shushing him.

He turned to Bea and me for help. "Why are they blowing the whistle?"

"Because the goalie didn't touch the puck," said Bea.

"Why does the goalie need to touch the puck?"

"Well, a player on the other team could touch the puck, too," I said. Mother looked at me proudly.

"I still don't understand."

"It's icing, Dad." Bea rolled her eyes.

"Icing?"

Nobody responded. Just then, Gretzky brought the puck behind the opponents' net—"Gretzky's office," the commentators called it. He hovered, waiting for someone to make a move. Suddenly, he darted with the puck, shot it in front, and scored! I jumped up and gave Bea a high-five. We hugged Mother and danced around screaming.

"Did you see that, Dad?" Bea asked.

Father tried his best to follow the game, but he simply wasn't interested. He retreated behind his newspaper but sat next to Mother, smiling every time she got excited. One day, he came home from the picket line with a gift for Mother. A key chain with Wayne Gretzky on it in his signature blue, white, and orange Oilers jersey.

"Just what I always wanted," Mother joked. "A picture of my boyfriend."

Scholar

THAT YEAR, WINTER WOULD NOT RELEASE ITS GRIP on the land around us. The cold air followed Father home from the picket line, and the chill he brought with him climbed our backs. The strike had locked down the community, and it felt like the town had been overrun by men. Men crowded the post office, the mall, the streets, but mostly in their cars, smoking, and the Oriental Palace, as Uncle Joe was the only one who didn't throw people out hours after they'd nursed their last beer. They would idle, pace, or make small talk with whoever was nearby. Some were drunk, even in the middle of the day, while others just chain-smoked. Some were off in the mountains in their snowmobiles, their wives at home worried about avalanches.

As the strike and the winter hung on, Mother entered a trancelike state, sometimes sitting motionless on the couch four hours, watching the day's endless reel of soap operas. Her face would be pointed at the television, expressionless, the only sign that she was alive was the occasional blink of her eyes. Even in her daily tasks, Mother became a lethargic bear who had mistakenly awoken early from hibernation. I watched as she folded the clothes into our dressers deliberately and with great care, trying to prolong the experience as if she were savouring it, as if she dreaded what was to come afterwards.

Around this time, Auntie Miriam went to Calgary to visit family and brought back something, or rather someone, that brought Mother back to life. She introduced her guest at a dinner at our home.

"Alfred is my cousin Agnes's husband's brother. He came here as a visitor but doesn't want to go back to China. He's a writer, but the Chinese authorities do not approve of his writing," Auntie Miriam told us. "My cousin's home is quite small, and they have a new baby, so I invited Alfred live with us for a while."

Alfred wore a track suit and had a boyish face with the worn expression of an old man. He spoke very little English, and only Mother could converse with him at any length in Mandarin. After trying awkwardly to join our conversation, Alfred pulled out a book. Mother and Auntie Miriam, who hadn't seen each other for weeks, were free to talk about him right in front of him. Alfred became a silent fixture, like the empty plates on the table.

"He's very brave. He's been through a lot in China," Auntie Miriam said.

"He must be scared," Bea observed.

"Being in a small town doesn't scare him. He's a solitary person and sits in his room writing a lot."

"It's admirable that you're giving him sanctuary," Mother said. "It's always good to help those in need, especially our own kind."

"Brave?" Father said. "This man is thwarting the law. Why doesn't he get in line and apply for status like the rest of us? I don't understand what the problem is?"

"Ah Loy, why are you being so cruel?" Mother admonished. "Have some compassion for someone who is facing jail and other terrible things in China."

"Swee Hua, for all the glorious things you like to tell me about China, now you're advocating giving safe haven to someone trying to escape this sacred home you have never been to," Father pointed out.

"I know China isn't perfect. I have never pretended it was. But to sacrifice your own kind needlessly? That is cruel," Mother argued.

"What makes you think this person is so special that he should be exempted from the proper channels that we all used? We have all suffered and had difficult times. If he is deserving, Canada will accept him," Father concluded.

"Ah Loy, it's not so simple, Auntie Miriam interjected. "Agnes tried to sponsor him, and the application was rejected. Her family has paid a lot of money to lawyers to try to get his permanent residence status here. Nothing has worked. Alfred is making a refugee claim now."

"I trust the system. We're in a democratic country that respects rules. We should, too. Maybe he is not deserving," Father said.

"How can you say that? You know nothing about this man!" Mother exclaimed.

"How can you defend someone you don't even know?" Father countered.

"Ah Loy, believe me, this man deserves to stay in Canada," Auntie Miriam asserted. "The system doesn't always work in our favour. Look at my own family. My grandfather was toiling on the Pacific Railway while my grandmother was stuck in China with three children. All because of the law. My father, his only son, was the lucky one to come here, but only after paying the hefty price of the head tax. How can you think that Canada will always come through for us?"

"That was in the past, Miriam," Father said.

"Well, the present is no different. If we don't take care of our own, who will?" Mother asked.

"Ah Loy, when your father left China and came to Brunei, don't you think he was deserving of refuge there?" Auntie Miriam asked. "Don't you think the law in Brunei was unjust and cruel? This is the same, isn't it?"

"It's not the same. My father was forced to leave to save his life."

"Alfred's life depends on staying, too."

"No, he chose to leave. He chose to thwart the law in China, as well as the law in Canada."

"Ah Loy, do you think I deserve to be a citizen of Canada?" Auntie Miriam asked.

"Of course. You were born here," Father replied.

"Would your opinion change if you knew my mother was only able to come to Canada using another Canadian woman's birth certificate? That I was only born here because my mother took this risk to get here?" Auntie Miriam asked.

Father was silent for some time. "What your mother did wasn't right, but I understand why she did it."

"Miriam is helping family. I don't understand why you can't see that," Mother said.

"Yes, yes, Miriam is helping family. But that doesn't obligate us—obligate Canada—to allow Alfred to cut in line. I waited patiently while my application was processed at the High Commission."

"You're different. You weren't waiting to see if someone would take your life," Mother said.

"Swee Hua, how can you say that? My life was in limbo every day I was living in Brunei. At any time, someone could decide to kick me out, to take everything away from me. My life was not as secure as you make it out to be."

"Ah Loy, we're not talking about you here," Auntie Miriam said. "I understand why you're skeptical. I was too when I first met Alfred. But he is genuinely in danger. My brother-in-law translated his writing for me. He did not ask for this. We take for granted that we can say and write anything we want in Canada. Alfred naively thought he had the same freedoms."

"Instead of criticizing, maybe you should talk to him," Mother suggested. She touched Alfred's arm and spoke to him in Mandarin.

"Swee Hua, what are you doing? Please stop," Father said. "I'm not here to interrogate him. I'm entitled to my opinion. Of course, your relative is welcome in my home, Miriam, but that doesn't mean I have to agree with how he's trying to cut corners with our system." Father got up from the kitchen table and went outside to smoke.

Alfred asked Mother if he had offended Father. She said that he only reminded Father of back home.

Alfred was planted at Woo's Confectionery while he was in Sparwood. He worked behind the counter, and when it wasn't busy, he drew. Sometimes when Mother was visiting Auntie Miriam, we sat and watched Alfred as he marked the paper with determined strokes of his pen in all directions, forming blocks of artwork on the page. Alfred's English was rudimentary, so he used hand gestures and charades to communicate with us. He seemed like a big kid dressed up as a visiting uncle. Like my po po when she came to visit, he wasn't afraid to talk to us even though we didn't share the same language.

Alfred invited Bea and me to paint on our own pieces of paper. He took our hands to show us how to make a stroke. The motions were deliberate, with set rules. Up to down, left to right, lifting the pen at the right moments. We learned simple characters at first: kǒu and rén. Alfred also showed us that we could use our bodies to make characters. Standing tall with our legs wide and arms out to the side, we were dà, or big. We laughed in delight and urged Alfred to show us more.

Alfred knew how to make us look at something differently. He drew elaborate pictures and pointed out things in his intricate drawings that were subtle but hilarious. My favourite was when he transformed a drawing of a horse into the character for horse, or mǎ. Sometimes when Alfred retreated to his own work, I would see the spark leave his eyes and the smile disappear from his face. Suddenly, he would become older. Like Mother, he could wear many faces.

When Auntie Miriam and Mother descended from the upstairs apartment, Mother was both pleased and ashamed when she saw our work. We didn't understand the conversation, but Mother appeared to be making excuses and apologies for why we didn't understand Alfred's language and why our calligraphy was so juvenile.

Mother had lengthy, hard-to-follow conversations with Alfred that she would translate only intermittently. Sometimes, they talked like old friends, laughing, patting each other's knees, and finishing each other's sentences. In more sombre moments, I saw them embrace, hold hands, or just sit silently, leaning into one another. Mother was so engrossed in Alfred's tales of life in China that she sometimes forgot that Bea and I also wanted to hear his stories. I softly touched her hand to remind her not only to translate but also that we were there, watching.

Alfred once told us that the lantern festival had just passed, and he was sad to be away from his family during the celebration. He told us about the flavour of the sweet buns filling their mouths as they lit and released lanterns into the night sky towards the first full moon after the Lunar New Year glowing upon the river in his village. Mother translated that all of his cousins and his two brothers did not live in the village anymore. They worked in the cities and only saw each other at the new year that everyone returned home for a reunion dinner. Alfred said that his oldest brother always brought a box of kites for the village children to fly. The sky would be dancing with colours. He loved the affectionate protests of mothers in the village that their grown children were too skinny and worked too hard. And he loved hearing women shout across the lanes to inform everyone that someone was home. At night, Alfred and his brothers and cousins would set off fireworks on the rooftops. Each household would try to last the longest, saving their largest explosions for last. Once the fireworks were spent, music would stream into the streets and people would come out to dance, even in the cold. Neighbourhood quarrels were set aside, and riches were shared. Then the men would sneak away and don their lion costumes and prance among the crowd, slithering in and out of each home, spreading good luck and prosperity for the upcoming year.

Alfred's eyes welled with sadness because this was the first year he'd missed the celebration. He worried he might never experience another Lunar New Year with his family. He lamented that there was no end to his journey, no certainty of where he would go, except that he knew he could never go home again.

This brought tears to Mother's eyes. She turned to me and said, "I used to love making paper lanterns with my family and setting them free in the starlit sky. I should have gone home more often, to pay respect to my elders. All those years lost being here."

"We can celebrate here, Mom," I offered.

"I want to make lanterns," Bea agreed.

"It's not the same," Mother said, brushing us off. She turned to Alfred and spoke to him in Mandarin. They embraced, their tears braided in a grief and longing unknown to me.

Table

BEA AND I JOINED MOTHER, AUNTIE MIRIAM, AND ALFRED for the trip to Calgary for his refugee hearing. We had to leave before dawn to reach downtown in time.

Alfred's lawyer, Elaine Wong, met us pulling a large suitcase behind her. She wore some blush on her cheeks and a suit with a blazer that gave her shoulders some height. Mother told us to address her as "Ms Wong." Bea and I were not to fidget, talk, or do anything disrespectful.

Ms Wong spoke Cantonese and some Mandarin, so she welcomed another Mandarin speaker in Mother to ensure that the translation at the hearing would be accurate. In the waiting room, she asked Mother to translate: "Alfred, you made your claim at a lucky time. The Supreme Court of Canada ruled that all persons claiming refugee protection are entitled to a hearing, and the government created the Immigration and Refugee Board. The Supreme Court brought some justice to the refugee system by obligating the government to hear directly from all refugee claimants in their own words. It is so new that this is only the second time I have appeared here as a lawyer."

"This is only your second time?" Auntie Miriam asked.

"Yes, but I've been doing immigration cases for five years now. This is new for everyone—the lawyers and the government. We're all in the same boat. Before, you had to write everything on paper and applications. Now, everyone will have a chance to speak before the board, including Alfred. Nothing is more powerful than the testimony of fear from someone who lives it. To have the opportunity to air one's grievance is rare, especially when it could lead to a positive outcome. This is a good thing, and we will make the most of it."

"So, this is a court process? We're going to be in front of a judge?" asked Auntie Miriam.

"It's technically not a courtroom, but it's similar. The hearing is less formal, and there are fewer rules. We will appear in front of board members, not judges. It's a bit like a serious conversation over a large table. Don't worry. Alfred's story is very compelling, and I believe if they hear his words, he has a better chance than if they simply read them on paper."

I was deeply impressed by Ms Wong. Here was a Chinese Canadian woman speaking with authority and confidently guiding Alfred in what sounded like a complicated process. Like Auntie Miriam, she spoke perfect English with no accent. I was in awe of her.

A security guard approached and directed us to enter the hearing room. It had four long tables positioned to make a square. The security guard told everyone where to sit. "He's just like Uncle Joe, telling his friends where to sit at a mah-jong table," Mother whispered to Auntie Miriam. Auntie Miriam giggled. The guard pointed at the north end of the table, where the people who held Alfred's fate in their hands would sit. Ms Wong was sitting on the east side, a representative of the Immigration Minister was sitting on the west, and Alfred was sitting to the south. Ms Wong spread her papers around her. Alfred mentioned to Mother that he felt too far away from his lawyer. Ms. Wong overheard and said that she was close enough to intervene if necessary.

The guard told the rest of us to sit in the chairs lining the wall behind Alfred and instructed us to stand when the board members entered the room. We were joined by an elderly woman who introduced herself as Gwen. She would interpret the proceedings and sat in the chair next to Alfred.

The security guard left the room and the door at the opposite end opened. A hush came over the room, and three people entered. The first was a large man, balding and sweating. The second was a tanned man with large spectacles who towered over the other two. The third was a woman with curly brown hair and stunning blue eyes. They were all dressed in suits and had large bundles of paper with them. Mother, Auntie Miriam, and Alfred looked fearful but obedient, like they had been summoned to the principal's office.

The questions at first were mundane. Alfred had to relay his name, where he was from, how he came to Canada, and where he stayed in Canada. Bea was bored and started reading a book next to me. It seemed to me that the adults in the room were asking very mundane questions that had nothing to do with why Alfred wanted to stay in Canada. Finally, things got interesting, and we started to hear things about Alfred that I had never heard before.

I learned that Alfred was a university professor in Chinese literature who also wrote fiction. He was married, but his wife died in a car accident. It was difficult to follow. The long staccato pauses for interpretation interrupted not only the flow of the story but also any personal touch that Alfred wanted to provide. I was surprised at how cold the three board members were, unaffected by Alfred's life. They reminded me of the robotic windmills I had seen near Lethbridge in the summer: large, imposing figures at one end of the room, blinking, breathing but doing nothing else. They waited silently as Alfred stopped talking to blow his nose and dab his eyes. He put his face in his hands and trembled. Even Gwen didn't know what to do. I could hear her whisper to Alfred but didn't understand what she said. I wanted so badly to go to him, to hug him. Mother and Auntie Miriam were holding hands, clutching each other tightly. Mother gave me a stern look to keep quiet and stay still.

Ms Wong started to move towards Alfred, but the large bald man put his hand up. "Mr Wang, please tell us why you are afraid to go back to China," he asked.

Alfred spoke a few sentences, and then a board member interrupted him so that Gwen could translate. "I am a wanted man. I will be imprisoned, tortured, and maybe killed if I return. Because of my writings, because of my thoughts. They're looking for me, and there is no place to hide."

I sat upright in my seat at these brutal words. When Auntie Miriam and Mother had talked about Alfred not being safe in China, I hadn't realized this was what they meant. An intense fear grew in me for Alfred.

Mother whispered to Ms Wong that Gwen was not interpreting Alfred's story accurately, but the board members did not care or do anything about it when Ms Wong told them. Mother's face crumpled when the woman board member with curly hair said that Alfred wasn't a journalist, that he was just making up stories, and belittled him for making his writing seem more important than it was. Mother shifted in her chair when the board member with glasses accused Alfred of unwisely writing material that he knew would displease the Chinese government and concocting his story when he saw what Canada had to offer. She held her face in her hands when none of the board members looked Alfred in the eye as he recalled how he was being followed, how he received warnings from a publisher.

It was Ms Wong's turn. She asked how Alfred knew he would be mistreated by the Chinese government. Alfred recounted stories he'd heard from friends and colleagues about people who were arrested, detained, and had disappeared because of their writing.

"Why do you think these stories are real?" Ms Wong asked.

"Chinese culture has been dying for some time now. In my opinion, the Chinese government is not interested in preserving the great things we have accomplished or creating a thriving environment for cultural thought and growth. Everyone fears the government, and this has affected how people work, act, and feel. New generations of Chinese people are without cultural education and only care about status and money. Chinese people are stuck in the days of the emperor, where one person ruled, except now it is a group of people. They still think they are great, when all they are interested in is conquering those around them who they think are barbaric. Really, they are the barbaric, hateful people. I don't want to be associated with them, and I will devote my life to becoming anything but Chinese."

Mother let go of Auntie Miriam's hands and folded her arms across her chest. Her lips were pursed so tight they disappeared, and her eyebrows were furrowed. I, too, was shocked by Alfred's words.

Ms Wong then provided a closing argument. She spoke with confidence and authority, holding her ground when she was questioned. I was hypnotized.

After the hearing, Ms Wong said, "Alfred, you did well. It's out of our hands now. I hope you all can enjoy the rest of the afternoon." She gave him a hug before she left.

Auntie Miriam hugged Alfred warmly, but Mother stood by barely acknowledging him. When he went to the washroom, Auntie Miriam said, "What's the matter, Swee Hua? You didn't say anything to Alfred."

"Honestly, Miriam, I can't look at him anymore. I can't believe he would say such horrible things just so he can stay in Canada."

"What are you talking about?"

"Did you hear how he talked about Chinese people?"

"Pfft. Swee Hua, you shouldn't take it so personally."

"How can I not take it personally? *You* should take it personally! He insulted all of us. He gave those ang mo lang more reasons to look at us like barbarians, like people with no capacity for reason or love. He betrayed us!"

"You're really being too dramatic, Swee Hua. He had to say something to convince those people that he needs to stay."

"Did he? Did he need to disown his own kind, his own people, himself? There is no honour in that. He went too far."

Alfred did not have to wait long. Less than two weeks later, Auntie Miriam asked Mother to translate the decision, which flowed over two pages.

> *The claimant, Wei Wang, is a twenty-six-year-old Chinese national who claims refugee protection on the basis that the People's Republic of China, as the agent of persecution, will punish him for his political opinion as expressed through his alleged writings of two novellas.*
>
> *We agree that Mr Wang's situation does not reach the threshold necessary for refugee protection. First, it is not clear that Mr Wang is the author of the writings provided. Mr Wang confirmed that none of the writings he shared had his name on them. Second, Mr Wang confirmed that the writings are fiction, and that they do not directly incite or call for political action on the part of readers. News articles provided by Mr Wang's counsel discussing political dissidents convicted of inciting subversion and receiving prison sentences illustrate very different circumstances. The persons in those news stories were openly and clearly organizing protests and other acts of resistance against the Chinese government.*
>
> *Finally, the panel believes that Mr Wang was seduced by Canada, having come as a visitor. While it is true that refugee claimants may become refugees after they leave their country of origin, in this case, Mr Wang's delay in making a claim speaks to the lack of credibility of his fear and also lends credibility to his admission that he has come to love Canada and therefore desires to stay in Canada.*

As Mother read the letter, Alfred looked as if a ghost had entered his body. Hopeful anticipation drained from his face, and he shrank into a pale, empty vessel. Bea and I couldn't fight back our tears. Auntie Miriam looked outraged.

I didn't understand. I was sure, after watching the hearing, that Alfred had won. I was convinced by Ms Wong's performance. I could only conclude that no matter how polished Ms Wong was, how much she sounded like the ang mo lang, or how many pieces of paper she flashed in front of them, they would never see her, or Alfred, as one of them. The three short paragraphs of the decision made me question Father's reverence for this orderly country. Looking at Alfred's devastated face, I didn't feel like the laws were working. I didn't feel like the rules were fair. I didn't feel like everyone had the same chance.

Weeks later, when Ms. Wong confirmed that an appeal to the federal court was dismissed, Auntie Miriam came over to discuss with Mother how Alfred could obtain sanctuary in Canada.

Alfred sat sullenly at one end of our kitchen table, with Mother and Auntie Miriam at the other. Bea and I sat on either side of Alfred, snacking on some cookies Mother had made that day.

"Swee Hua, please," Auntie Miriam begged. "Alfred is virtually stateless, like Ah Loy was. I can't do this without you. I need someone who can speak the language. I need someone we can trust, who won't run and gossip with everyone about this."

"You're asking a lot of me. You're asking me to help you and Alfred break the law. Isn't that what got him into trouble in the first place?" Mother argued.

"He didn't set out to break the law in China. Besides, you agreed that he would be treated unfairly in China, that the laws there are wrong."

"Yes, but why should I help someone who can't even stand Chinese people?"

"Swee Hua, that is ridiculous. Alfred loves China and Chinese people. What you heard in the hearing was just an expression of his political viewpoint. Why do you think Alfred writes what he does? In the hope that people back in China will listen and change their ways."

"That is not what he said."

"Listen, wouldn't you say anything to save your life. Why are you abandoning your friend now?"

Alfred finally spoke up, and Mother shot short phrases at him in Mandarin, slammed her hand onto the table, and then collapsed into a chair. Alfred replied, his voice choked, tears streaming down his face. Shouts and pleas went back and forth for a few minutes.

"Swee Hua, please. What is going on?" asked Auntie Miriam.

"Let me think about it, Miriam, okay? I have heard his explanation. Give me a few days," Mother finally said.

A few days later, Mother shared a piece of nian gao that she'd made and began to tell me about Alfred. "I'd forgotten about these until Alfred told me he had a craving. They remind me of my childhood, and I want you to know the taste, too." The dense cake was moist, warm, and sweet.

"I couldn't stand to listen to Alfred talk about us that way. I know he wasn't talking about me, but we're all Chinese. If he talks like that, others will, too. We are not what he says, Lily."

My mouth was full of nian gao, so I just looked at her, the warmth of the pastry comforting me as Mother's unease ran up my back like a shiver.

"But I don't think I could live with myself if I didn't help. What will happen to him? He is still one of our own."

Mother took a sip of her coffee. "Miriam is right. Alfred was desperate at the time. He seems remorseful. He told me he didn't plan to say those things, that it just came out. I should forgive him, right?" Mother didn't wait for me to respond and picked up the phone to call Auntie Miriam.

Despite Father's objections, Mother translated for Auntie Miriam as they sent Alfred into hiding. It was like Alfred had entered an afterlife, and my mother was Meng Po, the lady of forgetfulness, whose task is to make sure that the souls who are ready for reincarnation do not remember their previous lives or they'll stay in hell. She was leading Alfred to the underworld, readying his soul for rebirth.

Alfred left my life as swiftly as he'd entered it. Like a joyful dream, or like a tornado that whirled into town leaving widespread damage behind. We never mentioned Alfred's name again, partly to protect him, but also because it was too painful.

Bitter

THE PHONE RANG WHILE FATHER WAS SLEEPING after finishing a night shift. I heard him get up from his nap and swear before he answered. Mother had forgotten to switch the ringer off before leaving with Bea to get some groceries. I was left at home, sick with a fever. The tone of Father's voice changed from loud irritation to quiet concern as he listened to the person on the phone. I could only hear muffled Hokkien. He hung up and didn't go back to bed. From the number of cigarettes that flowed through his hands, I could tell it was bad news. Still, he didn't say anything as he helped Mother put the groceries away. I promptly forgot about the call when Bea gave me some sour keys she'd brought from the store.

A month later, Bea and I were doing homework when the phone rang. Mother picked it up and spoke in her loud overseas-call voice in Hokkien she used when she was talking to someone in Brunei. She repeated something over and over, and then she started to yell, cry, and stomp her feet. After several minutes, she slammed the phone down and collapsed onto the floor. Father came home at that moment, and when Mother looked up, she had hatred for him in her eyes.

"Chee hong gia, bastard! Lu chao kang, nasty man!" she shouted.

He stood at the door, frozen like the icicles forming on the eaves-trough. Mother rose, grabbed her tea mug, and threw it, tea and all, at Father. He ducked and the mug hit the front door, leaving a dark liquid and ceramic mess behind him.

"E see liao, she died!"

Father did not look surprised. He bent down to gently put his metal lunch box on the ground and slowly rose, showing his hands as if he were a hostage negotiator. Bea and I were paralyzed. We didn't know whether we should comfort Mother, or if she would lash out at us, too. Father moved carefully towards Mother in the kitchen.

She held her palm up. "Mai chin chiah kin! Don't come closer!"

Father obeyed. "She was already gone when they called," he whispered.

"She was not!"

"Her brain was not functioning. There was nothing you could do."

"She was alive."

"Not in the way you want her to be."

"I could have gone to say goodbye.".

"She would not have heard you."

"How do you know?"

"It would not have changed anything."

"Not for you, but maybe for me. Maybe she could have heard me one last time. Now I will never have that chance. Now I will never know. You are so selfish. You didn't want me to go back. Why? She is my mother."

"She was already gone. You are a mother, and you are needed here."

"Were you so afraid that if I went, I would not come back?"

Father said nothing.

Mother spit in his face and retreated to her bedroom. We didn't see her for the rest of the day.

Father suggested that Mother go back for the funeral, but it was too late. A cold war descended in our home and communication between my parents became minimal. Mother was far away, always staring off into the distance. She took less care to comb her hair or change out of her pyjamas. Sometimes it would take a few tries before Mother responded to my calls for her.

It was an unusually wet spring, depressing and grey. When Father was out of the house, Bea and I could hear Mother crying in her room.

One day, Bea and I found her outside, lying in the flower bed in the backyard, singing in Chinese. Mud surrounded her and blooming pink poppies drooped next to her, resting their heads on her shoulder. There was a snail on her neck. Bea picked it up and threw it far away into the grass.

Bea and I looked at each other. I knew that my sister was viewing something she shouldn't see. I saw her lip quiver as she tried not to cry.

"We need to get Mom inside," I told Bea. She nodded. We tried to drag her, but she was too heavy.

"Mom!" Bea sobbed. She could not hold in her tears anymore. I wanted to pull her away from Mother and tell her to go inside, but I knew I couldn't do this alone.

"Mom, please," I pleaded. "It's raining. It's cold. Come inside. Bea is going to get sick."

Mother just kept singing her off-key Chinese song.

"Mom! Get up!" I yelled. "You need to come inside. We can't carry you!"

Mother's song came to an end, and that seemed to break her trance. She slowly looked around and noticed we were on the ground with her, soaking wet. She hugged us clumsily. The daisies underneath her lay flattened in the grass, their white and yellow petals crushed into the ground. Mother placed her hand in a shallow puddle and her jade bracelet clanged against the interlocking brick pathway. Rising out of the flower bed, she stood and asked why we were outside. It was as if she hadn't heard our cries before. Bea's tears were invisible as the rain soaked her face. Mother walked towards the house, oblivious to our distress. We splashed through the backyard and followed her inside. She took a shower and went to bed, leaving us alone.

I dragged Bea into the laundry room, where she just looked at me limply. I told her to take off her wet clothing, and then dumped them into the washing machine with my own. We took a bath, and I tried to lighten the mood by bringing out the bubble bath like we were little kids again, but Bea started to sob as the hot water gushed from the tap. I wiped her down gently with a washcloth, lifting her arms to wash them, and then touching the cloth to her face, wiping her tears away. I washed her hair, and then used the plastic bowl in the tub to wash the suds away. She sat in the water while I did the same for myself. After I dried myself and put my pyjamas on, I helped Bea out of the tub, dried her, and dressed her. She looked at me blankly and did whatever I told her to do. I was afraid that if I stopped moving, the image of Mother lying down in the garden would come back to me and I would start to cry. I blow-dried Bea's hair and then my own. When I was finished, Bea looked at me and said, "I'm hungry." I took her by the hand, and we went downstairs.

Bea and I made mee goreng, adding what we found in the fridge: lap cheong, bok choy, eggs. Bea sliced the lap cheong, while I washed the bok choy. She watched me crack the eggs into a pot to poach where our noodles would soften. We were surprised by how good our concoction tasted. After our meal, we cleaned up the kitchen, and then kept cleaning. Ashtrays were everywhere. After we dumped the ashes in the garbage, we washed them all and left them to dry. Finally, I grabbed a few *Archie* comics and took Bea into bed with me. We sat shoulder to shoulder as we read.

Later that night, we woke to Mother crying again. We crawled out of our bed towards her bedroom. Through the crack of her door, we saw her sitting on the edge of her bed. Tears were streaming down her face. She let them slide down over her chin and onto her neck. Bea wanted to go in and hug her, but I stopped her. The sight of Mother's sorrow and loneliness pushed me away from the door, and I brought Bea downstairs, as far away as possible from Mother's sobbing. I sat Bea at the kitchen table again, poured two glasses of milk and brought out cookies we had baked with Mother a few days before. We sat side by side in front of the bay window, watching the rain get heavier, letting the rhythm of the pelting droplets drown out our Mother's grief.

The next morning, Bea and I were groggy from a night of restless sleep. Like Mother, we drifted around the house in a daze. The tension and the mourning made the air thin, and Bea and I wanted to escape, opening the door to gasp for breath. Hilary's home became our refuge in the days that followed.

One night, Mother asked how dinner was at Hilary's and I told Mother that I liked her cooking better. She smiled and hugged me tightly. After Bea went to bed, Mother let me stay up with her to watch a movie on TV. It was rare for me to be alone with her.

"You are a good jie jie," she said. "Remember to always take care of your sister. I am so proud of how much you have grown and how responsible you are. Always listen to your father and your aunties and uncles, even if they ask you to do difficult things. It's always good to respect your elders. And as you get older, you will need to take care of them, too. It's hard to be a jie jie, but I know you can do it, Lily. You are such a smart and good girl."

I wanted nothing more than for Mother to praise me and to love me. I hugged her, and she held me tight, stroking my hair. I let her embrace me, hoping that I would be enough for her to become herself again.

Eventually, I couldn't keep my eyes open any longer. It was late, and I felt safe, snuggled next to my mother. The last thing I remember was Mother smelling my hair at the top of my head and rubbing her ankle.

Bea and I came home from school just as a storm had rolled in. The thunder was fierce, and lightning hit a tree at the end of the block as we disembarked from the bus. We watched aghast as a flash of light pierced the sky, and the body of the tree split in two. Bea started to cry, and we ran all the way home.

When we got there, Mother wasn't home. Bea and I watched television, built a fort with our blankets from our bed, and brought our flashlights into our cave to read stories to one another. When our stomachs rumbled, we went to the kitchen and found piles of baked goods on the counter. We were snacking on muffins when Father came home after a twelve-hour shift. He placed his metal lunch box on the counter next to all the baking and tore off his baseball cap.

"Where's your mother?" he asked.

"We don't know," Bea said. "She wasn't home when we got here."

Father looked perplexed. "You've been home for five hours and you don't know where Mom is?"

He went upstairs and jumped into the shower. When he emerged, I felt a sudden coolness in the air. Bea and I stayed in the living room playing with some old sock puppets, trying to ignore the stillness around us. We heard cupboards and drawers being opened and closed, things being thrown about, and the stomping of Father's heavy feet. I heard him pick up the phone and call Auntie Choo Neo. He was yelling frantically into the phone in Hakka. He put the phone down, and then everything was silent for a long time.

Eventually, Father started crying upstairs. Then, his sobs turned into pained moans. I held back my tears, knowing that Bea was watching me. We held each other tight and didn't move.

I knew Mother was gone.

鬼
Ghost

AUNTIE CHOO NEO TOOK OVER THE HOUSE WITH PLEASURE. She rearranged things in the kitchen, and when Bea and I protested that Mother had put something in its place for a reason, she would snap, "Well, she's not here anymore, is she?"

Auntie fixated on the banana tree in our kitchen. It had always held a prominent place in our bay window because Mother had said it reminded her of home. For days, Auntie kept muttering about how she needed to move it out of the house. When Uncle Stephen came by she demanded he get rid of the plant immediately. "We can't leave that gui kia de he le chiu, that ghost in the tree, here. Boing he le lah sap, throw that dirty thing away!" she ordered.

"Choo Neo, you are being ridiculous," Uncle Stephen grunted as he lifted the plant. "You need to help me."

"I'm not touching that lah sup tang, garbage can. We don't need to see her anymore, and taking that tree out will guarantee it."

"Those old ghost stories are making you paranoid."

"I'm not paranoid, lah. I've told you time and again that she was Pontianak." I knew Auntie meant the ghost in Malaysian folklore who is believed to be the spirit of women who died while pregnant or in childbirth. She believed that Pontianak lived in banana trees during the day and roamed around at night.

Auntie Choo Neo continued complaining about Mother. "Her hair was too perfect, and she always looked too sweetly at my brother. When she lost my brother's only son, I know she died. You were not there, Stephen. I saw the blood drain from her face. We've been living with a ghost all this time, and now she has gone back to where she belongs. I've been telling Ah Loy that he is much better off without her. Our only worry is whether the girls are of this world or not."

Uncle Stephen tilted his head towards Bea and me where we sat at the kitchen table. Auntie Choo Neo hadn't even noticed we were there. She smacked Uncle Stephen over the head and whispered in her loud way, "Aya! You knew all this time and you didn't say anything? Kah kin, hurry up and get this out of the house."

"Mom is not a ghost!" Bea shouted.

Uncle Stephen fumbled out of the kitchen with the banana tree.

"Aya, I was just talking, Bea. Sit down and eat," Auntie Choo Neo replied.

"She is coming back. You better put that plant back where it belongs." Bea ran to stop Uncle Stephen. He placed the heavy pot in the foyer, just at the threshold of the front door. Auntie Choo Neo went to take Bea's hand, but she ripped it away out of Auntie's grasp.

"Put it back!" Bea yelled.

Auntie Choo Neo slapped Bea in the face, and then pulled her into her chest. Auntie's voice was firm. "Listen, Bea. Your Mother is not coming back. Do you see any of her clothes left? Her jewellery? Her precious belongings? She took everything. She is not on vacation. She is not coming back. The sooner you understand, the better for all of us. She left. I am here now. Show me some respect. No one else is feeding you dinner tonight. Only me. Do you see her here? What kind of mother is she to leave you here?"

Bea started to cry and ran over to me. I put my arm around her and started to cry, too. We didn't finish our dinner, and Auntie Choo Neo didn't say anything more to us that day. That was the last time I heard Bea defend our mother. It was as if Auntie Choo Neo's words had permanently pierced her heart.

Weeks went by and there was no sign or word from Mother. Father never talked about her, acting as if she'd never existed. She became a ghost to us.

Even though she was gone, I saw her everywhere. When I tried to rip a sheet of plastic wrap, I was reminded of Mother's swift hand, jerking the translucent sheet against the perforated edge and snapping it into place over a bowl, leaving no wrinkles or waves, just the reflection of a glasslike surface. The twisting, tangling, and knotting of the plastic in my hands reduced me to tears.

The macramé that held her plants, the crocheted tablecloths, her apron, the wok on the stove, the laundry piling up, her tennis racquet, the dress Po Po gave her. One day, I saw the bandages she had habitually wrapped around her ankle lying on the floor in my parents' bedroom. She had shed them like a skin she didn't need anymore.

I should have studied harder in school, should've been kinder to my sister, should've cooked the rice before Mother asked me, should've been quieter when Father was sleeping. We all gave her so many reasons to leave. As the weeks passed, I blamed everyone and held my resentment tightly in my chest.

At the end of August 1988, mere months after the strike ended, layoffs were announced and hundreds of employees were let go. Weeks later, the mine was shut down. Disappointment draped over the town more heavily as news of lost pensions, built over many years by labouring men, sank into the abyss the mine left behind.

An exodus from Sparwood ensued. Block after block, for-sale signs dotted the landscape like candidate signs during an election.

Father resisted leaving as long as he could. I think he hoped that Mother would return, and he worried leaving would make it hard for her to find us. Over time, his hope folded like an umbrella. More than that, I think Father wanted to prove Mother wrong. He wanted to show that we could stay, thrive, and build a permanent life in Sparwood.

I was sitting at the kitchen table when Auntie Choo Neo told Father, "Swee Hua is not coming back, and you need to accept that. It's time to leave, Ah Loy. Let the girls begin a new school year in a new school. Don't wait until it's too late to leave."

Long after Uncle Ming, Uncle Roy, Uncle Paul, Uncle Sam, and even Auntie Choo Neo left, Father held out. It was only after confirmation that Father had lost his pension from twelve years of work in the mine that we joined everyone in Calgary. Uncle Stephen had found work at a construction company and asked his boss if he would hire his brother-in-law. Father reluctantly agreed to take the job. We sold our house for a pittance, left the mountains, and came with a few belongings to the grassy foothills of a large city.

On moving day, I teared up looking at the empty house. The cavernous rooms seemed larger, and my memories of our home were already beginning to fade. I saw Mother sitting on the couch, stroking her ankle. I smelled her cooking and heard her jade bracelet clanging against the countertop. I sat in the foyer and cried. Bea sat next to me, clutching her stuffed tiger, and cried, too. When Father came to fetch us, he didn't say anything but took our hands and led us one by one into the van, holding back his own tears.

Watching the town get smaller behind me in the rear window of the van, I said goodbye to the Ktunaxa Nation. I thanked the town for its hospitality and pledged to remember my time there as a guest. Driving through the ghost town of Michel, I wondered if Sparwood would survive. The Michel Hotel, a pink colonial building, fading in the dust, was the only reminder to those passing by that there was ever life there.

When we left Sparwood, we left much more than our house, furniture, and unwanted belongings behind. The valley consumed my mother tongue, and I started to let myself forget Mother, too.

Part 2

現在
Now

子
Child

SHE CAME WITH THE NORTH WIND, during the change of seasons. It was the last day of summer. Long after the sun had set and the moon rose, my contractions began. They were short, pinching pains in my abdomen that paused for several minutes. I thought I could sleep through them, but just as my head relaxed on the pillow, they thundered through my belly, and I found myself wide awake, clutching the side of the bed. I crept out of the room, leaving John snoring on his pillow.

My daughter was coming early. I wasn't ready. My sister wasn't planning on driving from Montreal for another week. I hadn't yet finished writing memos on the immigration cases I was transferring to the lawyer who was taking over my practice during my maternity leave.

By the time John's alarm clock woke him up, the contractions were less than a minute apart, so we headed to the hospital. As another contraction swept over me, I waved away the lecture John gave me for not waking him sooner.

When we arrived, John told the nurse, "She wants an epidural."

"Honey, you're quite far along now," the nurse said, after examining me. "I don't know if we can give you an epidural."

"If I'm not fully dilated, I want an epidural," I insisted.

The nurse looked at me, and then at John, whose eyes were pleading. "Okay, I'll get the anesthesiologist."

A young man who looked like he was no more than eighteen years old came into the room. "Are you ready?" he asked.

The contractions were so painful that I didn't care who adminis-tered the epidural. I nodded and he instructed me to lean forward and stay still. He directed John to hold me in place. As I leaned forward, the pendant on my necklace swung in front of my face. Auntie Choo Neo had given it to me last week. It was a jade image of Guan Yin, the goddess of compassion and mercy revered for being a bringer of children. I had grabbed the necklace out of her hands and told her I would put it on later, but she insisted I wear it immediately.

"Aya! I put it on for you," she said. "No argument, okay? How are you going to put this on yourself? Look at this small clasp. I will do it."

I didn't have the heart to tell my aunt no. She was already wrap-ping the gold chain around my neck as she brushed my hair out of the way.

Somehow, I had forgotten I was wearing it. In fact, bent over as the needle slid into my back, looking at Guan Yin, I was certain I had taken her off. I tucked her inside my hospital gown while asking her forgiveness for hiding her away.

Thirty-six hours and two vacuum-suction attempts later, my daughter was delivered. The nurse brought her over and gently placed her on my chest. Silent tears streamed down my face. All my numb-ness and pain fell away like a leaf floating from a tree. A warmth came over me, and my body no longer shivered through the thin hospital gown. When the baby grabbed John's finger tightly for the first time, he looked at me with a large grin.

I gazed at my daughter, elated to meet her. She had a lot of hair for a baby. I couldn't help feeling disappointed at how dark it was, how broad and flat her nose, how she looked so much like me.

Four months after Mother left, I woke to wetness and saw blood on my sheets. I ran to the washroom and saw more blood on my under-wear. I started to cry and sat on the toilet for a long time, wishing for Mother.

Auntie Choo Neo came to the bathroom door and asked if I was inside. She practically lived at our house with Mother gone. I didn't answer, hoping she would go away. She knocked on the door and told me to open it. I opened the door slightly. She handed me a clean pair of underwear, a box of sanitary napkins, and some newspaper. She told me to put on my underwear with the napkin on the bottom and wrap the soiled pair in newspaper before putting the whole package in the garbage.

"Don't use toilet paper to wrap it, lah! Use the newspaper! We are not rich here, remember. We only use toilet paper for ourselves, okay?" She closed the door and left.

I spent the next few days avoiding Father and Bea. I didn't want them to know what had happened. I hid in my room reading, and when Bea tried to cajole me into playing, I snapped at her. She cried and ran away.

My first period was heavy, and the cramps were unrelenting. I was lying on the living room floor in front of the TV before dinner when Auntie Choo Neo yelled at me to get up and set the table. Seeing my discomfort, Bea said, "Auntie, I think Lily is really sick."

"She's not sick! Being a woman is not easy," Auntie Choo Neo informed us both. "Get up!" she shouted as she nudged me with her foot. "The table will not set itself."

On the fourth day of my period, Father implored me to get changed, as we were going to Uncle Paul and Auntie Betty's goodbye dinner. Father had become even less social without Mother, but our friends were leaving Sparwood. Uncle Paul had been laid off, and they were moving to stay with family in Kelowna. I pleaded with Father to let me stay home, telling him I was sick. But he gave me one stern look and I knew it was non-negotiable. "Becoming a woman means taking on more responsibilities," he said.

I was horrified. Auntie Choo Neo had told him. I wanted to wash the blood away and everything that came with it. I felt like I was an exposed open wound, and Mother should have been there to take care of me.

At the Oriental Palace that night, the mood was sombre. The chatter at the large round tables was subdued when Auntie Choo Neo announced to everyone, "Lily has started menstruating!"

I stood there, dumbfounded. Rage started to climb from the floor up through my body. Auntie, who was so careful to prevent me from hearing any talk about Mother, was now broadcasting the most humiliating news all over the community. I was angry at all my aunties, who revelled in this new gossip, who had abandoned Mother. I wanted to yell, "I'm a woman now! Tell me everything! Tell me the truth! I know you have so much to say about Mother."

But they didn't know where Mother went either. If they did, I would have heard already. That's why her disappearance seemed not only drastic but permanent. She deliberately cut herself off completely from her family, her friends, from everything in Sparwood, so we couldn't find her.

Auntie Choo Neo's declaration enlivened the conversation among the women. They started talking about their own first periods, laughing uproariously. Hilary looked at me in amazement. Bea asked Carmen what a period was, and Carmen only snickered. Worst of all, the boys started whispering and laughing, taking turns throughout the evening trying to touch my back to see if I was wearing a training bra. I hid in a corner with my back to the wall. Hilary and the other girls kept playing and ignored my sulking. I felt like they were avoiding me, afraid they would catch their period, too.

If Mother were there, she might have brought me to her side while she played mah-jong. Or she might have been onstage, singing vibrantly. But she was not there. Looking at the stage cluttered with boxes of empty takeout containers, I started to let go of her, shedding her like my body was shedding a moon's cycle for the first time.

Bea arrived at the hospital a few hours after I gave birth. She rushed in, sweeping aside the curtain dividing the room, and bellowed, "Surprise!"

A woman on the other side of the curtain muttered, "Shit. Seriously?"

"You're here," I said, slowly pulling myself up to a seated position. I was urgently reminded of the throbbing pain in my pelvic region and winced. After just having fallen asleep, the jolt of my sister's entrance felt like being startled awake to an emergency. Coming down from the shock, my body felt heavier, clunkier, harder to move.

"You don't look happy that I'm here, Lily," Bea observed.

"Sorry if I'm not bouncing out of the bed to greet you," I snapped. "I just spent the last forty hours in labour and learning to feed a newborn."

"Speaking of which, where is the little bambino?"

We both turned to the recliner in the corner and saw John, groggily holding the baby. She was sleeping, undisturbed by her aunt's hurricane of an arrival. Bea took her niece in her arms and cooed at her.

"Have you named her?" Bea asked.

"No, we've been struggling with that," I confessed.

"Good! I have a few thoughts. And it would be good to keep the big reveal for the red egg and ginger party."

I laughed quietly, leaning back against my pillow. "Slow down, Auntie Bea. Who said anything about a red egg and ginger party?"

"Excuse me?" Bea was surprised. "We didn't have a baby shower, and I totally understood that. It's bad luck to celebrate before the baby arrives. But I think it would be good for this family to celebrate something for once now that she's here. And I want to show off my new niece."

"Listen, Bea. I don't think my friends would get it, you know? They've all pitched in to buy us a new stroller. And John's work colleagues sent over all of these great baby books. My colleagues also got us a gift certificate for this place that delivers great meals. We didn't need a shower, and we don't need a party. Everyone has been so generous already."

"What's there to get, Lily? People eat, they bring gifts or red packets, and we all hold the baby."

"I just would rather that we didn't."

"Why? You know that Auntie Miriam, Auntie Choo Neo, and all the other aunties have been waiting for this."

"Well, I'm not about to do something to please other people. It's not for me. It's so provincial and tacky, asking people to bring money in red envelopes."

"It's not tacky. It's tradition. It's part of our culture."

"Not mine. We're Canadian, Bea."

"What's that supposed to mean?" Bea handed the baby to me. "I'll leave you to it. I'm calling Dad." She parted the curtains and walked out.

Even though Bea had left, I felt like there was still a red egg in the room among the bouquets and cards. I didn't want it there, taunting me. I didn't want my daughter to be part of that peasant tradition.

鼎

Cauldron

WHEN I HAD ARRIVED AT THE HOSPITAL, the weather was still warm. Leaving, I felt the north wind nip at my bare toes in my flip-flops. John had brought my leg warmers and a coat, and the hospital had given our daughter a knitted hat for the walk to the car. I looked up and the full green canopy of summer had given way to crispy yellow, red, brown, and orange leaves. It was as if I had travelled through time. The fall season in the Sparwood mountains was muted, softer, and predominantly yellow. Even after the many years I had spent in Ontario, planting myself here after university, I was entranced by the way the trees looked. Enflamed.

At home, there were flowers, cards, and a dry warmth from the recently turned-on furnace. News of the birth had spread, but the house was quiet. Bea didn't know we had been discharged, because John wanted our homecoming to be our private family event. As a historian in Asian studies, she had decided to use her time here in Ottawa to visit the national archives to conduct some research and find a quiet place to polish a paper she was writing.

The rich, earthy scent of root vegetables simmering in chicken broth greeted me. John had made a pot of Ukrainian borscht.

"I ran into Borys. He brought this gift over. It's a mini vyshyvanka!" John said.

"It's adorable, though she won't be able to wear it for a couple of years."

"I know, but it's cute, isn't it?"

"It is," I confirmed, and took the fine white shirt in my hands to admire the red embroidery.

"You know, maybe we should get one of those cute cheongsams I saw in Chinatown for the baby? She can have her pick of outfits," John offered.

"Nah, she doesn't need anything like that," I said.

"Why? I want her to know she has two cultures."

"It's just that I think the cheongsams are tacky."

"Okay, well, I also saw that Chinatown Remixed is happening this weekend. You know, that local art festival I was telling you about? Maybe we should go?"

"She's a baby, John. She doesn't need to do things like that. Besides, I'm not really up for it. I'm just so tired, you know?"

"Borys also told me that next week the Orthodox Church is having a Ukrainian dinner and the choir is performing. I guess I should tell him we probably won't make it."

"Why? We never miss it."

"Yeah, but you just said you weren't up for going out."

"I'll be up for the dinner. I never miss a chance to eat varenyky." John and I laughed and hugged.

John went to the large pot on the stove, and I sat down at the table next to the bassinet where the baby was sleeping, looking at the flyer Borys must have given John. The savoury dumplings were what brought us together in university.

It was the fall of my second year in undergrad at the University of Calgary. The second week of school was clubs week, and I was meandering through the tables in MacEwan Hall promoting club after club when a pair of jovial guys shoved a small steaming plate in my face.

"Sour cream?" one offered.

"Uh, what is this?" I answered.

"Perogies!" the blond guy said enthusiastically.

"What?"

"You've never heard of perogies before?" the first guy said, incredulous.

"No, I—"

"Potato dumplings. Don't let this guy bother you. He's a bit of a jerk," the guy with dirty blond hair interjected. He motioned me to the other side of the table and scooped a spoonful of sour cream onto my plate.

"Try it," he suggested.

I cut off a corner of a pillowy dumpling with my fork, dipped it into the sour cream, and placed the bite in my mouth. "Mmmm, this is really good!"

"You've seriously never had these before?"

I noticed the cardboard sign on the table that read, *Ukrainian Students' Society*. "No, I don't have any Ukrainian friends."

"Well, now you do. My name's John."

"Lily," I said and smiled.

"If you become a member, you get a discount at Perogy Night."

"But I'm not Ukrainian."

"You don't have to be. You just have to enjoy *being* Ukrainian."

I laughed. "But I don't know how to *be* Ukrainian."

"Don't worry, I'll be your personal guide."

Before I knew it, John had signed me up and paid my fee. Before I left the table, he put a membership card in my hand and asked if I would meet him at the Den later. This cute guy was grinning at me with a dimple in one cheek. I couldn't say no.

As I walked away, my friend Gabby appeared with two shawarmas in her hands.

"I waited for fifteen minutes and figured I would get you one. Now I see what was holding you up!"

"Thanks, Gabby. I'm starving!" I declared, finishing off the perogies and grabbing the shawarma from her hand.

"Thanks for sharing," Gabby said. "Uh-uh, you're not getting off that easy! Who was that cute guy you were talking to?"

"His name's John. He was just recruiting me to join the Ukrainian Students' Society."

"Is that all?"

"Well, I tried my first perogy ever."

"Are you serious? You've never had a perogy before? Okay, wait, focus. What else?"

"I'm meeting him at the Den after his last class today."

"Lily! That's so exciting!"

My first date with John happened so quickly that I didn't have time to prepare or overthink it. Gabby and I had lunch together, and then I went to class. Before I left, she gave me the rose-coloured cardigan she was wearing, adorned with pink pearl buttons, to cover my shirt stained with the garlic sauce that dripped from my shawarma.

"For your date," she said. "Call me as soon as you get home."

I laughed and hugged her before walking to the Den, where I waited for twenty minutes before John arrived. He apologized and informed me that I had learned my first lesson: Ukrainians are known for being late. Ukrainian time, he called it. I wasn't impressed but forgave him after he told me he was delayed because he was helping a panicked first-year student find her class through the labyrinth of hallways connecting the buildings on campus. He joked he was glad he never took up pre-med like this tearful new student. We decided to order some nachos and beer.

After clinking our glasses together, John said, "So I haven't seen you around. I'm guessing you're not a poli sci student like me. What are you taking?"

"You are correct. I'm in management but ..." I avoided John's gaze and grabbed a chip from my plate.

"But?" John said, catching my gaze as I admired the long eyelashes framing his green eyes.

"I guess it wasn't my first choice, to be honest—as a major."

"If it's not your first choice, then why are you doing it?" John asked as he filled our glasses from the pitcher of beer.

"My dad. He wants me to have a good job after university. It's the practical choice." I shrugged.

"I see. And what would you have liked to take instead?"

"I guess I would have probably liked to have taken political science."

"It's not too late," John said. "You could still add and drop classes for another week."

I laughed it off, but I made a mental note to think about what he had just said later.

Changing the topic, I asked, "So why are you a member of the Ukrainian Students' Society?"

John leaned into the table and started talking with his hands more. "Well, for starters, I am Ukrainian, but it's more than that ... I went to Ukraine when I was in high school. My grandfather took me, and it was the first time he had returned to his homeland after he immigrated to Canada as a political refugee. Ukraine had just become independent."

"So that trip made you think more about your connection to Ukraine?" I leaned my face into my hand as I perched my elbow on the sticky pub table.

"Something like that. I remember watching my grandfather cry when he was back in his village. He told me he never thought he would get to go back, that he would ever see an independent Ukraine. The country is young and growing. Clubs like ours are fun, but they're also lifelines for Ukrainians abroad to keep culture, language, and kinship alive far from home."

As I listened to John, I felt envy for his connection to his grandparents. "So do you speak Ukrainian then? I mean with your grandfather?"

"Yeah, I grew up speaking it with my parents, too."

"Wow. But I guess you don't use it beyond your family?"

"Well, I use it when I speak with other people who can speak Ukrainian. People say Ukrainian is a peasant language ... to put us down. So many languages around the world are dying, cast aside by dominant languages and cultures."

"I didn't mean to offend you."

"Oh no, you didn't. I guess I wanted to explain why it's so important."

I hesitated, and John waited for me to speak. "That's so funny that you say that. I actually get it. I understand this obscure Chinese dialect. Nobody has ever heard of it."

"What's it called?"

"Hokkien ... All my life, I saw it as a peasant dialect, too."

"I bet more people speak it than you realize. Just because there may be fewer of you, doesn't make it less valuable."

"I never thought about that ... I should be more careful. Honestly, I just got kind of tired of explaining to people what Hokkien is and why people don't know about it, why it isn't Mandarin or Cantonese." I pushed the plate of nachos to the side of the table as the server came by.

"You don't need to apologize for it."

"I guess it does come across that way ... I don't know. I just have never really felt at home with this kind of stuff."

"What do you mean?"

"Well, I don't need a reminder that I'm Chinese. People treat me differently because of how I look. To be honest, you can blend in ... You don't have random people making negative assumptions about you based on how you look."

"I know I can't understand that, but if I may, all the more reason to be with people who share your identity. I find it really comforting to be with people who understand ... certain things that we may share."

"Yeah, I get that ..." I sipped my beer. John made it sound so easy, but it wasn't for me.

When our glasses were empty, John invited me to attend a talk about the Arctic the following day put on by the Political Science Department. Through the semester, John and I held hands on dates between political science and Ukrainian Students' Society events. I eventually switched majors, and by the time the first Perogy Night was held that year, we were officially dating. I sought refuge with John and his culture. He was so knowledgeable about it, so at ease and proud of it. It was a novel feeling, the feeling of embracing something that was not the mainstream. I was relieved by how my foreignness wasn't the topic of discussion. I could hide behind John's enthusiasm for his own background.

In our kitchen, I walked up to John and hugged him from behind as he added mushrooms to his borscht. He turned around and asked, "What was that for?"

"Remember when I had my first perogy?"

"Of course," he said, and kissed me.

女
Woman

JOHN RETURNED TO WORK AFTER A WEEK AT HOME with the baby and me. The house was quiet, and the sun was high in the sky, the light penetrating the front bay window. I wrapped a blanket around the baby and me, cocooning with my daughter, tipping my head down to sniff the top of her head. Intoxicating. I was so happy to be home and wrapped up with my little girl. I sat for a few minutes, letting the sun bathe us through the window. I looked at her face and felt like I was peering into an old mirror. Her dark hair, wide nose, and full lips reflected memories of faded pictures I had seen in childhood. Cradling the baby in one arm, I got up to get my old baby photos.

The photo album creaked loudly as I opened it. I saw myself as a wrinkled newborn with large tufts of black hair and smiled looking at the wafts of hair on my daughter's tiny head. In one photograph, my father cradled me in one arm and, in his other hand, held my birth certificate, something he was never given when he was born as a stateless child.

In another photo, Mother held me high with both arms raised straight above her head. She was looking up at me, laughing, as drool seeped from my smiling mouth and I reached for her with my star-shaped hands. I could not stop staring at this photo of Mother and me. As I embraced my week-old daughter, I could not imagine ever leaving her.

I flipped through the snapshots of my early life, and so many questions started popping into my head, questions I wished I could ask my mother. I didn't know if I was breastfed or if my mother relied on formula. I didn't know what my mother thought of pacifiers. I didn't know if she slept with her babies or set us in our cribs. I didn't know if she felt as afraid, unprepared, and naive as I did.

In recent years, I had watched my friends with their newborns as their own mothers arrived to help. They folded laundry, washed dishes, and held the baby while the new mothers showered or drank a cup of hot coffee. I longingly imagined the questions and answers exchanged between these mothers and daughters, the tender guidance as well as the unsolicited advice that fuelled the customary tension between a mother's old methods and a daughter's modern ways.

I thought of my childhood best friend, Hilary, who worked part time as a pharmacist and had a two-year-old daughter. Remarkably, after all these years, we were neighbours again. Hilary had married a scientist who worked at the National Research Council in Ottawa. She told me that her mother claimed that Hilary was potty-trained before she was a year old. Hilary had rolled her eyes, pointing at her toddler still in diapers, and declared that her mother was out of her mind. Another time, Hilary's mother suggested that she place her daughter on her stomach to sleep, because the baby stopped crying whenever her mother put her down that way. She reminded Hilary that she had done the same when Hilary was an infant. Hilary was horrified by this advice, which contradicted the guidelines for avoiding sudden infant death syndrome. She vowed never to have her mother babysit during nap time again.

When Hilary told me about her mother's antics, I said, "She's just trying to help."

"Helping by being a thorn in my side," Hilary scoffed. "She always has to point out that she was a better mother than I am. Like it's a competition, right?"

I laughed along with Hilary's indignation, even though I wished I could complain about my mother's foreign and old-fashioned ideas. I wanted my mother to reminisce with me about when I was a baby. I wanted her to tell me how to swaddle my child. I wanted her to annoy me with ridiculous anecdotes about how well my sister and I slept and firm views about what to do about the baby's crying.

I looked down at my sleeping daughter. Even though I revelled in our first week home, the sleep deprivation anchored me with a deep sadness. The wound of my mother's departure felt fresh and deep. I was terrified and longed for her support. But when I thought about why Mother wasn't here with me, teaching me and comforting me, the magnitude of her decision to leave her children behind devastated me. When the baby howled for me, and pounded and scratched at the skin of my chest hungrily, I vacillated between tremendous anger at Mother's selfishness and profound sadness as I thirsted for her presence.

Mother had disappeared more than two decades ago. Over time, her presence in my life began to feel like a relic. She was like the old, beaded bracelet I treasured at the bottom of my old ballerina jewellery box, something I thought about once in a while, an object that only I could appreciate. My memories of Mother were scratched up and faded like the beads, yet I still wanted to keep them. As the years moved by, I looked at the bracelet and those memories less and less, preoccupied by the present. Until now.

Now, Mother's departure replayed like a recurring nightmare, foisted upon me, conjuring sharp pangs of regret that I had ever loved her. The pain twisted so tightly, forming a pulled braid that ignited a migraine, unravelling into outbursts of rage, leading to unexplained clashes with my family that I worried I could never recover from.

As I fed the baby, I wondered what parts of Mother were inside me. What kind of mother would I be? Could I resist turning into her? Becoming a mother had reignited my questions about her. Where was she? What had happened to her?

A week after we came home from the hospital, Father came to meet his new granddaughter. He came with two large grocery bags, walked directly to the kitchen, and placed his own soup pot on the stove.

"Is the baby sleeping?" he asked, looking around for her.

"Yes, she's upstairs. Do you want to see her?"

"Let her sleep. I'll see her later."

"What are you doing, Dad?"

"Jiu gai." He saw my confused face and reminded me, "It's for new mothers."

After Mother left, Auntie Choo Neo did most of the cooking for us, but eventually, even Father couldn't rely on his sister all the time. He was forced to reach into the deep recesses of his memories to recall how his own mother had fed her children. Perhaps out of necessity, his cooking was different from Mother's. I regarded it as the kind of food Chinese villagers or peasants must have eaten. Unlike at Hilary's house, where her mother expertly made her delicious Cantonese cuisine, we didn't have the same variety of meats, exotic mushrooms, or seafood. Father favoured offal, tofu, eggs, pork, and chicken. And a lot of root vegetables like yam, turnip, carrots, and a few flowering vegetables like okra, eggplant, and bitter melon.

My love for Father's cooking was a well-kept secret. When I was growing up, I was aware of how different Hakka cuisine was from not only Canadian food but also other Chinese cooking and feared people would see it as inferior, or gross. Hakka food was a guilty pleasure that I indulged in by myself in the privacy of my home.

A few years before, during my second week of articling for an all-service law firm, I was running late for work and knew I didn't have time to make my lunch, so I grabbed leftovers from dinner the night before. Juk, as I called it, or congee. Saddled with student debt, I didn't want to spend any money on buying lunch. That day, while eating lunch in my shared office with a fellow student, I was reminded why preserved duck eggs were fondly called "thousand-year-old" eggs.

"Oh! I think your food has gone bad," my officemate declared. "It's all black and grey!"

I looked down into my Tupperware and said, "No, that's just how it looks. It's just preserved eggs."

"Are you sure? I would hate for you to get sick."

"I'm sure. I've eaten these many times."

"Okaaay! I'm off to get something fresh downstairs. You sure you don't want me to get you anything?"

"No, thanks." After she left, I had lost my appetite. I shoved the Tupperware back in my bag and vowed never to put myself in a situation where I would have to bring my food out in public again.

Father was a slow and loud cook, and now he was banging around the kitchen with various spatulas. I was so sleep deprived that I just sat at my kitchen table without offering to help, watching him mince copious amounts of ginger, the yellow pieces glistening on the cutting board. Then he chopped an entire chicken, deftly moving the cleaver over the board forcefully and rapidly. The pounding against the wooden board was a familiar metronome that my body hummed to unconsciously. Father dropped the ginger, spices, and chicken into his soup pot and slowly poured in the rice wine at intervals. Rice bubbled in my rice cooker, the lid dancing in a lively, wet tempo. Father left his concoction on the stove to simmer and sat down with me, leaning back in his chair. He smiled, satisfied, content, at peace.

"So does my granddaughter have a name yet?" he asked.

"We still haven't decided," I confessed.

"So, no birth certificate?"

"Well, she needs a name first, Dad."

"What are you waiting for?" he demanded. "That piece of paper is the most important thing in her life. You know I never had one. It was like I was invisible, a ghost, or worse, just shit on the ground."

"Dad, why are you being so crass?" I said with an uncomfortable snicker.

"Lily, this is no laughing matter. You need to get her birth certificate right away. It's her life. It's proof she is Canadian, that she belongs here."

"Honestly, Dad, there's no rush. It's not a big deal here."

Father shifted closer to me in his chair, as if I needed to hear him better. "It *is* a big deal!"

"Dad, calm down."

"Listen, Lily. It may not seem like a big deal to you because you were born here. You don't know what it's like not to have any status. Don't ever take it for granted. Laws could change tomorrow, and then people born here may not be able to get citizenship. That is the reality. Nothing is certain."

"Dad, I'm a lawyer, I should know. The government isn't going to change laws that drastically."

"I am very disappointed to hear you say that," Father huffed. "You're right, as a lawyer, you should know better. You should be more aware that things won't always stay the same."

"Aren't you being a little melodramatic?"

"Lily, you're always telling me that the laws are changing all the time for your clients, and it's hard to keep track of everything. That the government is finding ways to restrict people from getting status, and you're afraid people won't be able to stay here."

"Yes, that's true. But it doesn't affect people like us, Dad."

"Don't think you're immune to this, Lily. It could happen to people like us, too. Not every country gives citizenship to people born in their country. Didn't you tell me about that young man who lost his Canadian citizenship?"

"Yes, Dad, but that was under very different circumstances."

"Just do it. Go and get her birth certificate. For me," Father begged. "There is nothing worse than being without citizenship. It's like being homeless. It's like you aren't human. You can't do anything. You are nothing to anyone. Please. I had to live like that for a good part of my life. I don't ever want my grandchild to live even one day being stateless. I don't ever want her to know what it's like to be nobody, to suffer because she doesn't have a piece of paper or identity."

"Okay, Dad. Don't worry. I'll do it," I promised.

"Good. Do it right away. Next time I see you, I want to hold that birth certificate in my hand. You're lucky you have the power to do this for her."

I nodded. "John and I will talk about it when he gets home."

Father turned his attention back to the jiu gai. It had been a long time since I had seen him this worked up. I had viewed applying for my daughter's birth certificate as an administrative chore, an item on my to-do list, like going to the grocery store or getting the oil changed in the car. For Father, it was a much more important task. My daughter did not yet exist in the eyes of the state. Her legal life was in limbo, and I controlled when it would begin.

"Dad, did you make this soup for Mom when she had me?" I asked.

"I don't remember," he said, but I knew he did. Father's slow and careful movements as he prepared the ingredients revealed he needed no recipe. He not only enjoyed the ritual but had done it before. I didn't understand why he wouldn't recall this memory for me.

While Father stood in front of the pot, stirring with a large wooden spoon, I thought back to the days when I spied on him while he was trying to find Mother. I remembered late-night phone calls when he thought Bea and I were sleeping. Most nights his raised voice or broken sobs woke me up. I tiptoed to the doorway of my room and peered through the banister downstairs to watch Father pace, the coiled-up phone cord trapping him within a small patch of carpet. For several months after she disappeared, he searched for Mother every night he wasn't working. He called everyone he knew in Canada and all over Asia. He pleaded for any information in English, Hakka, Hokkien, and even in his broken Cantonese and Mandarin. Sometimes I understood what he said, but other times I could only guess. I heard him say, "It's not for me. For her girls, please help me find her." Father, a man struggling to keep whatever pride he still had, embraced this demeaning task. He didn't care about the shame that came with it. He just wanted to find her.

After many months and countless calls, he stopped. Father didn't just stop calling; he cut off contact with everyone. The tap had been shut off for good, and a wrench in very strong hands would be required to open Father up again.

Decades had passed, and Father built a new life for us all after Mother left. He became a single parent overnight and never complained about it. He provided the necessities and worked long hours, but he had no energy for anything else. Whenever Bea and I asked to play a game with him or go for a bike ride, he would brush us off and tell us to play with each other. At the time, we were hurt by Father's rejection, but now I could understand the exhaustion that comes with being a parent, and I could imagine the mental energy needed to overcome the trauma of Mother leaving.

In that moment, watching Father standing over the stove, I saw the grey in his hair, the wrinkles around his eyes, and wondered which ones I was responsible for.

When he retired, Father followed his daughters across the country, perhaps to make up for the lost time in our youth when he wasn't fully present with us. He chose to live in Ottawa, when I decided to firmly plant my feet there, and when Bea secured a job as a professor in the History Department at McGill University. He told everyone that it was a privilege to live in our nation's capital, that it made him feel more Canadian. When Uncle Stephen passed away, Auntie Choo Neo had no reason to stay in Calgary and moved to Ottawa too. I realized that Father was not rooted out West but had tethered himself to us, wherever we were.

Over the years, Father never strayed far from Bea and me. I watched him cope and hoped that he had healed. Perhaps Father could now face the past.

"Dad, do you know where Mom is?"

Father looked at me like I had stabbed him in the back with the cleaver he had used to chop up the chicken.

"I can't help but think of her. Now that I'm a mom, she's been on my mind a lot."

This explanation didn't elicit any response from him. The silence was broken by the popping of the button on my rice cooker. I felt like my time was up and prodded Father with an imploring look. He dished up some rice and jiu gai onto a plate, brought it to me at the table, and told me to eat. I waited for Father to serve his own plate, but he didn't. Instead, he took his apron off and shuffled to the front door. I watched in disbelief as he took his coat off the coat rack, slipped into his boots, and opened the door. I stood up, but before I could take a step, he was gone. He left without meeting his granddaughter.

Tears streamed down my face, landing on the edge of the plate Father had set before me. I watched as the drops flowed towards the centre, where the steaming rice lay.

疋

Bolt of Cloth

THE BABY WOULDN'T SLEEP. A month into motherhood I felt like I had gained no insight into caring for a baby. I tried swaddling her tighter, pushing a rolled-up muslin blanket under her, switching the side she was lying on, and playing rain sounds on the CD player. Nothing would settle her down for her nap.

Today, I planned to sit down and read the latest case dealing with immigration law that had come out of the Supreme Court of Canada. I never forgot the way Elaine Wong had conducted herself during Alfred's immigration hearing. Her impressive advocacy skills prompted me to study immigration law to understand the disappointing decision in Alfred's case. Later, I joined a firm that worked to obtain immigration status for people in Canada.

My colleagues told me the court had provided some helpful reasoning on what the "best interests of the child" meant in immigration applications, based on humanitarian and compassionate grounds. It had come out the week before, but I had been so tired in the evenings that I couldn't stay awake to even peruse the summary. I was looking forward to my alone time with this judgment and my highlighter.

The court's decision affected how children abroad could be reunited with their parents in Canada. Sitting on the edge of their seats in my office, so many of my clients would push onto my desk pictures of their children in another country and ask when they would be able to see them again. I saw the pain in their eyes but always gave a professional and unsatisfactory answer. What could I do? Sometimes, I explained the law. Other times, I said we just had to wait—wait for some faceless, nameless bureaucrat to decide. It felt awful having nothing concrete to offer someone wanting to hold their child. In some cases, I had to give bad news: their application was refused, or their appeal was denied. Sometimes, I would let my emotions bubble over and agree with my client bluntly that, yes, the law was unfair, or yes, it was ridiculous they had to wait so long. Some of my clients appreciated the candour, but some became more despondent. On those days, after they left, I composed myself and stayed at work for hours, searching for anything that could turn the tide for them.

Occasionally, I wondered if Mother showed pictures of us to someone, maybe a lawyer, far away and asked what her options were for reuniting with her children, only to find out it was hopeless. These irrational fantasies of Mother suffering without us comforted me, even as I knew she could come home whenever she wanted. I couldn't bear to think of a scenario where she was glad to be without us. Sometimes these thoughts fed my anger—her suffering was punishment for leaving us.

The only thing I was certain of was the suffering of those she left behind. Before moving away from Sparwood, I tried to find Mother on my own. One day after school, I told Bea I had to stay to do some homework in the library. Instead, I walked to Woo's Confectionery. When I opened the door and the bells jangled, it was as if Auntie Miriam knew I would be coming. She locked the door to the store, turning over the open sign to indicate it was closed. After shedding a few tears, I summoned up the courage to ask, "Auntie, do you know where Mom is?"

Auntie hugged me and gave me a chocolate bar. "Oh, Lily. No, I don't. I wish I did." She sighed. "Your mother didn't even say goodbye to me." Then it was her turn to cry a little. I realized that Mother had abandoned Auntie Miriam, too.

For a time, I believed Mother had left us thinking Auntie Miriam would be a better mother for Bea and me. And sometimes I wished I was Auntie Miriam's daughter. Mother was foreign not only to my home but also to me. Her accent, her Hokkien words, her weird penchant to rip off her socks as soon as she came into the house, and her lament for the lack of fresh meat at the grocery store. She asked if I was embarrassed by her. I said no, but if I am honest, I was annoyed when she didn't change or notice her mistakes. I saw the tilted heads when she spoke, the raised eyebrows when she asked for the tripe from the butcher. I wished she blended in more, like Auntie Miriam, confining her Chineseness within the borders of her mind. Maybe Mother sensed this. Auntie Miriam's grandfather had risked life and limb laying down track all across British Columbia for the Pacific Railway, and the veneer of Canadian esteem stuck to Auntie Miriam.

In the months after Mother's departure, I increasingly went to Auntie Miriam when I needed a hug or had a new question. What was the last thing Mother had said to her? Had she received a letter or a phone call from her?

Then, one dark and rainy day, I decided that Auntie Miriam knew all along where Mother had gone, that she was putting on a convincing act. I went to Auntie Miriam's store, doubts swirling in my head, tears dripping from my eyes.

I pointed at Auntie Miriam and moved closer to her. "You're a liar. Just tell me. Tell me where she is. Tell me where you're hiding her. I know you helped Alfred escape. You must have helped Mom, too!"

Anyone else would have kicked me out. I was on the precipice of adolescence, shouting rudely. Instead, Auntie Miriam mustered all her compassion for me. She brought me into her arms, even when I pushed her away, patiently answering all my questions, even though she had already done so, many times before.

Auntie Miriam dried my tears and said, "Lily, your mother may never come back." Auntie always listened to me, and she never talked down to me. "I would hate for you to waste your life waiting for her. This will be a hard time for you. This may be the hardest thing you will have to endure. You will have to be more independent and take care of your sister. I'm so sorry you are going through this. I wish you didn't have to. You have every right to be angry. To be honest, I am angry at Swee Hua, too. I don't understand why. I just don't."

Slowly, I came out of my trance and realized that Auntie Miriam was not hiding Mother from me. She had only ever been kind to me. "I'm sorry, Auntie ..." I muttered.

"Don't be sorry, Lily. It's only natural to have all these feelings right now. You know, I've had many questions, too. I've tried to find Swee Hua, but I've had no luck. And you're not the only person to come to me."

"What do you mean? My Dad?"

"Yes. We have tried, Lily. Your Mother does not want to be found."

The baby was not content to sleep in her bassinet, so I relented and put on my baby carrier. I wanted so much for her to sleep separate from me, unattached, untethered. I needed a few moments just to lounge on the couch and do something that felt normal. I took the long piece of soft cloth and wrapped it around my waist, slung it over my shoulders, and tied it tight. I picked up the baby and placed her inside, spreading the cloth over her body and head. She smelled like the nian gao and braided bread Mother used to bake, just out of the oven, and soon enough, she snuggled into my body and started to snore. I swayed my hips leaning against the kitchen counter as I read the decision. After a few minutes, I decided to move to the table, but the baby started fussing. It was hopeless. I had to keep moving, and I couldn't read while doing that.

Pacing between the kitchen and the living room, I caught a glimpse of the first snowflakes of the season through the windows and contemplated going for a walk. But I talked myself out of it, reasoning it was too cold for the baby, even though I knew this was only the beginning of winter and there was more cold to come. My baby album on the coffee table caught my eye and I picked it up to put it away. As I lifted the lid of the box that was home to the album,

I grew intrigued by what else was inside. It had been so long since I had rummaged through the box I had carted from dorm room to apartment and now to my house. With the baby wrapped against me sleeping soundly, I started to pull out the box's contents. There was my high school diploma, photos from my high school graduation, and my yearbooks. There were certificates for Kiwanis competitions and a bundle of old letters from my childhood friend Caroline Anderson. There were my report cards and school photos from elementary and junior high placed neatly in a scrapbook. Then I pulled out an accordion folder I didn't recognize. The last time I had opened the box I was frantically packing to move out of Father's house to go to university.

The folder looked older than the rest of my things and had a few circular coffee mug stains imprinted on one side, overlapping one another, as if this folder had sat somewhere for some time being used inadvertently as a coaster. I unwound the thin string wrapped around a small cardboard circle to keep the folder shut and lifted the flap. Inside were papers of all sizes, so I went to the kitchen and spread them out on the island counter. There was a photograph and a letter-sized sheet of light red paper that looked like it had been folded several times. Had Mother intended to bring these with her? I picked up the photograph first. It was Mother. She was young and standing next to Po Po. They were both smiling, and it looked like they were in an airport. I looked at the back of the photo and saw Mother's name etched in Chinese characters. I had never seen this photo before. It looked like it had been taken from a frame, since the edges of the picture were not faded. Who framed it? Where? I didn't remember seeing it in my house or Auntie Choo Neo's.

The light red document was written partly in English, but most of it was in Malay. I recognized Mother's name, and under Sijil Kelahiran was the translation, "Birth Certificate." At the top of the page it stated, "Bukan warganegara." There was no English translation of this, so I used my phone and read: "Not a citizen."

I was stunned. I had known Mother was born in Malaysia, but she had always said she was a citizen. She had often proudly reminded us that she had this status and Father didn't. Even as a child, it struck me as a bit cruel, making it seem as if Father came from the wild jungle while she was from a more refined place.

I held the document and stared at Mother's name. Why had she left this behind?

貝
Shell

THE EMPTINESS OF THE WEEKDAY while John was at work echoed in my head like a migraine. The drone of the silence was broken up by the unending cycle of crying, feeding, swaddling, and rocking the baby. And the countless loads of laundry. It had only been six weeks since she was born, but I was filled with dread and sorrow that my body had not yet returned to the way it was before pregnancy. I had not expected it to be the same as it was, but I thought it would have been my own again by now. I was exhausted by the constant feedings, by this little being grasping at my body so frantically all the time.

Perhaps I would feel better if I could feed her from a bottle instead. The baby took easily to the bottle, but my lactation specialist, all my friends, and everyone else told me that breast milk was best, so I tried to keep formula to a minimum, even though I secretly wished I could stop breastfeeding. I tried pumping, and then feeding her the breast milk with the bottle, but the machine gripping me felt unnatural and the time it took made me rethink the utility of the process when I still had to feed the baby when it was all over. I surrendered, abandoning the pump for good.

I was nursing the baby as usual when I heard the front door open.

"I could be naked right now!" I declared.

"But you aren't," Bea replied. She had texted me earlier in the week, saying she would be by for lunch.

"I gave you a key for emergencies, not so you can come and go like you own the place."

"You're feeding the baby right now. It wouldn't have been much fun for you to come and answer the door. I was doing you a favour."

An aroma tickled my nose and I perked up. "What's in your bag?"

"Oh, I just picked up some food from Auntie Choo Neo. Something she whipped up. But seeing as you're busy, maybe I'll just go back to Auntie's and eat it there."

"Don't be a brat. Hand it over." I peered through the glass container. Chili crab. My favourite.

"After you're done feeding my niece, you can get your hands dirty with this," Bea said.

I took the baby off my breast, popped a pacifier in her mouth, swaddled her, and gently placed her in the bassinet perched on the kitchen table.

"Isn't that supposed to be bad for the baby?" Bea asked.

"What do you mean 'bad'?" I glared at my sister, hands on my hips.

She didn't cower. "I heard that pacifiers deter babies from breastfeeding."

"Well, I don't care. Otherwise, she'd be stuck on my boob for the entire day. Or crying." I pointed at the baby shifting in the bassinet as if she was trying to get comfortable.

"Maybe she needs that."

"I don't need that, and that's good enough for me." I put my hand on my chest, looking up as I held back the tears that came more readily these days, wishing I could just put some noise-cancelling earphones on and lie on the couch for a moment to sleep.

"Aren't you going to change her? There's spit-up all over her neck there." Bea nudged me and tried to reach the baby, but I elbowed her away.

"I wiped it already. Will you stop?" The weight of her judgment was tugging the bags under my eyes, allowing the tears to pool there.

"Stop what?"

"You're worse than Auntie Choo Neo. Maybe you've been spending too much time with her." My voice quavered.

"Now that's going too far."

"You're asking for it. You're so judgmental in the worst way. You don't even have a baby!"

"Ugh! I'm not an idiot, you know. I have friends with babies. And I'm just trying to be helpful."

"Well, be helpful by serving up the crab."

Bea saw the tears I wiped away from my eyes and finally stopped. I turned my back to her for a moment to carry the bassinet to the end of the kitchen table. I waited for her to say something more, but she didn't, and I sat heavily at the table. Why couldn't she just offer to watch the baby while I slept? I wanted so badly to close my eyes.

The baby agreed to sleep in her bassinet, while we dug into Auntie's chili crab. The sweet and spicy sauce coated my fingers, and I gladly licked off every savoury droplet. We ate in silence for a few moments, passing the nutcracker, seafood picks, and forks between us.

After sucking a juicy chunk of meat out of the shell, Bea pointed at my ratty bathrobe and asked, "So is this your new getup?"

I didn't look at my sister, annoyed that she was pushing my buttons again. "Why bother changing? The baby just spits up on me. And it's not like I need to be anywhere."

"Well, maybe you should get out of the house with the baby?" Bea stabbed her crab leg with a seafood pick, trying to fish the meat out.

I put down my empty shell and sighed. "I'm super tired. I don't think you realize how little sleep I'm getting."

"I see other moms out and about."

"Well, I'm not other moms."

"Okay, touchy! Maybe you're practising confinement," Bea provoked.

"Me?! Yeah, right. Confinement is another way to keep women down in patriarchal Chinese culture." I pounded a large leg with a mallet on the wooden cutting board between us.

"I know. And yet, here you are, seemingly embracing this outdated custom," Bea goaded. "I'm surprised you're not outside prancing around, thumbing your nose at the very idea."

"Why would you say that?"

"Confinement is one of the most common Chinese traditions around childbirth. Keep the baby away from the bad, snatching spirits by staying inside and hiding away. It's almost like you're doing it unconsciously. You haven't even washed your hair. Staying true to all the tenets of this practice, I see."

I dropped the piece of crab leg that I was fighting to open and seethed through my teeth, "Shut up! I know what you're doing. Your reverse psychology won't work on me."

"Well, it sure looks like you're doing what every Chinese mother does."

"We all know that ghosts don't exist. Those uneducated and poor women in Asia don't realize it's their poverty and their country's low health and safety standards that are responsible for their babies' deaths. Superstition won't protect anyone."

"Your attitude is so hostile. What if your daughter grows up and asks you one day about her background? Are you just going to ignore her?"

"It's not her background. She's Canadian."

"What if she asks you why you didn't do a red egg and ginger party for her? Are you just going to deny her these experiences?"

"She's a baby. She won't even remember. It's not important to me."

"What about us? It is important to her family, to Dad, Auntie, and me." Bea got up to peer over into bassinet. "Look at her. Her hair is so thick and black. It's amazing that any of John's genes made it in there."

"Why are you saying that?"

"The truth hurts? Just because you don't like being Chinese doesn't mean she won't."

"I'm not going to hide it from her." I placed a section of crabmeat in my mouth.

"You can't hide it anyway." Bea laughed. "It's pretty obvious she's Chinese. But you're not going to show or teach her anything about her culture?"

"She can seek it out if she wants to when she's old enough," I tossed a clean shell into a large metal bowl, the clanging echoing against the table. I winced, fearing the baby would wake up.

"Because it's so easy," said Bea.

"Well, we didn't get taught anything, did we? And we're just fine."

"Dad and Auntie did the best they could, but they couldn't do it all. I hated having to figure things out by myself, and I would hate for my niece to go through that."

"You know, that's actually not true. Mom did teach us a few things."

"Why do you have to bring that woman up?" Bea pushed her plate away and threw a napkin on top.

"Mom? Why not? Not everything was bad. Why do you always have to try to forget we had one? You're the one who thinks it's so important to remember where we came from. Well, we came from her." I scraped the body of the crab for the remnants of meat, ginger, and chili sauce.

"That's right, Lily. We *had* a mom. She left her responsibilities and forgot about us." Bea was vigorously wiping her hands with the few napkins left on the table.

"We don't know that she forgot about us."

"You're a lawyer. Look at the evidence. All she taught us was how to be a bad mom."

"You're just remembering the end. Mom was good before she left. She taught us how to cook Chinese food. All the words we know in Chinese are from her. Dad didn't teach us anything. Mom made us celebrate different holidays, like the Mid-Autumn Festival, even though Dad thought it was silly."

"You have a selective memory. Dad cooks Chinese food, and he'll go along with anything Auntie Choo Neo celebrates, including Lunar New Year. I really hope you're not taking any lessons for being a good mom from our mother. All I remember is her crying a lot, lying around in despair, and neglecting her duties. Kind of reminds me of you right now."

I stared at my sister, dropping the nutcracker, its jaw stuck on a trapped piece of crab. "Maybe this is why you're alone. Your heart is stone cold. You can't even feel for your own mother."

"Feel for her? What about us, Lily? She definitely didn't feel for us when she abandoned us. Maybe it's a good thing we're having this conversation now. Keep going this way and I'll be raising your baby."

"How can you say that? You know what? This lunch is over. Get out!" I yelled, pointing at the front door.

"Gladly." Bea violently pushed her chair back and stomped out.

I gazed at the empty shells spread before me, unsure what to do first: wipe my tear-streaked face or wash my sticky hands.

舌
Tongue

"AYA!" AUNTIE CHOO NEO EXCLAIMED, grabbing the baby from me. "Lu jin niao siao! Clever one! Already causing problems."

A week after I fought with Bea over plates of Auntie Choo Neo's chili crab, Auntie decided to make an appearance herself.

"Come in, Auntie. Do you want some tea?"

"Yes! It will go nicely with the scones and clotted cream I brought. A good British treat for breakfast."

"Thank you, Auntie. How nice of you," I said dutifully and placed a few scones from the box on plates. "Would you like me to put some cream and jam on your scone?"

"I'll do it. We have lots of time to eat."

"Okay ... Auntie, you remember I have my appointment with the nurse at ten, right?"

"Aya, you act like I don't know what it's like to be a mother! I don't mind if she's here while I'm here."

I smiled, realizing my aunt would always come and go as she pleased. After talking softly to the baby while watching me eat, Auntie Choo Neo handed her back to me and started spreading cream and jam on her own scone. "Your father's upset with you," she informed me.

"I know," I replied.

"There's no sense in looking for someone who doesn't want to be found."

"I'm not looking for her, Auntie."

"Are you sure? It sounded like you wanted to know where she is."

"I just want to know what happened. I thought he might want to talk about it."

"There's a Chinese saying: 'The tree has been made into a boat.' Do you know what that means?"

I shook my head.

"What's done is done. We can't turn back time, and we can't change anything. Let things lie. Your mother cast her life in a new direction. We don't know why, and there's nothing you can do about it. Bo pian lah, you have no choice. Besides, we don't want the ghost of your mother to snatch this baby."

I was shocked by my aunt's superstitious talk. I knew it was futile to pursue the discussion any further. Father and Auntie were not interested in opening the past, and I didn't have the energy to fight them. Still, it bothered me that everyone treated Mother like she was a ghost wandering around in purgatory. We weren't allowed to talk about her in case her wayward soul returned to taunt or curse us.

"Now, Beatrice wants to settle a date for the red egg celebration. You can say no to her, but not to me. Winston has married that seow char bor, crazy woman, denying me any grandchildren. This is my only chance to be a proper po po," Auntie declared.

My eyes filled with tears. I was so wrapped up in my own selfish need to have a mother that it hadn't occurred to me until this moment that my daughter was missing a po po. It touched me that Auntie Choo Neo wanted to fulfill that role. When I was young, Auntie Choo Neo was a force to be feared, and her manipulations were terrifying, but in her old age she had become softer and warmer.

When Father was at his lowest point after Mother disappeared, Auntie took care of everything. She packed our lunches, signed our school forms, did the laundry, shopped for the groceries, and made dinner. It must have been hard to step in to raise two girls on the cusp of our teenage years, but she became our mother without saying so out loud. And while she complained loudly and often about the extra work we created for her, she never seemed to need our approval or thanks. She did it selflessly, though sometimes in her own cantankerous way. At the time, I hated Auntie Choo Neo, resenting her for taking on Mother's role, thinking that made it easier for Mother not to return. My bitterness grew during my teenage years, as Auntie tried to control me with strict rules and punishments. Whenever she was around, I couldn't hang out with my friends or go where I wanted. She confined me to my homework, my piano lessons, and my chores at home. I didn't appreciate her then, but she was doing what any parent does—trying to protect us, teach us, and guide us into the world of adulthood.

It wasn't until I went away to university that Auntie Choo Neo started to soften. She finally showed her love for me, shedding tears that I was leaving home. She cleaned my dorm room twice over and took me shopping for new outfits to wear during my first week at school. Then, as I was busy with my studies, Auntie Choo Neo stuffed my tiny beer fridge to the brim with my favourite dishes, including ayam masak oh soup and kyu niuk, braised pork belly with potatoes or taro. She would appear on a weekend to take me for a haircut and even try to have girl talk with me, asking if I had found a nice Chinese boy to marry. Appalled, I would stuff my face with the cuttlefish I loved to snack on.

Now Auntie Choo Neo deftly handwashed all the dishes the scones touched, even after I opened the dishwasher for her. As she wiped the counter, I said, "Auntie, of course you can be the baby's po po. I'm so happy she will have one."

"Good. Now, as Po Po, I must insist we set the date for the red egg and ginger party." She pushed me towards the table again, sat down, and pulled out her phone.

"Auntie ... Honestly, I don't feel comfortable doing that," I hesitated.

"Why?" Auntie exclaimed.

"I ... um ... I really ..." I stammered.

"Spit it out!" she demanded.

"I don't really feel like it's something that's part of me, something I fully understand, something that can be meaningful to me," I tried to explain.

"It's not about you. This is for this niao siao," she said, squeezing the baby's cheek.

"What about me?" I shot back. "I'm her mom. You and Dad had your turn. What if I want something different for my daughter? What if I think it will hold her back?"

Auntie Choo Neo said nothing. I was shocked she didn't have an immediate comeback and watched warily as she refilled her teacup.

She took a deep breath and said steadily, "Sometimes you do things not for yourself but because you honour your elders, your traditions, and your ancestors. Just because your mother left, it doesn't mean you have to abandon who you are."

"You're not making sense, Auntie. My feelings have nothing to do with my mother."

"I am not blind, Lily."

"It's not about her," I insisted. "I don't want to pretend anymore, okay? I don't need to perform just so we fit the stereotypes. And I don't want my daughter to have to pretend just to make everyone around her feel comfortable. Why make things more complicated?"

"Pretend? We're not doing this for anyone but our family. And if you don't know what to do, so what? That's what your family is here for, to help you. There is always something you will not know."

"No offence, Auntie, but I don't want to hand over the education of my daughter to anyone blindly, including my family."

Auntie Choo Neo gave ground. "Okay, lah. Listen. Let's do the red egg your way. It doesn't need to be traditional. It doesn't even have to be Chinese. But we can have a celebration, right? Some food, some family. That's all your father and I want."

I couldn't ignore the kindness and devotion Auntie Choo Neo had bestowed upon me for so many years. "Okay," I relented, "but everything has to be approved by me and John."

"Of course!" she exclaimed triumphantly. After pulling out her calendar and prodding me to pull out my phone, she helped me set a date for the red egg and ginger party. "It won't be on the hundredth day, but it will be with family. All the aunties are so busy that this was the earliest date." To my consternation, she had already consulted with the aunties who would be travelling from Vancouver, Calgary, Kamloops, and Sparwood. "We will celebrate then," she concluded with satisfaction.

Auntie Choo Neo got what she wanted, always businesslike. As she briskly got up to leave, she pulled a gift bag from her large purse. "Just a little something for my niao siao. You need to name her so I can call her something different."

The nurse arrived right after Auntie Choo Neo left. The baby was born tongue-tied, and her frenulum was cut to help with her feeding. The nurse checked to see how it was healing and helped me find the right nursing posture for my baby and me. After twisting into many different positions, we cast away the nursing pillow and instead propped up the baby more vertically, having her rest against my body with her legs between my legs. Once we found a posture that worked, the nurse fell back onto the sofa and asked me if we had settled on a name.

I laughed sheepishly. "Honestly, I haven't had time to think about it. Sleep, food, and a long hot shower are top of mind."

Suddenly, I felt a cold wind brush my neck, as if someone were tapping me on the shoulder with icy hands. I thought back to how Father had implored me to get the baby her birth certificate, how I had promised to take care of it. All my drama with my family, my exhaustion, my desire to find some semblance of my old life had pushed that crucial task out of my head. I was confronted now with guilt so large that I couldn't move.

"Are you okay?" the nurse asked.

"Yes, sorry. I just remembered something I need to take care of," I said.

"No need to apologize. I remember when I had my first. It was all such a blur. I'm surprised, though. Usually, people love choosing a name for their baby." She searched my face. "There's no short list?"

"To be honest, this pregnancy was unexpected. I wasn't sure if I could ever be a mom."

"Well, you have one day left to decide! You have to submit your forms to the province tomorrow. She won't be able to access health care, and you won't be able to get the child tax benefit. It will just make life more difficult."

I knew she was trying to be helpful, but the nurse's comments were not comforting. I felt like a terrible mother. I couldn't even get myself organized enough to submit my baby's paperwork on time. With my clients, I had always provided documents and disclosure ahead of schedule. With my own daughter, I was scrambling and running out of time.

My preoccupation was not just to find something that would roll off the tongue easily. People make so many assumptions when they read or hear a name. They guess where the person has come from, where they've been. They imprint in their minds a version of that person that may not be based on anything true or accurate. Crafting my daughter's first impression to the world made me feel like the forms I had were pinned to the table with a paperweight. I couldn't drag myself from under the burden and was overcome with the power I held to unleash over her future.

I had waited long enough. It was time to tackle this problem head-on.

After the nurse left, I held my daughter and looked at her. She had spit up all over herself and I had to change her. I noticed the gift bag Auntie Choo Neo had left. Inside was a cheerful yellow-and-orange onesie. I was grateful I didn't have to climb the stairs to find a new outfit for her.

I placed the baby on a quilt that Auntie Elizabeth had made. Hilary had brought it over when I was in the hospital. I hadn't had a chance to thank them yet. The new onesie had mitts in the shape of lion paws. I chuckled at how babies needed to protect their faces from their own tiny sharp fingernails. There was also a hood, which I placed gently over her head so that the ears and mane of a lion flowed around her face. I tucked her into a carrier strapped to my body, the mane tickling my neck. As my daughter fell asleep, I called her "my little lion."

Curious, I pulled out my phone and searched for names that meant "lioness." Hundreds of results appeared. I called John. "How do you say 'lioness' in Ukrainian?" I asked.

"What are you talking about?" he said.

"The baby's name," I explained. "She's wearing this really cute onesie that makes her look like a little lion."

"Give me a sec." I heard typing, and then, "Leonida."

"Okay, how about we put Leonida on her birth certificate, but we call her Leo for short?"

"I like it!"

"Great! Leo."

Pleased, I pulled a baby book out of Auntie Choo Neo's gift bag. Opening it, I marvelled at the soft yellow petals jutting forward from the thick pages, delicately framing the face of a lion meant for a young hand to touch.

Enclosure

THIS MUST HAVE BEEN WHAT MOTHER FELT LIKE when she was living in Sparwood. I was only a couple months into being a mother, but I was already questioning how life had brought me here. Did she fantasize about unlocking the shackles of marriage, children, and housekeeping, releasing herself of the weight?

I didn't set out to practise the Chinese custom of confinement. The dips in my mood and the intense feelings of sadness started to come to me more frequently, and then the winter north wind led to my self-imposed quarantine with the baby. I began to understand Mother's fear of the cold. It was as if all my courage had seeped out of me with the afterbirth. The thin, slippery layer of snow on the ground and the wisps of flakes falling from the sky looked like shards of glass that I had to protect my baby from. The need to cocoon made it easy for me to stay in my bathrobe, shuffling around in my slippers. I was conflicted, however, battling bouts of claustrophobia and guilt.

In my work as an immigration lawyer, I saw the heartbreak of parents separated from their children, yet I was looking for every opportunity to separate myself from my child physically. I didn't want her clinging to me or saddling me down. The carrier, the feedings, felt like an oppressive stranglehold that I could not wrestle away from. How could I not be happy to be home with this baby, a miracle that some people struggle so hard to bring to their families? I thought about going outside for stimulation and fresh air. The four walls of my house felt like a prison, yet I didn't have the energy to break free.

John saw my decline, but his efforts to get me out of the house during the day were futile since he had to be at work. So he summoned Hilary to help. One day she appeared at my door with her two-year-old daughter, Abigail. She saw me in my bathrobe and ushered me into my bedroom, throwing a nursing shirt and a pair of yoga pants at me. "Put these on," she instructed. "All the moms are wearing these comfortable getups these days."

I was too stunned to resist. Hilary told Abby to stop playing with my baby monitor and gave her a board book instead. Hilary then tackled the baby. She put Leo in her puffy down-filled one-piece and strapped her into the stroller, tucking a few fleece blankets around her. I was amazed at how quickly Hilary moved and how she seemed to know where everything was. She inspected my diaper bag and decided its contents would suffice.

"Kanket!" Abby shouted.

"That's her word for blanket," Hilary translated, then opened the door and yelled, "Let's go! The playgroup starts in a half-hour, and it's at least a twenty-minute walk. It can fill up, and they close the doors to latecomers."

Hilary had become a fast walker as a mother, and I hadn't gone anywhere with purpose in quite some time. I struggled to keep up on the frozen sidewalks. Although the air was cool, I was almost blinded by the brightness outside. The strong sunlight reflected off the snow crystals coating every surface, and I was taken aback seeing my breath on this crisp morning. Although I was surprised by how difficult it was just to step out the door, it did feel good to be out, the open air instantly lifting my mood.

I glanced at the storefronts on Somerset Street in Chinatown. The Chinese signs were worn, with Vietnamese signs scattered among them. The arch that stretched across the road welcoming us to the neighbourhood was like a diamond-encrusted tiara placed on top of a grimy paper-bag princess. Gems like Shanghai Restaurant and May's Garden remained, but Chinatown had seen better days. I often wondered where the Chinese people in the suburbs now ate, and how long it would be before this urban Chinese community shrank again.

Hilary handed me a travel mug. "It's magic," she said.

"Coffee?" I asked.

"Yes, but it's called 'magic.' I just discovered this new coffee shop in a bike store, of all places. It will change your life forever. Just the perfect ratio of milk and ristretto."

I took a sip. The bold, strong but sweet flavour gave me the reassurance I needed.

We pushed our strollers, and my feet began to remember what it felt like to move on pavement. Hilary allowed me to walk silently with my thoughts for a while. Only when we were a block away from our destination did she say, "I take Abby to this playgroup because I know a few of the moms but mainly because the woman who leads it does a great circle time. Even I'm enchanted! Another benefit? There's a Chinese playgroup there."

I laughed. "My kid is only a couple months old. What's she going to get out of it?"

"Who cares?" exclaimed Hilary. "It's what you get out of it. You get to hang out with me for the morning. After this, we're going for lunch at that pho place on the corner of Booth. Then we'll hit that new bubble tea place."

I smiled. Hilary knew me so well. She had planned the perfect day according to Lily, and it was nice to think that I could indulge in a few of my favourite things.

We parked our strollers in the stairwell and climbed up with our babies and bags. Shedding our outerwear and unpacking our gear took as long as the walk. Abby ran into the familiar room and grabbed a toy stroller, pushing it around and cooing, "Baby!"

I followed Hilary, grabbing a set of toy keys for Leo. She took my elbow and pointed out a woman whose long brown hair looked professionally blow-dried. I admired her cable-knit cardigan and ankle boots. We exchanged warm smiles.

"Madhu, I want you to meet Lily." Hilary seemed to know everyone. "She's a childhood friend of mine and she has a new baby. Her first. She's a playgroup virgin, haha."

"Nice to meet you, Lily. Welcome." Madhu was distracted by her son trying to escape the room. "Gotta run!" Hilary told me that Madhu was a lawyer too, so we might have something in common to chat about other than our kids.

Then Hilary abandoned me on the mat to retrieve her coffee at the other end of the room. She ran into a mom who'd just made it inside before they closed the door for the morning and stood there chatting for some time. I sat cross-legged with Leo in my lap. She was drooling happily on the new toy in her clutches, so I pulled out my phone to check my email.

A woman with light brown hair that skimmed her shoulders and straight bangs framing her eyebrows sidled up to me. She looked ready for a fall workout, in tights and an expensive merino wool base layer top I had been eyeing to go cross-country skiing in. "Hi there. I'm Meg. I haven't seen you here before."

"Yeah, this is my first time," I replied.

"My, that's a young one!"

"Yes, she's just eight weeks old."

"You only have one on your hands?"

"Yes, for now."

"Oh, okay. Well, I was wondering if you and your employer would consider taking on a toddler, too. I'm looking to share a nanny. I head back to work in a month, and I'm having the worst luck finding someone suitable."

I was stunned, and fascinated. I hadn't realized that Leo could pass as a different race from me. I had been fixated on her dark hair and eyes, but watching her jerky arms move as she rattled the plastic toy keys, I noticed that her skin was much fairer than mine. "Oh. Well—"

"Listen, don't say no yet. Just think about it. I'm happy to talk to your employer about it. I'm really easygoing, and my daughter over there is a delight."

I followed her pointing finger to see a sturdy curly-haired child push another child. The woman laughed dismissively. "They're at that stage where they're just testing so many limits."

"I'm sorry, but I'm not a nanny. This is my baby."

"Oh, shit! Why didn't you say so earlier? You just let me ramble on and on."

The woman got up, and I sat there dumbfounded. I couldn't take my eyes off her. She looked back at me and decided it was time to leave the playgroup.

The facilitator called after her. "Going so soon? We haven't had circle time yet." The woman carried her screaming child out the door.

Hilary raced over with one of her friends. "What happened? What did you say to her?"

"She was trying to find a nanny share and—" I started to say.

"Noooooo!" Hilary exclaimed. "You're not saying ...?"

I nodded.

"It must be because your baby is a halfie," said Hilary's friend.

Hilary gave her a look that could sour milk. "Excuse me, Kay? Did you just call Leo a halfie?"

"I, uh, didn't mean anything by it. I mean, she's mixed ... I'm sorry, I don't know your name. It's obvious she's not, you know, pure Chinese," Kay stammered.

"Stop right there," Hilary said. "Just stop."

After the playgroup, as Hilary and I walked west on Somerset, she looked over at me cautiously. "Sorry about that."

"Why are you apologizing? It's not your fault," I said.

"I promise you, playgroups are not usually that eventful. Any drama is usually caused by the kids!"

"Don't worry, you haven't scarred me. That's life, right?"

"It shouldn't be like that. We shouldn't have to deal with that."

"I don't want to make a big deal about it. Besides, she left. I'm over it now."

Hilary could always tell when I was lying, but she also knew I didn't want to talk about it anymore, even with her. I was afraid of what would emerge if I dwelled on it. I had worked so hard to keep the memories of similar episodes, the feelings they provoked, at the bottom of a crater within me. I didn't want any cracks to form, to let even a bit of steam out, for fear a thick lava would bubble to the surface.

"Tomorrow I'll take you to the Chinese playgroup. It'll be fun, and we'll have more in common with the people there," Hilary said.

"I'd really rather not, if you don't mind."

"Why? What else do you have planned?"

"I just don't want to have to explain for the thousandth time why I don't speak Cantonese or Mandarin, even though I look Chinese. Besides, I'm not in the mood to hear people call me Ri-Ree instead of Lily. Honestly, I have no idea what my parents were thinking."

Hilary laughed at my imitation.

"Nobody expects you to speak Chinese at the playgroup. Some do, but you don't have to. Besides you *are* Chinese!" Hilary replied.

I rolled my eyes. It was so easy for her. She had no idea what it felt like to be an outsider in the community that everyone else thinks you belong to. "What kind of bubble tea are you going to get?" I asked, changing the subject.

It wasn't Hilary's fault. I knew that. But I sometimes wished I were her.

寸

Inch

THE LOUD CLANG OF THE MAILBOX WOKE ME from a languid nap. I rose like a disgruntled bear, its hibernation interrupted, and lumbered to the front door. Leo's birth certificate had arrived! The long form, on a yellow-tinged piece of paper, had a typewriter-like font. I knew Father would want to see it and sought my phone to take a picture but stopped myself abruptly. I rummaged through my mind for the last time I had seen Father. I could smell the jiu gai and the steamed rice and realized he still hadn't met Leo. I hadn't heard from him in weeks. The aftertaste of my guilt jerked me out of the dregs of my drowsy state.

Father lived a short drive away in a modest bungalow with Auntie Choo Neo. On dry days, Father would cut the grass while Auntie weeded the flower beds. After a snowfall, he used his snow blower while she shovelled the steps. On days when nothing needed fixing, I would find them in Chinatown or T&T, having their coffee and reading the newspaper.

When Uncle Stephen died and Auntie Choo Neo chose moved to Ottawa to live with Father, I was comforted. Father became even more of a loner as he aged, and Bea and I worried about him constantly, but now that Auntie was with him, we knew they took care of one another.

I could hear the doorbell ring through the quiet house. A small sun-faded red Chinese knot hung from the mailbox, a reminder to celebrate Chinese New Year and preserve the ties that bind us. Father and Auntie must have had it for years.

Father opened the door, and I was relieved he acted like nothing had happened between us. While I unzipped my coat, he took the car seat, brought it in the centre of the living room, and gently untucked the blanket around the baby. Father unbuckled Leo, untangling her arms from the shoulder straps, and expertly put his hand behind her head before lifting her. He placed her on the couch and unzipped her outerwear, releasing her flailing arms and legs. He smiled, smelled the top of her head, and whispered to her. Seeing them together, I smiled so widely. For the first time in weeks, I felt pure joy. I told Father her name was Leo and handed him her birth certificate. He beamed, clutching both firmly. I let them have their moment together and went to put my coat in the closet and peer into the kitchen to see if Auntie Choo Neo was around.

When I came back, Leo was asleep. I watched Father walk around the living room with the tiny bundle in his arms and remembered when my sister and I would snuggle under his arms while watching television. Before Mother left, he wasn't very affectionate, but her absence forced him to comfort us. When he sat on the couch, we would attach ourselves to his sides. He never pushed us away, and as we grew older, as he learned to enjoy the closeness, we were the ones who pulled away. He must have missed that, but now he had Leo.

"Where's Auntie?" I asked.

"Out with her knitting group," Father said. "Leo has your hair. You had so much when you were born."

"Yeah, I don't think John ever had hair like that." We both laughed.

"We used to tie it up at the top."

"I know. I've seen the pictures."

Father pulled out his cellphone and asked me to take some pictures of him and Leo together. He held Leo gently and smiled, and then moved around the house for more photos in the same pose: standing with the sleeping baby cradled in one hand, her birth certificate in the other. I laughed; he had done the same, decades before, with me.

Father sat down in his armchair, perching his arms on the armrest to create a cradle for Leo. "I used to come home from the night shift early in the morning, and you would be standing in your crib waiting for me. I didn't want to wake your mother, so I would bring you to sit with me while I had my coffee and some breakfast. We would read the newspaper together."

"I don't remember that."

"You were small. Back then, you spent more time with your mother, so maybe you remember her more."

I was grateful Father had recalled some memories for me. It didn't escape me that he brought up Mother. It was a kind gesture that Father would not have given me before.

Father took Leo with him to the kitchen to make himself a cup of coffee, and fatigue hit me hard. I fell asleep on the couch and awoke an hour later with a large blanket cocooning me. Father had sent me a text, telling me he took Leo for a drive in my car to see Auntie Choo Neo at a coffee shop in Chinatown called Raw Sugar.

I felt well rested and wandered into the kitchen, snacking on baos from a pastry box on the counter. Then I decided to venture down to the basement to see if Father had kept anything from the past. He had gotten rid of many things in his move across the country and there were only a handful of boxes in the furnace room. One box had some old files; another was stuffed with a lifetime supply of work gloves and coveralls, things Father hadn't used since he retired. A third box was filled with Christmas decorations. Another held gardening tools and seeds.

The last box I opened, however, had three photo albums. Inside were pictures of Mother and Father early in their marriage, before I was born. I saw their bell-bottoms, their hairstyles—my father's Elvis pompadour, my mother's flipped-out ends—and smiled. I found my parents' wedding photo: Father in his suit and Mother in a rented dress, posing with family. There was Auntie Choo Neo, thinner but with the same tight smile. Her son, Winston, a little boy at the time, was standing in front of her holding a toy. I flipped through the pictures, saw the smiles and the embraces, and marvelled at how young and beautiful everyone looked. One photo at the end of the last album caught my eye. It was the same photo I had seen in my house a few weeks ago, of a young Po Po standing with Mother in an airport. This must have been taken when Mother was leaving Brunei. I pulled back the cellophane sheet and took out the picture. This photo didn't have a faded border like the photo in my house, and there was no writing on the back.

I heard keys jingling in the front door, so I placed the picture back in the album and closed the box. There was nothing else here that belonged to Mother or the past. I ran upstairs, not wanting Father to know I had been snooping through his things.

I came home from Father's house motivated to see what I could find out about my mother on my own. It was clear that I was not going to get anywhere with Father, Bea, or Auntie Choo Neo. I strapped Leo onto me in the baby carrier and brought my computer to the kitchen island. As I swayed my hips, I typed "Swee Hua" into the search engine.

I pressed enter and the list that ensued was enormous. Of course—"beautiful flower" is a common name for girls. There was a jewellery store chain in Sarawak, Malaysia. I saw a few LinkedIn and Facebook accounts. I clicked on all of them, even when the last names didn't match. None was Mother. They were young people working as lawyers, architects, teachers, doctors, property managers, hotel managers, and owners of restaurants and corporations. I also read some obituaries, but they were for other Swee Huas, who lived, loved, and left those who cherished them behind.

I spent hours on the internet and read dozens of pages of search results, only to confirm my mother's name was not rare. And perhaps what Auntie Miriam had said to me all those years ago was still true. She did not want to be found.

When Leo started fussing, waking from her nap, I closed my laptop. As I was pulling the baby out of the carrier to feed her, John came home. He looked particularly dapper, with a sharp pink tie and his hair blown slightly to the side by the wind. Next to him, I felt frumpy in my nursing top splattered with spit-up. I realized this was the first time in a long while that I had paused to really look at him, not in passing on my way to tend to the baby, or with eyelids tugging at me to sleep.

"How was your day?" John asked.

"Okay," I replied.

"Just okay?"

I looked at John's familiar, caring face and resolved to tell him what had been consuming me the last few weeks. "I've decided to look for my mother."

"I see." John said and sat down across from me.

"Ever since Leo was born, I can't stop thinking about her. I feel her everywhere, like she's following me, or haunting me."

"You never really talk about your mom. I feel like I don't know much about her."

"Sometimes I feel that way, too. For a long time, I just suppressed all my questions and emotions because I couldn't do anything about them. My dad, Auntie Choo Neo, and Bea never wanted to talk about her. They still don't."

"I can understand wanting to know. To be honest, I'm surprised this didn't came up sooner. Every time I tried to ask you about her, you changed the subject or just ignored me. At first, I thought you were hiding your family from me. That you weren't serious about me," John recalled playfully.

I tugged at his arm, pulling him closer to me. "You're right. I was afraid of what you'd think of them," I confessed. "Do you remember when I first met your baba? That's when I knew you could handle my family."

"Ah yes, the epic shopping trip with Baba."

"I think we'd been dating for around six months. You told me we had to run some errands for your baba before we hit the movie theatre, because she couldn't drive. What I didn't realize was that you weren't just doing the errands for her, you were taking her on those errands." I wagged my finger at John.

"That's right! I tried to tell her we only had time to go to the butcher, but she insisted on hitting the bakery and every grocery store in between."

"I remember how she was back-seat driving you the entire way, telling you the exact route she wanted you to take, despite any road-work or traffic. She refused to listen to your suggestions. I remember her clutching her coupons, ready to hand them over to the cashier. And I remember you looking at your watch, calculating the time we had left before the movie started. I loved watching you squirm. And then, just when we thought she was done, she wanted you to take her to the pharmacy."

"She left the most important stop for last! I couldn't leave her without a week's worth of meds." We laughed, and I admired how she'd outsmarted us both.

"At least she bought me that great sandwich for lunch at that bakery," I said.

"I think that sandwich saved the day. We were both starving!"

I grinned at the memory, relishing the sparkle in John's eyes. I could tell he missed his baba. "We missed our matinee that afternoon, but I never laughed so hard at how your baba had the whole day planned out, with one of us on each arm. I had never seen you blush so much."

"Baba loved how you started picking up Ukrainian from our con-versation. She thought you were so smart."

"That was one of my favourite dates we've ever had. And not just because I genuinely loved how your baba had you wrapped around her little finger, but because I realized even you have an Auntie Choo Neo. I knew I didn't need to feel embarrassed about her. Even though I couldn't understand everything she said, your baba lectured you the way Auntie Choo Neo did with me. Baba called the shots and didn't let anyone push her around, just like Auntie. More than that, though, I recognized how she, like my aunt, dealt with being in a new country by elbowing her way around the best she could."

"You never told me that before," John said, taking my hand. "Although I did notice that after meeting Baba, suddenly the door to your home was wide open to me. At the time, I thought that we had just reached the six-month milestone. It didn't occur to me that Baba was the reason. But now I realize that I also felt a familiarity with Auntie Choo Neo when I first met her."

"Did you? She was so mean to you!" I said with an apologetic grimace. "Do you remember how she kept commenting on how pale your skin was? You held your own, though, as I knew you would."

"Yeah, I could laugh it off because I knew what she was about. You're right, just like Auntie Choo Neo, Baba was never shy about sharing her thoughts and opinions. She obviously knew what was best for everyone! Plus, she loved shopping and dragging us with her."

"The only difference is that Auntie Choo Neo would demand we stop at her favourite convenience store to buy a lotto ticket," I added. We bent over laughing.

"Listen," John straightened and turned serious, "I'm happy you want to find your mom. It can't be easy to be in the dark about so much. You must have a million questions about why she left and why she never contacted you."

"I think I'm ready to find out now, even if my family isn't. The trouble is, I'm at an impasse," I admitted.

I stood up, having finished burping Leo, and handed her to John. He took her in one arm and wrapped the other one around my shoulders. "It may feel like you're at a dead end, but you've only just begun looking for her. Don't be discouraged yet."

齒
Tooth

I HATED TO CANCEL MY PLANS to meet with my colleagues for the first time since Leo was born. I had wanted to hear about how things were going at work, but the baby was inconsolable.

That night, as I was trying to calm her down to put her to sleep, I couldn't take it anymore. "Why are you so terrible right now?" I asked the baby in desperation.

John must have overheard me. "Lily?" He walked into Leo's room. "Why are you saying that?" He took Leo from my arms and said, "Look at her, she's chewing her hands and drooling more than usual. I think she's teething. She's in pain. I'll get some ice and put it in a cloth for her. Can you grab the Tylenol?"

I was chastened by how easily John decoded her cries. I went to the washroom to riffle through the medicine cabinet. A half-hour later, Leo was sleeping serenely in John's arms. He set her down in the crib and closed the door.

"How did you know?" I asked him.

"I didn't. I just made an educated guess." He shrugged. "She was crying differently. I think she was really in pain."

I nodded. "Why does this process have to be so painful? Didn't teething babies give cavemen away to predators?"

John laughed. "Are you okay? You were pretty hard on her."

"I was just so tired of her crying. And I couldn't figure out what was wrong."

"It's probably harder for you to see because you're with her all day. It's tiring."

"Don't you think I should have known? I'm her mom."

"Don't be so hard on yourself. We're a team. We figured it out in the end."

"You figured it out."

"Sometimes there's nothing to figure out." He put a gentle hand on my arm. "This was just one incident, Lily. You're her mom, and you provide her with more than I can right now."

This didn't comfort me. I felt wholly inadequate as a mother, exhausted and irritable. I looked down at Leo, sleeping quietly in her crib. Something was preventing me from getting close to her, connecting with her. The sense of detachment scared me.

The next day, Leo was still battling her tooth. I had already given her Tylenol and offered her some toys I had put in the freezer, but nothing was helping. I put her in the carrier, tried to feed her, even offered her my own fingers to chew on. Nothing made her stop crying. I had to call my law partner, Vishal, and tell him that Leo was not cooperating and that I couldn't bring her into the office.

"Lily, forget about work for now! You're on maternity leave. Don't worry, we haven't forgotten about you."

"No, I know. I just thought it would be nice to reconnect with the team and hear about what everyone's been doing."

"Work will always be here waiting for you. Don't worry. Enjoy your time with your daughter. I've got to run, but we'll see you soon."

I dragged my feet back into the kitchen, where I had left Leo, sobbing in her Jolly Jumper.

"Okay, monkey, let's go for a walk. Maybe it will distract you from your teeth." I sighed, saddened by the missed opportunity to reclaim a part of my life that I missed so much.

Outside, there was a light dusting of snow and the air was cool, but I was warm in my parka. Leo, in the carrier strapped to my body, seemed to enjoy the swaying of my steps. She settled, and I tried to make them slow and deliberate. I had nowhere to go but found myself in Chinatown. Thoughts of my mother seeped into my head. Was this how she felt when she was with us? She was far away from her home and wanted so badly just to see it again for a brief moment. I longed for my old life, my work, my routine. I wanted so badly to be part of something other than the world of motherhood. It must have been more difficult for her, missing her home, her family, her culture.

The guilt I felt for having these thoughts overwhelmed me. I worried that I would turn into Mother, that I would transform into a ghost and neglect my family. I wondered if I was fighting something innate, inherited, uncontrollable.

I pulled out my phone and called Auntie Miriam. I was ready to do more digging. Someone out there must know where Mother was.

"Hi, Auntie Miriam!"

"Lily! I'm so sorry for not calling earlier to check on you. How are things? Did you get the package I sent you?"

"Yes, thank you. I'm so sorry for not acknowledging it sooner. That's why I'm calling. I wanted to thank you. I got it a few months ago. I love the outfits you bought for Leo. They'll be great for the summer."

"I forgot to note in the card that Joy made the one with the tulips."

"Oh wow, she made that dress? It's beautiful. I saw her label on it, so I assumed it came from her store in Vancouver. I'll have to send her a note of thanks. She must be doing well."

"She's doing great. She told me to tell you that you have a lifetime discount at her store."

"Oh, that's so kind of her!"

"So how's it going? I can't believe you girls are all grown up and having families of your own! It feels like yesterday that you were rushing into my store to eat candy and read *Archie* comics."

"I'm okay, Auntie. Still learning the ropes. I can't believe how much work being a mom is, and I've only just begun this journey."

"You forget the work and remember the good times. Trust me. It will get easier, too. You probably don't remember, but your mother made it look easy. It was like she had two little sisters with her all the time."

I laughed, and we were silent for a moment before she continued. "Oh, Lily, I'm sorry. I didn't mean to do that."

"No, it's okay. It's funny that you bring her up actually, because I've been thinking about her a lot lately. That's really why I'm calling."

"You must miss her. I miss her, too."

"The last time I asked you about her, you said you didn't know anything. Is that still true?"

"I really don't know anything, Lily. I wish I did. Swee Hua left no trace. Back then, I called the person who helped us get Alfred to a safe place, but she claimed that your mother didn't contact her. Even if your mother did ask Cathy for help, she wouldn't tell me. That's her job—to keep secrets. I think your mother didn't want to burden anyone with having to keep things from you."

"Hmm. Yeah, I was hoping something might have changed."

"Swee Hua knows me. If she had contacted me, I would have tried to convince her to come home. She also knows I would have told you where she was."

"Do you think it's worth contacting that Cathy woman again? It's been many years, so maybe she could give me a clue if she knew anything."

"Oh, Lily. Some years back, Cathy suffered a stroke and now lives with her daughter in Calgary. When I visit my cousin Agnes, we sometimes go see her. She can't talk anymore and is a mere shadow of herself. It's quite tragic. If she knows anything about your mother, it's impossible for us to know now."

"I'm sorry to hear that, Auntie. That's terrible news."

"You know, I thought Swee Hua might leave for a few weeks, or a few months, but then she would come back. Not in a million years did I think she would leave for good."

"I thought she would come back, too," I said quietly. "I know this sounds silly, but I had all these crazy ideas in my head back then that Mom ran away with Alfred," I confided.

"The thought crossed my mind too, Lily. Your mother and Alfred were two peas in a pod, but I think they were just friends."

"You think so? I just remember how close they were."

"Remember, your mother was the only person Alfred could have a full conversation with because no one else spoke Mandarin like she did. I just don't think either of them would have done something like that. Besides, after taking Alfred to Vancouver, none of us ever saw or heard from him again. He had to go into hiding, Lily. I often think about him, too."

I sighed, and we both laughed to fill the stillness on the phone.

"Auntie." I took a deep breath. "I need some answers. Do you know of any way I could find Alfred?"

"Oh, Lily ... Hmm ... You know what? Let me ask my cousin Agnes. It's been a few years since we've talked about him. Maybe she does know something by now. Alfred was her brother-in-law, after all. I can't promise you anything, but let me see what I can find out, okay?"

"Oh, thank you, Auntie! You have no idea how much this means to me."

"Don't thank me yet, okay? Just send me some photos of Leo. Choo Neo has already sent out the invites for the red egg party, and I can't wait to come visit."

"It will be so nice to see you, Auntie. Thank you for answering my questions."

As I hung up, I looked around and realized I had walked all the way to the river. So I decided to continue down the path a bit more to take in the vista, the bridge stretching from one side of the wide body of rushing water to the other. For the first time, I felt a sliver of hope.

A few weeks passed with no word from Auntie Miriam. Then one day, while I was juggling Leo in one arm and handing the fishmonger at Kowloon Market a tilapia to gut and clean with the other, I could feel my phone vibrate in my pocket.

Auntie left me a voice mail. "Lily, I'm sorry it's taken me so long to get back to you, but I decided to go to Calgary to ask Agnes in person. I have news. Call me back."

I tapped my foot, waiting impatiently for the fishmonger to finish. I grabbed the fish, a bunch of coriander, green onions, ginger, and garlic and ran to the cash register. Frazzled, I secured Leo into her stroller with her pacifier and dialed Auntie Miriam.

"Auntie! Sorry for missing your call. I was just out getting groceries. I'm walking home so I apologize for all the background noise."

"Lily, no need to apologize. I'm glad you called. Agnes does know where Alfred is. You won't believe this, but he's actually in Ottawa!"

"What? How can that be?"

"It's incredible. After all this time, he's practically your neighbour. Agnes gave me his phone number. I can text it to you."

"Why didn't she tell us before?"

"I asked her the same thing. Apparently, Alfred was so afraid of being found and sent back to China that he didn't get in touch with anyone, including his brother, for many years. Even after he reconnected with his family, he made them swear they would never tell anyone. Agnes only felt it was safe now that he's obtained Canadian citizenship."

"Did you ask her about my mother?"

"Yes. Agnes said that Alfred never mentioned anything about her, but that doesn't mean he doesn't know anything. You should call him."

"I will, Auntie. Thank you for this. So much."

When I returned home, I didn't wait. Leo was on my hip, drooling on my shirt, when I called Alfred. I got his voice mail. I hadn't prepared what I was going to say, so I hung up and tried again later that day. The same thing happened. I hung up again.

When John got home, I told him my news.

"Maybe you should leave a message. Nobody picks up the phone on a number they don't recognize anymore," he pointed out.

"I know. I just don't know what to say."

"Maybe keep it simple? Tell him the truth—that you just learned he's in Ottawa, too."

"What if he doesn't call me back?"

"He definitely won't call you back if you don't leave a message."

I handed Leo to John and left a message for Alfred.

日
Say

JOHN DECIDED TO GO ON PARENTAL LEAVE to give me a reprieve from the loneliness and exhaustion of motherhood. I watched with admiration, and a little jealousy, as he delighted in providing every little thing Leo needed. He made it look effortless. He was gentle, comforting, structured. He cleaned, cooked, all more efficiently than I did. I marvelled at how he attended deftly to our daughter and two pots of simmering stew on the stove.

Then one day, as I was sitting on the couch with my feet up, I looked at the two people in my family. John had just finished reading and singing a Ukrainian folktale to Leo, who smiled at him from his lap. He talked with her in his language, and she babbled back. I felt like I was looking at two strangers.

Then Leo said, "Ta Ta."

John pointed at himself in astonishment and said, "Tato!"

"Ta Ta!" Leo screamed in delight.

"Did you hear that? I think she said her first word! She called me—"

"I heard that! What a milestone. I wish I'd recorded it," I said.

My chest was tight, like the walls were closing in. I was unable to breathe and ran to the washroom to cry. Already I was feeling inadequate as a mother, but realizing I lacked the ability to share my mother tongue with my baby put me over the edge. Was it my fault that I had nothing to pass on to her? Did I have anything to give? She had said Tato before Mama. The distance between us tugged at my heart. My tears were flowing, but my fists were clenched. I sat on the edge of the bathtub with my head between my knees, sobbing but also raging. I was angry at Father for washing away any language or culture he had when he came to Canada. I was angry at Mother for leaving us here without someone to teach us anything about who we were.

Then it dawned on me: this was how Mother felt. Isolated from family who could help her and teach us, she left when she felt we didn't need her anymore. She must have watched Bea and me and realized that we were lost causes, strangers.

I thought of the time a few months after Abby was born when I came by to pick up Hilary to go to a movie. Auntie Elizabeth had greeted me at the door. She was in the middle of reading a book strewn with Chinese characters to her infant grandchild.

Hilary raced down the stairs, pulling on her parka.

"We're not in a rush," I said. "The movie doesn't start for another hour."

"I know, but it might be nice to walk in the mall a bit. Let's go. Ma, she's sleeping! You don't need to read the book to her!"

"Aya, she is listening to my voice. She will learn more this way. Besides, you're not teaching her anything!"

Hilary rolled her eyes. "My mother doesn't see the irony in the fact that we talk in English all the time," she said after shutting the door behind us. "Sometimes she catches herself and starts speaking to me in Cantonese, and then makes me do the same. But as soon as she wants to criticize me, she makes sure I understand by speaking English."

"Your mom means well," I said. "I love how she's reading to the baby."

"Well, maybe she's right. I can't teach Abby as well as she can. Don't tell her I said that, though. I don't want it to go to her head."

Sitting on the edge of the bathtub, I felt sadness for the loss of something I couldn't touch but could feel its absence, like an essential internal organ. It wasn't actually that I was jealous of John. I was glad he had that richness to give Leo. I was angry that the choice was made for me long ago, angry at myself for not realizing sooner that I could have done something about it before Leo arrived.

Sinking to the bathroom floor, I resolved that it would be better for Leo to spend the rest of her time at home with her tato. He had much more to offer her than I ever could. I needed to be more than a mom for a while.

Going back to work was easy. I hadn't felt so alive since Leo was born. I was in control again, comforted by my competency in my professional world. Although guilt crept into my heart, the adrenalin from standing up in court in my black vest and robes and white tabs, no matter how ill-fitting, was exhilarating.

My colleagues complained about wearing the robes, but I liked how they were supposed to make us look anonymous, unidentifiable, so that only our words would have an impact. It fed my longing to blend in, to fall in line, to have a particular standing. I revelled in the camouflage the robes gave me, seeking to hide in the heavy cloak, but sometimes I would be greeted by people as if I were the clerk in the courtroom, there to transcribe or assist the judges, and I would be reminded that I was not invisible. Still, the weight of the wool kept me grounded and blocked any self-doubt. I was proud to say I was a member of the Law Society of Ontario.

My first day back in court came a few weeks after I returned to work. My colleague Nadine gave me a case that she had done all the written work for. "I've submitted everything to the court. All you have to do is argue it. Good luck!" she said.

"Are you sure you don't want to argue it yourself?" I asked.

"No, I'm going on vacation. Finally!"

The judicial review was straightforward. The main argument was that a member of the Immigration and Refugee Board made an error in law. The presiding judge was more engaged than usual and peppered me and opposing counsel with questions. I relished the dance and never tired of going to court. Every case was different, and every appearance unpredictable. Counsel and judges brought up questions that I hadn't prepared for, forcing me to think on my feet. Now I had an extra spring in my step and a more confident lilt to my voice. Any misgivings anyone had about my early return were erased when they saw my performance during my oral argument.

I never forgot the power that I saw Elaine Wong wield all those years ago. Even though she didn't succeed in Alfred's case, I felt that she was a sorcerer of some kind, that her role as a lawyer possessed a kind of magic.

When I was studying for my immigration law exam, I often thought about how Alfred might have won his case if he had come forward just one year later. The 1989 Tiananmen Square Massacre happened the June following Alfred's departure from Sparwood. Chinese dissidents were recognized as refugees more readily after human rights organizations documented the wrongs perpetrated against people in China. As we watched the turmoil unfold on our television, Auntie Choo Neo furrowed her forehead, worried for the people on the streets, tsking in disbelief.

I'll never forget Father's reaction. "This is why I've never been to China," he declared. "Look at how they treat people there. I'm so glad I live in a democracy, where I have citizenship and rights."

If Mother had been with us, she would have defended China. She would have said things were more complicated. She would have blamed the disturbing news on the West's portrayal of the events. She would have said that awful things happen everywhere. She would have implored Father not to abandon his kin.

Standing here in court sometimes felt surreal, and I wondered what Elaine Wong would say if she could see me now.

On my way to the robing room after the hearing, I saw a Chinese man waiting at the entrance to the courtroom. He stared at me intently. "Lily?" he said.

"Hello, do I know you?" I said politely. He looked familiar. Was he an old client? I was embarrassed that baby brain had affected my memory.

"It's Alfred."

I was shocked. Could it be? Then I saw it. He was older, grey, with more wrinkles, but the boyish grin and round face were the same.

"Do you remember me?" he asked.

"Yes, of course!" He seemed shorter and thinner. "Your English is amazing."

"Thank you. Can I take you to lunch?"

After dropping off my files in my car, Alfred and I crossed Metcalfe Street to walk along Sparks. We settled on D'Arcy McGee's and ordered pub fare.

"How did you find me?" I asked. "I left you a message weeks ago. I had given up hope that you would call me back."

"I was so surprised to hear your voice, Lily. At first, I wasn't going to call you back. I still have that old fear of getting caught in Canada. Then I saw an opportunity to see you in person. I'm taking the paralegal course at Algonquin College and my instructor for the immigration law class advised us to attend a hearing at the federal court. I saw your name as the lawyer for this case and knew it was fate," Alfred asserted.

"I was surprised to hear you're in Ottawa now," I said.

"Yes, I moved here after I got married. My wife worked for Nortel until it sought bankruptcy protection, going belly up like the mines," Alfred replied.

I stared at Alfred sitting in front of me. "I can't believe we've been here in the same city. I've always wondered what happened to you. All of us in Sparwood were worried about you. How were you able to stay in Canada?"

"I went to Vancouver and worked for several years in the kitchens of noodle houses, away from the eyes of the authorities. I met my wife there. She's Canadian, like you, and taught me English. Her father owned one of the noodle houses that I was working in. We fell in love despite her father's objections and married so that she could sponsor me."

I nodded dumbly, marvelling at how far Alfred had come and how luck had brought him to where he was. Like Father, he was eventually able to shed his sallow skin of statelessness.

"My wife died last year. She had cancer. For many years, I worked odd jobs, teaching in Saturday Chinese schools, working in construction, cooking in restaurants. My writing stopped after my refugee hearing. That whole ordeal took my writing away from me. But after my wife died, I decided to become a paralegal to help others. And I've started writing again."

"Alfred, your story is incredible. I'm so sorry to hear of your loss. I would've liked to have met your wife. Do you have any children?" I asked.

"A daughter. She's in university right now in Toronto. But enough about me! What about you?" Alfred queried.

"Where do I begin? Well, I moved to Ottawa for a job, and my father and Auntie Choo Neo followed me. I can't wait to tell them you're here."

"And you're a lawyer!" Alfred said excitedly. "Your father must be proud."

I smiled. "Yes, can you believe it? Elaine Wong inspired me to become an immigration lawyer."

"She was very commanding. I remember that, too." Alfred looked down at his napkin, folding it into smaller sections.

"I'm sorry, I didn't mean to bring up bad memories." I rested my hand on his arm.

"No, I think she did what she could. It's just hard to believe you've grown up! And what about your sister?" Alfred said, the sparkle returning to his eyes.

"Bea's a history professor in Montreal. Oh, and I have a daughter, Leo. In fact, we're having a delayed red egg party for her. You should come! Auntie Miriam will be there. A lot of people you knew from Sparwood will be there. I'm sure everyone would love to see you."

Tears welled in Alfred's eyes, and we hugged. After a quiet moment, Alfred ventured, "You called me to talk about your mother, didn't you?"

I nodded in anticipation.

"I know where she went," he said.

I didn't know what to say. My suspicions were correct. After all these years, it was Alfred who held the key. I looked into his eyes and plunged headlong into the past.

赤
Red

FOR MANY YEARS, I had wild ideas about where Mother was and what she was doing. Some were painful, like she was off on some tropical island in Asia with a new husband and children, laughing and eating durian and mee goreng. Other fantasies were more comforting but just as painful, like Mother was toiling away in a faraway country as a seamstress, begging a lawyer to help her find a way to reunite us. When I was a teenager, I saw a gaunt woman meandering on the street in downtown Calgary. She had long black hair and was smoking a cigarette, the fumes rising in front of her dark-circled eyes. She reminded me of E gui, the hungry ghost, a malnourished spirit haunted by starvation and the insatiable need to fill the emptiness within. I imagined she wore Mother's face. Was she astray somewhere with her memory lost? Would I recognize her if she was standing in front of me? What if she needed help and I hadn't tried harder to look for her? These guilty thoughts tormented me in nightmares for weeks after I saw that spectral woman. I fought hard to push them out of my head in my youth, alternately tending and hiding the wound.

Now, sitting in the pub with Alfred, it was like a knife had suddenly gashed open the scar. The prospect of learning the truth about Mother induced a bout of hyperventilation. Alfred looked at me with concern and waited, saying nothing for some time. After I had regained my composure, Alfred gently placed his hand on mine and said, "I'm so sorry. I should have known that this would be a painful topic."

"Alfred, please. It's not your fault. You're right, it still hurts after all these years. I think I just needed to ready myself. I've been asking everyone about my mother. I thought I could get some answers from my father, but either he doesn't want to talk about it, or he doesn't know."

Alfred nodded. "Your father doesn't know, but I do. Do you want to know?"

I closed my eyes and took a deep breath. "Yes."

Alfred told me that when he first moved to Vancouver to work in a Chinese restaurant he was depressed and abused by the owner. He was forced to work twelve-hour days with no time off for little pay while he boarded in a small room above the restaurant with three other men. He didn't go outside because for fear of being caught. There were no books for him to read, and he was never alone. For an introvert like him, it was torture.

He had been there for about six months when he saw Mother come into the restaurant. She ordered a bowl of soup and kept looking towards the kitchen. Apparently, Cathy had told Mother where Alfred was. He requested a cigarette break, went into the dining room, gave Mother a surprised but delighted look, and motioned for her to follow him out back.

I imagined a worn, tired Alfred, a dirty apron wound around his skinny waist, a cigarette dangling from his thin lips, the wrinkles now deeper around his eyes. Mother, I envisioned, was wearing her high-heeled boots, since it was rainy and cold, and a wool coat with a fur fringe, clicking out the restaurant door and around the side.

"What are you doing here, Swee Hua?" Alfred asked.

"I'm leaving Canada. Do you want to come back to Asia with me?"

Alfred scoffed and lit his cigarette. "Don't you think if I wanted to leave, I would have done so by now?"

"Maybe you haven't thought it through. You wrote for a reason— to change the way the world works. Don't you think our world, our culture, is worth saving?"

Alfred looked sharply at my mother. "Why are you here? Where is Ah Loy? Where are the girls?"

My mother drew deeply on her cigarette and looked up at the sky, tilting her head as if to pour the tears back into her head. "They're not here. They're better off."

"What do you mean?"

"I mean, they're still in Sparwood."

"Are you leaving Ah Loy?"

The tears now flowed freely onto her face, smearing the heavy eye makeup she wore, trying to hide the sleepless nights she endured. "Yes."

"Why, Swee Hua? Why?"

"Listen, I don't have time to explain this to you. I've made up my mind. I can't stay here in this dead, cold place anymore. I feel like I'm going crazy. I need to go home. Nothing you say will change my mind."

"Okay, listen. I can't stay out here long. Meet me at the Marco Polo tonight. Do you know it?" Alfred inquired.

Mother nodded. "I know exactly where it is."

"Okay. Nobody knows me as Alfred here, and I'd like to keep it that way. Call me Wei when you see me."

When Alfred finished work that night, he was exhausted, but he waited until everyone had gone upstairs or left to go to the mah-jong tables or bars down the street, and then he walked for a few minutes down Pender Street towards the Marco Polo's neon sign. In the six months of Alfred's sojourn in Vancouver, he'd noticed how much those bright lights had dimmed. When he'd first arrived, he was amazed at how vibrant and busy Vancouver's Chinatown was. Now, a few flickering bulbs clung to the sides of the buildings like forgotten relics, waiting to die out. It was as if Chinatown were disappearing right before his eyes.

By the time Alfred arrived at the Marco Polo, the 10:30 show was well under way. A melodious voice singing one of Teresa Teng's signature ballads, "Yuèliàng Dàibiǎo Wǒ de Xīn," or "The Moon Represents My Heart," hypnotized the room. Alfred hadn't heard the romantic song in some time, and the sweetness of the voice was eerie. He looked at the stage to see if somehow the Marco Polo had done the impossible and brought Teresa Teng to Vancouver's Chinatown. They had, after all, hosted the Platters in the past. To Alfred's amazement, it was Mother.

Alfred described the rouge on her cheeks and lips, the red polish on her long fingernails, and the fluffy curls of her hair topped by a crown of gleaming fake jewels. Wearing a sequined evening gown, Mother glided across the stage with her arms outstretched, casting a spell over the crowd. The notes escaped her pouting lips effortlessly, beckoning waltzing lovers to the dance floor.

Alfred told me that it was poignant that he entered the Marco Polo to that song. The popularity of Teresa Teng was a sign of modernization, as well as cultural innovation, showing the world that Chinese music was richer and more diverse than just the revolutionary songs. The song Mother sang represented a decadence that the Communist Party tried to quell, but the government could not prevent it from seeping into the country.

Mother's set ended with "Goodbye My Love," an iconic song about a promise not to forget someone after they had passed.

After her set, Mother changed her clothes and joined Alfred at the bar. Eyes were on the couple, since everyone wondered why the famous singer Pearl had come out tonight for the first time to join someone for a drink. The bartender, protective of Mother, glared at anyone who looked like they were contemplating interrupting them.

"Swee Hua, I had no idea you were performing here," Alfred said. "I had heard about the magnificent Pearl but of course didn't know it was you."

"I needed to make some money, and this was the easiest way for me to do it," Mother explained.

"I wish I had known. I would have come sooner."

"I know," Mother said, and they embraced. "Wei, listen. I've been talking to Cathy Yee. Do you remember her?"

"Yes, she was my fixer. She got me the job at the restaurant."

"She is very resourceful. She got me this job here and has been helping me plan for the future. I'm going back."

"What do you mean, Swee Hua?"

"When I heard those critical things you said about China at the immigration board, I realized you were in a difficult position. But your writing inspired me. It made me think about reconnecting with my homeland," she said.

"Which homeland would that be?"

"Brunei, anywhere in Asia. Anywhere but here."

"But your home is here?"

"But my roots are there. I feel at home there. Isn't that worth reclaiming, protecting, preserving?"

"You and Ah Loy and the children have built something here in Canada."

"I know Ah Loy thinks he's at home. He is comfortable disappearing, being the dutiful servant. But I don't want that. I don't want to forget my home. And not just for a Canadian passport."

"Swee Hua, I'm so surprised to hear you talk like this. I thought that seeing what I went through would make you realize what a complicated endeavour that would be."

"You're living like a cockroach here, Wei. Come back with me. Reclaim your dignity. We're not welcome here, and I refuse to die here."

"But what about your family?" Alfred asked.

"Ah Loy betrayed me. I can't look at him. I can't live with him anymore." Mother told Alfred about how she missed the opportunity to say goodbye to her mother before she died.

"What about your daughters?" Alfred inquired.

"They're doing well. Despite Ah Loy's faults, he is a good father. I can't be a good mother unless I am at home with myself. I hope to come back for them one day," she said.

As Alfred reported my mother's intentions, I had no words. I was fighting really hard to stop the tears welling up in my eyes. After a few moments, they just came down and I used the pub napkins to wipe the wetness from my face.

Alfred said that he learned from Cathy that Mother had indeed left Canada after obtaining a permanent resident card for Brunei. After a few months, he received a letter from Mother. It included a picture of her wearing an apron and standing outside a kopitiam. Her hair was blowing sideways, and he could see large rain clouds in the background hovering over the bamboo awning of the open-air coffee shop. Mother wrote that she had found a job with her aunt who owned the kopitiam that sold the area's famous chicken rice. She expressed regret that Alfred had not come with her but said that she finally felt at home.

Why didn't she write to us? I imagined what it would have been like to receive a postcard from my Mother in Brunei. How might my life have changed had I only known where she was and what she was doing? Would I have been less sad, less insecure, less dramatic in my youth?

Alfred wrote back expressing warm regards and well wishes for her new life. A few months later, he received another letter. Mother wrote that she had gotten into an argument with her aunt at the kopitiam. After the falling out, she went to her older sister, Ah Lian, in Brunei and asked for a job. Ah Lian's husband owned a mechanic's shop and hired her as an office manager. For a time, she was content, but Ah Lian's husband started making advances towards her.

"Your mother wrote me that her sister called her names and said ugly things to her. She taunted her by saying she was an unwanted, illegitimate child. That your mother was not really her sister."

"I knew as a child she didn't always get along with Auntie Ah Lian. What happened to her?" I prodded Alfred.

"Your mother left Brunei. In her last letter to me, she said she was working in another kopitiam in Ipoh. I wrote her back several times, but my letters went unanswered."

Never in my wildest dreams did I think Mother would go to another foreign country to try again to plant seeds, something Father was trying to do for us here in Canada. It stung to hear that Alfred knew more about Mother's whereabouts than anyone in my family. Why did she cut us off? Why didn't she reach out to us?

Alfred wrote down the name of the kopitiam in Ipoh on my napkin and said, "I'm sorry I don't know more."

方
Square

I CAME HOME FROM MY LUNCH with Alfred exhausted and spent. I threw my briefcase into my office and draped my garment bag containing my robes over my chair. John and Leo were napping, and I was glad that I didn't have to engage in conversation.

I went to the kitchen to fix myself a cup of tea. Furious, I wanted to throw the mug in my hand against the wall but thought better of it. A sleeping baby was not something you wanted to mess with. I gave up on the tea.

John found me splayed on the couch in my hoodie and jogging pants, crying.

"Oh no ... Bad day in court?" he asked. "Bad news for your client?"

I leaned towards the coffee table and grabbed a few tissues to dab my eyes and wipe my nose. "No, I had a great day in court. I just had an unexpected visitor."

John sat down on the couch with me, and I told him about my encounter with Alfred and the news of my mother. He listened in disbelief, rubbing my ankle.

"I just don't understand why she went there!" I blubbered. "I mean, I know she was born in Malaysia, but she never lived there. She had no ties, no links, nothing!"

"Lily, some things aren't black and white. They can't be neatly packaged within borders," John said calmly. "Obviously, your mother must have felt she had a tie there."

"How can you say that?" I was incensed. "She had spent the last decade of her life here in Canada. She has a family here, children. Aren't those ties important?"

"You can't speak for her," John said.

"Why? Why are you defending her?" I exclaimed.

"I'm not. I know she's done the unforgiveable to you and Bea. I don't know if I could forgive someone for doing that."

I nodded and pulled on the drawstring of my hoodie.

John continued. "I'm not saying she was right, but there might be something you aren't seeing or understanding. Would you judge me if I flew to Ukraine tomorrow to join the thousands demonstrating against the government to try to save an independent Ukraine from being swallowed up by Russia?" John asked.

"What are you talking about?"

John lifted his tablet from the coffee table and placed it between us. The images were disturbing. A large public square filled with thousands of people, winter coats, makeshift shields of corrugated steel, gas masks, yellow and blue flags mixed with the European Union flag, burning vehicles, protest signs, plumes of smoke, barricades, and soldiers with guns. "Our identity, culture, language are at risk by moving away from the European Union and into the corrupt arms of Russia," he said. I watched in horror as John scrolled through hundreds of pictures, letting me take it all in.

"Listen, I was born here in Canada. My parents were also born here. Yet my blood boils watching Yanukovych shoot people in the main square," John said. "If Leo wasn't here, you better believe I would be on the next plane. Why do you think I've been boxing up winter coats and medical supplies? When your people are suffering and fighting for their survival of course you want to do something about it."

"I had no idea you felt so strongly about what was going on. I didn't realize it was so personal. I thought you were just doing something humanitarian," I said, moving closer to him.

"It is humanitarian, but it's also a defence of our Ukrainian identity in the world." John's voice started to thicken, and I took his hand, surprised to learn he'd sheltered me from his inner turmoil in the last few months.

"My point is you can't know what your mother was thinking. Her fights, her sufferings are unknown to you. Her motivation, while foreign to you, may not have been foreign for her."

What John said didn't make me feel better, and he saw that. "Knowing this doesn't mean that you have to forgive her," he said. "It doesn't mean you have to accept her choice. It just means that you may not fully understand how and why she made that choice." He squeezed my hand and I nodded.

"There is just so much I don't know," I said. "We're just speculating, guessing."

"Maybe you should ramp up your quest to find her. Ask her yourself."

I stared at him in disbelief. "My mother obviously doesn't want to be found. If she did, she would have written, called. Something, anything." I threw up my hands.

"You said that Alfred doesn't know what happened after she went to Ipoh. Maybe you should find out."

"You mean go to Ipoh?"

John nodded. "I'm on parental leave now. You can take all that vacation you've banked. Maybe now is the right time."

"We're really going to go halfway across the world?"

"With a baby!" John said, laughing.

Part 3

見
See

入

Enter

"THERE'S A REASON WHY I CAME TO CANADA. So you would never have to go back."

Even though Father was opposed to the trip, he was helping me clean out my fridge for the sojourn abroad. Wiping down the shelves despite my protests to leave them be, Father berated Auntie Choo Neo for travelling with us.

Auntie defended herself and revealed she was a bit homesick. "I miss Winston. Besides, she needs someone to show her around, lah," she said, pointing at me.

I had not invited Auntie Choo Neo, and although I wanted help, I knew how she felt about Mother.

When I told Bea, she said, "Why would you go there? I'm surprised you're even interested."

"What do you mean?" I asked.

"Well, you hate everything Chinese."

"It's not Chinese there."

"Yes, it is. It's a mixture, but there are definitely a lot of Chinese people there."

"Well, it's really John's idea. We have some time and I love to travel. He's never been there."

"Funny how John is more into your culture than you are."

For now, all Bea needed to know was that we were going. I knew if I told her why, she would use any means, including upsetting Father and Auntie Choo Neo, to convince me not to. I didn't need a full-scale assault on my plan. I didn't want anyone's hopes or fears to bubble to the surface like the marrow coming out of the pork bones in Father's soup. I had enough of my own to deal with.

John's idea to travel to Ipoh lifted my spirits. I had lost confidence in my ability to judge people, to trust, and to recall the past in a way that I thought was accurate. Planning the trip distracted me from reconciling what I had heard from Alfred with my mixed feelings towards Mother. I wanted so badly to be right about Mother still loving us, and wrong about her moving on without us. Planning the trip also bought me time. I could divert my attention to the logistical tasks of travel instead of thinking about what the truth could be.

John and I thought it best that we accompany Auntie Choo Neo to Brunei, and then head to Ipoh on our own. We had a mere two weeks to find out a much as we could.

Flying with Leo was challenging. Why did a baby need so many things? But Auntie Choo Neo proved to be helpful, lugging gear, holding Leo, and just reassuring us things would be all right. Auntie expertly settled Leo, rocking her in the aisles of the airplane and gently placing her in the travel bassinet. As Auntie rocked the baby, I wondered if my own mother would want to do the same thing if she met Leo.

We were given immigration cards to fill out on the plane, and I dutifully filled in all the boxes. I had to complete one for everyone, including Leo. When I reached the box marked "race," I didn't know what to write for her. What was she? Why was this so important? So I listed her as Canadian. And felt guilty that I checked mine as Chinese.

When we landed in the capital city of Brunei, the thickness of the air enveloped me. It was a heat I had never felt before. My skin stuck to Leo's, and she burrowed her warm head into my shoulder, trying to escape the blazing kiln we found ourselves in.

Winston greeted us at the arrivals level, playfully waving a sign that said, *Welcome to Bandar Seri Begawan!*

I recognized him right away. The dimples and stray hair sticking up on the back of his head was the same as in the childhood photos I had seen. I also recognized the raised-skin scars on his arm, the markers Father shared that were self-inflicted as a way to move through the elementary stages of suffering in Buddhism as an attempt to reach enlightenment. Father told me he did this when he was young and foolish, and implored me never to do the same, clarifying that Buddhism actually abhors harm to anyone, including oneself. Like everything else from back home, Father didn't want to talk about Buddhism when I asked him questions about it. He said it was not important for me to understand. I marvelled at how Winston looked at once familiar and foreign to me. The scars signalled a kind of kinship but also acts of youthful rebellion and exploration that are virtually unknown in Canada.

Auntie hugged her son and said, "Jin gu boh kua dio, it's been a long time since I've seen you."

It was one of the few times I had seen her tear up. I realized that Auntie had been apart from her only son for years, her last visit right after I graduated high school. It suddenly occurred to me that Auntie Choo Neo had chosen to leave her child behind, too. She chose to come to Canada, but she had wanted to bring Winston with her. She'd begged him to come, but he refused. He was already a young adult at the time, set on making his way in the country of his birth, unafraid of the precarity of his lack of citizenship. Auntie was always convinced Winston would eventually come around, but he didn't. He held firm like the sea almond trees along the coast in Brunei, highly tolerant of difficult saline conditions, even blooming and fruiting periodically. I wondered whether Auntie regretted her choice. She was a beacon, awaiting Winston's arrival. It must have pained Auntie to let the years of separation go by, watching from afar as Winston married, started a business, and lived his life.

I wondered whether I would have a similar reunion on this trip. Would I look at Mother's face, hug her, shed tears? Would she be happy to see me? Did she have regrets? The anticipation was overwhelming, and although my tears were for Auntie and Winston, I longed so desperately for a similar encounter, a new beginning.

After wiping away her tears, Auntie Choo Neo didn't waste any time. "Ai yo! Look at you! So thin! You not eating?" Auntie's accent suddenly became thicker and more pronounced, as if she'd never left.

"Nice to see you too, Ma. Come, Come!" Winston motioned for us to follow him. "Leave your things. My driver will put them in the car."

John looked at me and mouthed, *Driver?* My cousin's comfortable life here made me wonder what my own life would have been like if my parents had stayed. We climbed into the shiny suv after John installed Leo's car seat.

"Ah, good for safety!" Winston remarked.

"You would know, lah, if you have your own seh kia!" Auntie Choo Neo retorted.

"Ma! Enough already. I told you that we are not interested in children! How many times already?"

"Or you cannot!"

"We can, Ma. But please, stop." Winston turned to John and me in the back seat. "Anyway! You all must be hungry. My driver in the other car is taking your things back home, and I'll take you for lunch. Lily, Ma told me you like kolo mee and karipap. I'll take you to Menglait, Gadong. Veronica is already waiting for us there."

John elbowed me and mouthed, *karipap?*

I whispered, "Curry puffs."

John nodded knowingly.

"My favourites. I can't wait!" I said, smiling.

Luckily, I had taken the diaper bag as we watched the other suv drive off with the rest of our things. The air conditioning was welcome, but it soon turned the vehicle into a fridge, and I was glad that I had the muslin baby blanket to wrap around my shoulders.

Winston parked his car in front of a strip mall and ushered us into a small restaurant teeming with people. We met Winston's wife, Veronica, who was already waiting for us at a table. He shouted something in Malay to the staff, and nods were exchanged. Winston turned to John. "You can handle spicy?"

"I love spicy," John said.

In minutes, the table was filled with all kinds of food. Flaky, puff pastry filled with potato and curried ground meat sat on a plate in the middle of the table. I had always thought Father mangled the name curry puffs because of his accent, but when I heard Winston order them, he said them exactly the same way: karipap. As I bit into one, I relished the crispy coating and made a mental note to apologize to Father for insisting he was pronouncing the name wrong all these years.

My mouth watered as I looked down at my kolo mee, a Sarawak dish of dried noodles tossed in a savoury pork and shallot mixture. But I also coveted Auntie Choo Neo's curry laksa. Her noodles were wrapped around the tiger prawns, balancing on the fish cakes, poking out of the coconut milk and lemongrass broth, taunting me. Veronica saw me eyeing it and prodded Winston to order me a bowl. Now I had two lunches in front of me. John asked if he could try my laksa and Winston interjected, "I ordered you one already, lah!" The entire table erupted in laughter.

A young woman my age walked into the restaurant, jet-black hair straightened to perfection. Her nails were manicured, and she was carrying a luxury Birkin bag on her arm. Her butterfly-sleeved, navy shift dress fit her like a glove, and she was in impeccable shape. It was like she had walked out of a magazine. She sat down at the table next to us and motioned to her Filipino helper to sit next to her with the baby in her arms. She reached over and stroked her child's cheek, and then greeted another woman entering the restaurant who also looked stylish and fresh. I glanced at the baby again. She could not have been much younger than Leo.

So, this was how ladies lunched here. Hilary and I wore yoga outfits and brushed off our stains with our pastry napkins, laughing at the bags under our eyes as our pregnancy weight rested against the table. I watched the helper and considered how all over the world these migrant women had to look after other people's children, while their own children went without their mothers. I wondered how many people I had put in that position in Canada, how many people I had helped get their temporary residence to work as a nanny. I felt conflicted about my role in facilitating the global exchange of women taking care of foreign children to earn money to take care of their own, in their faraway homes. I pledged to do more advocacy work to change the system so that caregivers could come to Canada with permanent immigration status and with their families on arrival. As I caught the helper's eye, she quickly turned away, nervous that she had attracted my attention. I suddenly became conscious of the fact that part of her job was to be invisible and ignored.

I turned back to the table, and Veronica pointed at my uneaten food. "No good?"

"Wo sukat! I love this!" I exclaimed.

Veronica snickered and elbowed Winston. "You need to tell your cousin that she is speaking Malay."

I felt heat rise in my face.

"Lily," Winston chortled as he poked me in the arm, "'sukat' is not Hokkien." My faux pas became a source of amusement at the table, and I felt foolish for trying to speak the local language.

"She did *not* learn that from me, lah," Auntie Choo Neo said.

Winston talked about our cousins and their excitement to see us, updating Auntie with all the juiciest gossip. "Ma, do you remember Ah Hoon?" He leaned in dramatically.

I let mother and son catch up while I searched on my phone one more time for any Swee Huas in Ipoh. None.

"Si beh siao! So crazy!" Auntie crowed. "Wa kah lu gong, I told you." She nudged me to get my reaction.

"Yeah, that *is* unbelievable!" I said, not following the story.

Winston seemed to know exactly who his mother wanted news about and provided just enough information for her to yelp in judgmental glee or laugh uproariously.

At no point during our meal did anyone mention Mother or her family. Even here, across the ocean, she was a taboo topic. But even though nobody would utter her name, Mother was on the tip of my tongue.

Private

A FEW DAYS INTO OUR VISIT, I was still jet-lagged, and Leo was both wired and exhausted. I threw her sleep schedule out the window and we took a midday nap. John and Leo were still sleeping when I emerged from the guest room at Winston's house to find no one else was home. I ventured outside and found my cousin's driver sweeping the driveway.

"Hello, miss. Do you need to go somewhere?"

I paused, and then said, "Yes, I do." In that moment, I decided to go to Auntie Ah Lian's house. I grabbed my bag and showed the driver an address on my phone. My mother's sister must know something.

I had tried calling Uncle Kong Tuan several times after I only received a busy signal calling Auntie Ah Lian's number. I called from the Hong Kong airport during our layover and when we first arrived in Brunei. Both times, Uncle Kong Tuan told me to call him back when I was settled. When I finally reached him to say I was ready to visit, he made excuses for why he was too busy to meet. I knew Mother had a difficult relationship with her sister, but I still hoped that they remained in each other's orbits.

I braced myself for how my relatives might receive me. I was uninvited, unwelcome, and unexpected. When I arrived, Uncle Kong Tuan was in his garden, tending to his collection of bonsai trees, flanked by a series of birdcages hanging under an awning. I startled my elderly uncle by showing up unannounced at his home and quickly introduced myself. Uncle Kong Tuan shifted nervously between the bonsai trees perched on wooden stools and motioned for me to sit at the outdoor table with him. I handed him gifts of maple cookies and a bottle of cognac.

"Will Auntie Ah Lian be joining us?" I asked.

Uncle Kong Tuan sighed and cracked his knuckles. "Your auntie died last year," he replied bluntly.

I stared at my uncle, crestfallen. Finally, I mustered, "Last year? Why didn't you tell us?"

Uncle said in an offended tone, "Tell you? Why should I tell you? I don't even know where your mother is. How should I have told you?"

A breeze triggered tingles in my spine, and I suddenly became aware of the cavernous gorge between my uncle and me. But I couldn't dwell on it. I needed to recover what I could from this meeting.

"Uncle, I'm so sorry for your loss," I said. "Had I known, I would have called you sooner."

"E bo ho, she was not well," he said. "Ken se, cancer."

Uncle told me about her diagnosis and quick decline. I listened and followed him inside his house as he scrambled to make tea and place a few wafer cookies on a plate. In the lull in the conversation, I asked him about his bonsai trees and his birds. He shared his bird calls with me, and his ritual for pruning his trees. When I felt I could, I asked the question I had come for.

"Uncle, you mentioned that you didn't know where my mother was. Do you have any idea where she's gone? That's why I'm here. I've come back to look for her."

Uncle tsked and cracked his knuckles again. "If you don't know, then how am I supposed to know?"

"I know she stayed with you some years ago. Did she leave a forwarding address, a phone number or a letter?"

"No," he said brusquely.

My heart sank. I felt the hope in finding my mother slipping through my fingers like the sand at Muara Beach. The news of Auntie Ah Lian's death was upsetting, even though I didn't have a relationship with her. Now I couldn't ask her what had transpired between the sisters. I wouldn't hear her childhood stories of Mother, even tainted by envy or resentment. I wouldn't be able to query her theories about where Mother may have gone or why. The only person who had known Mother since she was a child was now gone. No one else was left to tell me anything from her past. Even though I was physically closer to the place where I thought Mother might be, I felt further away from her than ever.

When I arrived back at Winston's house, I found everyone home and chatting busily.

"Where have you been?" asked Auntie Choo Neo.

"Just went to the grocery store to get some baby food," I fibbed, as I held the bag out in front of me.

Winston motioned for me to join him in the kitchen to put the food into the fridge. He eyed me warily, and I realized his driver must have told him the errand he was on. "Please don't tell your mother," I said.

Winston laughed. "You know Ma so well. So, tell me, how was your uncle?"

"Did you know that Auntie Ah Lian passed away?"

"Yes. Sayang, what a pity. I heard she was very sick in the end."

"Why didn't anyone tell us?"

"Ma knows."

"Li nang le kong sih mih? What are you all talking about?"

"In fact, your uncle came to me to ask where your mother was to tell her the news."

"Uncle didn't say anything to me about this."

"Maybe he forgot. Maybe he didn't think it was important."

"Maybe he still thinks I'm a little girl," I muttered. Winston gave me a concerned look and didn't deny it. I asked, "What did you tell him?" I was twisting the hem of my blouse, hoping there was news I had not yet uncovered.

"I told him wo m'jai, I don't know. I said I thought we'd be the last people your mother would come to for anything. Swee Hua knew Uncle Ah Loy was looking for her and this side of the family is loyal to your father."

"Does my dad know about Auntie Ah Lian?"

"I believe he does. I don't know why Ma or Uncle Ah Loy didn't tell you. But I can say that your mother's family jin kiam chye, is in a real mess."

I was not a child anymore, and I was disturbed by Auntie Choo Neo's insistence that I be sheltered from things, all these years later. Did she see me as a younger version of Mother, a fragile flower whose petals would fall to the ground if shaken by the news?

I was also frustrated that another avenue of information was now gone. Mother's aunt who owned the kopitiam, the only other person Alfred told me she had seen when she came home, had died years before I had known she had a role in Mother's story. I learned of her death when Father received a call late one night while I was a teenager. He was startled to hear a voice from Brunei. Auntie Ah Lian delivered the news that her aunt had passed away, thinking that she should let Father know in case he knew where Mother was. It was a short, awkward conversation in Hokkien. For me at the time, it solidified the notion that nobody knew where Mother was, including those in Brunei.

I looked at Winston, unsure whether to trust him. It wasn't as if Winston was unfamiliar with Mother. In fact, she had watched over Winston during his early years when Auntie Choo Neo was helping with the family business. He must have sensed my trepidation because he began to speak fondly of Mother, telling me stories about how she taught him to play tennis and took him to the movies.

"This is so frustrating," I complained. "Has no one heard from her? How can that be? Someone must know something."

"Truthfully, Lily? No one has heard from your mother in years. I think she did go see Ah Lian at some point, but it was a short visit that ended badly, from what I heard. I don't know what happened between them."

I was grateful for Winston's openness and willingness to talk about Mother, but the fact that he had not heard about her in years deflated me.

"Did you see my mother when she was in Brunei?"

"No. She avoided this side of the family. I was also younger at the time and wasn't involved with trying to find her or talk to her. I know Uncle Ah Meng tried to find her. Your father was frustrated that his older brother didn't try hard enough, but Uncle Ah Meng insisted he tried many times to find Auntie Swee Hua. I believe him. We only learned she was at Auntie Ah Lian's after she was long gone."

I was surprised by all the drama that had unfolded in my family. I still didn't understand what was so alluring here for Mother, especially when her own children were waiting for her in Canada. I tried to make sense of what Mother gave up to come back to this place. Winston saw my confusion and put an arm around my shoulders.

"So nobody knows where my mother is? Have you heard anything from anyone else?" I tried one last time.

"This place loves gossip. If she was around, we would hear about it. Honestly, Lily, I wish I had something more to tell you. It's like your mother walked off the face of the earth."

龍
Dragon

DURING OUR WEEK IN BRUNEI, Winston took us to Kampong Ayer, where Father grew up. I immediately recognized the houses on stilts, the green-and-gold-topped minaret in the distance, and the wooden water taxis whizzing by. Standing on the dock, I felt like the photographs from my childhood had suddenly come to life.

As we climbed into a water taxi, I realized that my cousin was taking me here out of duty, to bear witness, to see where Father was from. I was glad Leo wasn't with us on this river tour without a life jacket. As the sun shone, we careened under the wooden plankways and through the village, past shops and an array of colourful houses on stilts. Children in hijabs passed on their way home from school, and one boy expertly rode his bicycle in the opposite direction above us on the narrow wooden dock. The driver told us there was once a fire in a section of the village that spread quickly, since all the buildings on stilts were made of wood. The structures we saw were rebuilt with more fireproof material such as concrete siding and equipped with air conditioners and the latest appliances. The houses looked like the modest wartime bungalows in Ottawa, as if they were plucked out of any Canadian suburb and placed on stilts in the Brunei River.

We stopped suddenly and Auntie Choo Neo pointed upwards. "We grew up here! Your father and me. Look at that! All of us in that one small house."

It was now occupied by a family who dangled their laundry over the murky river, waving like flags. A fan was perched in a window like a bird, wrenching its whirring head to one side. I tried to imagine

Father as a young boy, living in this house on stilts, jumping into the river to swim.

Tears formed in the wrinkled corners of Auntie Chee Neo's eyes. "You know, when I was growing up, I hated this place. People would look at our home and know we were poor. It only had two rooms, and all four kids had to share one—me, Uncle Ah Meng, your father, and our baby sister, Ah Muey. All the villagers knew we were the odd ones here. Not many Chinese people lived in Kampong Ayer, but we had no choice. My brothers were so naughty we got kicked out of our rented house, and the only place we could live was among the Malay on the water. We used to shit directly into the river!"

I apologized to John for the vulgarity of Auntie Choo Neo's memory, but he just laughed.

"Do you miss it, Auntie?" I asked.

"No, Canada is my home," she said without hesitation.

After we took some pictures, Auntie gestured that we could go. Whizzing by, the driver pointed at a rock poking out of the river. Perched there, suntanning, was a large crocodile, mouth open, eyes closed. He looked regal, like the king of all dragons, resting before taking calls from his subjects. The wind swept our hair as the motorboat sped deeper into the jungle, away from the village. After a few minutes, we turned towards the shore and our driver pointed upwards. In the distance, we saw proboscis monkeys snacking on some green unripe fruit in the trees, watching us intently as though staking their territory and reminding us who really belonged here. I felt the lure of this place, as if the mangroves' claws clutching the earth underneath the salty water were trying to embrace me. Holding on to the side of the boat, I was surprised how a place could make me feel alive in a different way, seen and understood.

When we finished our boat tour, we stood on the shore and looked across the road to where the Sultan Omar Ali Saifuddien Mosque stood. The golden-domed palace-like structure reminded me of Father's position as a foreign and forgotten subject here, a minority who was openly unwelcome by law. In all his stories of Brunei, it was easy to forget that Father, raised as Buddhist, was living in a Muslim country. My family had chosen to focus on the fact that Brunei had previously been a British colony.

The air was oppressively dense and hot. My sweaty feet were sliding around in my plastic sandals. Mother and I had the same square feet without curves. Now I understood why she never wore socks.

Our weeklong visit was coming to an end, and Winston told Auntie Choo Neo that he wanted to take me to see Jerudong Park, the largest and most expensive amusement park in Southeast Asia. The Brunei government spent $1 billion to build it, and it was made famous when Michael Jackson performed a free concert there in the 1990s.

Winston was clever. We planned to meet up with my cousin on Mother's side, and Winston did not think Auntie Choo Neo would approve. But he also knew that she would have no desire to go to Jerudong Park.

In our spurts of conversation when Auntie Choo Neo was out of earshot, I learned that Winston had attended school with my cousin Priscilla, Auntie Ah Lian's daughter, who now lived in Singapore. Winston introduced us on WhatsApp, and we exchanged a few messages and spoke briefly. I told her I was sorry to hear Auntie Ah Lian had passed away and casually mentioned that it was too bad they she wasn't here in Brunei for a visit, that it would be nice to connect since I had come all this way. Priscilla offered to fly in to meet with us the evening before John, Leo, and I were set to depart for Malaysia. Her generosity filled me with hope.

When we arrived at the amusement park, Winston looked at his watch and rushed us through the admission gate. He was messaging frantically on WhatsApp, and then abruptly stopped. He told me we were meeting Priscilla in an open green space called Colonnade Field. Just then, prayer time was called, and everything at the park came to a standstill. People not praying flooded the field and set up picnic blankets everywhere, making our task of intersecting with Priscilla that much harder. Winston finally found her looking into her phone, and she greeted him with a kiss on the cheek.

"This is Lily, John, and Leo," Winston introduced us.

"Nice to meet you," Priscilla said and embraced me. She had Mother's dancing eyes.

"You know, Priscilla has a great singing voice, just like your mother," Winston informed me. It was like he had read my mind; in front of me was someone I didn't know but recognized.

Priscilla noticed Leo starting to fuss in her stroller and offered to take a walk so that the baby could fall asleep. Winston fell behind us, joining John and the stroller, while Priscilla led me on an aimless wander through Jerudong Park. At first, she let me gawk at the stillness of the park during prayer time. The roller coaster, carousel, and Ferris wheel still as statues.

After a few minutes, Priscilla linked arms with me. "I don't know what you've heard, but our mothers weren't the kindest of sisters to each other," she said.

"I know."

"Ma claimed her little sister got away with everything, that she was spoiled by Po Po. I also heard Auntie Swee Hua say the same thing—that Ma was the favoured child and got everything she wanted."

"I never met Auntie Ah Lian. My mom didn't talk about her often, but when she did it wasn't flattering. She would often say that Auntie Ah Lian was the older sister but didn't act like it. She said that our gong gong favoured her, and that she had a mean streak and bullied her."

"Your mother, my mother. Stubborn women who both thought they were right." Priscilla shook her head ruefully. "They had more in common than you know. Both were unloved by one parent. Both felt the other was taking something away from them. Both were unkind to each other."

"Could it really be true, or just bad talk from them both?"

"I saw it. I wasn't living at home anymore, but I visited when Auntie Swee Hua was briefly living with Ma. The jealousy, the yelling, the name-calling. It was as if they were children again. I couldn't believe it. I have a sister, so I know how hard it is to get along!"

"I have a sister, too," I said with a laugh.

Prayer time ended, and crowds of people shuffled into lines waiting for the rides to regain their momentum and awaken from their temporary inertia.

"Did you get a sense of why my mother left Canada?" I asked.

"No, not really. She kept her distance from me. I only saw her once for a couple days while I was visiting. All I can tell you is that she was very unhappy. At the time, I thought it was because she was not getting along with Ma, but it could've been something else."

"Did Auntie Ah Lian ever say anything to you about why she left?"

"She just told me that Auntie Swee Hua left on her own, and that she couldn't care less where she ended up. I told her that this was cruel and that she would not want me to treat my sister this way. She taught me and my sister differently."

"Same here."

"I'm sorry I don't know more. Maybe the next generation can do better." Priscilla smiled at me hopefully.

"Absolutely," I agreed.

"Listen, Lily, there's another reason I came. I have something for you." Priscilla reached into skirt pocket and put something in my hand. My eyes widened and I gasped. It was Mother's jade bracelet. It looked the same as when I last saw it, with a brown mark on one side.

Priscilla helped me twist it onto my wrist. "Ma had this, but I knew it wasn't hers. It originally belonged to our po po, but I believe Po Po gave it to Auntie Swee Hua. Ma told me it didn't really belong to her because she wasn't her true daughter. I remember Auntie Swee

Hua frantically searching for it when I was visiting. I even helped her look for it. When Ma died, I found it among her things. I thought maybe one day Auntie Swee Hua would return, and I could give it back. Instead, you're here. Giving it to you is the next best thing."

I hugged my cousin, touched by this gift. As I was embracing Pricilla, the giant rides around us clanged into motion, spinning, whirring, and squeaking. The sight of the Ferris wheel rotating reminded me of the windmills standing tall above the undulating grasslands near Pincher Creek.

Pricilla gently pulled away. "I know you must miss her. I miss Ma, too." It was both awful and comforting that Priscilla understood the void our mothers had left.

With Winston and John, we took turns going on the rides and watching a napping Leo. Throughout, my cousins happily told John and me tales of their childhood in Brunei. I envied the large family gatherings with buffets of food and the stories that the uncles, after a few drinks, would laugh over. A favourite story included a dramatic re-enactment of how they avoided working for my stern grandfather by hiding in the water under the docks in the Brunei River. I glimpsed another life I could have had. Father had kept too much from me.

However, I felt a shared experience in how we interacted with our elders. We laughed over our slapstick attempts to solve their internet and tech problems imitating their inherited gestures and mannerisms. It was the first time I had genuinely laughed out loud during this trip, and the first time I felt like I didn't need to explain or hide anything about my family. I soaked up our merriment and savoured my cousins' familiar lilting accents. They were absent from my past, yet now I felt like I was granted membership into a club I hadn't known existed.

My mother's bracelet looked familiar around my adult wrist, and I twisted around like she used to. I wasn't accustomed to the weight it brought to my arm, and the clanging sound it made against the bar strapped across my lap on the Ferris wheel delighted me. A second chance was being granted to me.

至
Arrive

NESTLED BETWEEN THE LIMESTONE MOUNTAINS was the town of Ipoh. Although its glory days of the boom from the tin mines were behind it, the city was still charming. Settled in the urban valley were low buildings with a colonial touch, their age betraying them. The windows of the buildings looked bruised and battered, their wooden shutters faded and warped from the heat. I imagined a shiny and vibrant array of colours among the buildings in Ipoh's heyday, the various gowns each building had donned now revealed through layers of paint that flecked off the edifices because of the monsoon rains, revealing old, and older, hues from a different time. Money from the tin mines, as well as members of the Hakka Miners' Club, had long fled. I wondered if there had been another girl like me, who had looked out of the back window of a car, saying goodbye to her hometown when her father lost his job at the mine. During her childhood among the pink mountains, did she know Ipoh was in danger of becoming a ghost town?

Our taxi driver informed me that the city was experiencing a renaissance, with artists attracted to the low rents for both apartments and studio space, and tourists eager to try tasty local favourites such as white coffee, chicken rice, and Hakka mee.

I asked the driver whether he had heard of Kong Heng, the kopitiam where mother had worked. Apparently, the place was still standing and hadn't changed since the 1980s. He told me his grandfather had taken him there every weekend, and there had always been a sea of people hovering around the tables like pigeons looking for crumbs.

The driver emphasized it was an authentic kopitiam, and that some of the hawker stalls in the open-air coffee shop were the same as when he was a little boy. He added that we should definitely talk to the auntie at the popiah stall, since she had been serving the Hokkien-style pancake spring rolls there the longest. And the uncle at the chee cheong fun stall, with its savoury rice noodle rolls, was a close second.

The next day I found myself wandering in the old town of Ipoh. The colonial buildings flanking the pink mountains reminded me of the forlorn pink motel in Michel, the ghost town on the outskirts of Sparwood. I stood before them, looking for the kopitiam Sin Yoon Loong, where I'd heard they had the best white coffee. Famous in this part of the world, the white coffee's nutty, less bitter taste comes from the shorter roast at lower temperatures with palm oil margarine, turning the bean a whitish colour. Here, the white coffee is not complete without sweetened condensed milk. When a cup was placed in front of me, I sipped the hot, creamy drink so quickly I had to order another right away. I also satisfied my craving for the region's signature kopitiam breakfast of soft-boiled eggs with kaya toast, buttered and spread with the sweet coconut jam.

I found a seat under a whirring ceiling fan to wait for my breakfast and checked my WhatsApp messages. Nothing. As I dove into my second cup of white coffee, I realized this was one of the rare moments I was alone on this trip, and I loved the silence within me amid the chaos of loud voices, cups kissing saucers, and motorbikes and cars honking outside. I was so tired. More than the travelling, it was because of the careful conversations I had to have with family about the past, the unruly emotions I had to wrestle with in response to the discoveries and non-discoveries, all while repeating the unending cycle of diaper changes, feeding, and coaxing Leo into naps. John and I had discussed the possibility that I was experiencing postpartum depression, but in my heart, I felt my heaviness was more than that.

Ever since Leo was born, I had felt Mother's presence everywhere, like her essence was a heavy cape wrapped around my neck, dragging me down. I couldn't stop thinking about her. She came into my dreams, often appearing as the beautiful, murky figure from my childhood, only to transform into a vampire-like creature with long black hair.

When I was feeling particularly sad, I would play out the memories where Mother seemed fragile, ornate, decorated with her jade bracelet. She was delicate, gorgeous, and sang like a bird. In these moments, I thought of her as being too fragile and weak, tired of performing. I wondered if being our mother led to her brokenness.

But if she was broken, she must have healed by now. For how could someone that broken make such a monumental trip again across the world; her fragility, I thought, was a state of being that existed only in Canada. Perhaps her seemingly frail existence in my childhood was not a sign of brokenness but a record of who she was at the time.

Other times, I saw her as a wilfully disobedient person. With an irritable resentment, I recalled her monologues, her debates with Father, and silently accused her of creating unnecessary crises and emergencies through the carelessness of her actions. She had whipped up her tantrums from irrational fears and deliberately caused trouble. She was selfish, giving no consideration to anyone around her.

Oscillating between these extreme perspectives of Mother, I was violently jerked up and down on a see-saw where, no matter what, my legs could not touch the ground or push away. At first, I attributed this inner struggle to my hormones during my teen years, during pregnancy, and now after giving birth. Then, my body wasn't mine, and it was operating on its own accord. And now, my body was taking the baby's interests as its primary concern. My body was always hungry, producing unending liquids, dripping with sweat and milk, simultaneously burning fat and producing it. I didn't see my waistline diminishing and bitterly could not stop eating in voracious fits. These were novel, unwelcome, and uncomfortable feelings, all stemming from a vain and selfish desire to retain something from my past. It was these compounding, overlapping, and troubling feelings about Mother that led me to this kopitiam. I had to find her, even if I was not sure I could forgive her. I was going to follow my strongest lead and dive into the most enduring relationship that Mother had not eviscerated.

I devoured the kaya toast and tapped my phone to see what time it was. The person I had arranged to meet was forty-five minutes late, and I did not feel guilty about starting breakfast on my own. I saw many people eyeing my table, coveting the seat across from me where my bag held court. I was about to lose hope when, finally, I spotted a woman approaching me. She had shoulder-length, straight, black hair, curled towards her face, and dark sunglasses. Her lips were a perfect shade of maroon, and she wore a white button-up blouse with smart fitted pants.

I stood up to greet Che Eng, my mother's best friend.

She embraced me and said, "My goodness, I can see your mother in you!"

I winced at the comparison and laughed a deflection. "You're too kind, but we both know my mother was much prettier."

To my surprise, Che Eng brushed my hair behind my ears and grabbed my shoulders. "She was a beauty, but she was annoyed by all the attention she got when we were young. She wanted to be more than her looks."

I forced a smile and motioned Che Eng to sit down across from me as I moved my bag off the chair. She continued, "You don't believe me, ah? It's true! Your mother was full of big ideas. She was a dreamer. And she was very smart and quick on her feet."

"Well, to me, she seemed beautiful, but ... fragile, and maybe restless, too."

"You were small. You probably could not see, lah. Your mother was not fragile. She was one of the bravest people I knew. She was the life of the party and always held court in any room. Not because she was beautiful but because she could debate with anyone about anything."

Che Eng hummed like she was remembering something and went on. "She also got us in a lot of trouble growing up. Swee Hua was always up for an adventure. I met a lot of smart and interesting people because she was so unafraid and curious."

She smiled, her gaze distant. I tried to imagine teenage versions of Che Eng and Mother, arm in arm in their wide-legged pants, gallivanting to parties and riding bicycles haphazardly around town. Che Eng's attention returned to our table when the waiter came by to take her order.

She ordered the half-boiled eggs special, and then leaned in towards me like she was ready to tell me a secret. "Children don't always know about the life their parents had before they were born. I thought Swee Hua would become a politician one day, or even a judge. It surprised me when she ended up ..."

"A housewife?"

"Well ... I know she was brave leaving home and starting a new life in another country. But I thought her world travels would lead to more."

I sat with what Che Eng had told me, unsure whether to believe this version of Mother existed. I wondered if we were talking about the same person, but then I thought about the glimpses I'd had of Mother in the Oriental Palace, during her performances, at the mah-jong table, where she felt comfortable to speak her mind and be herself. Perhaps Mother was putting on different shows for different people. She never told me about her plans or dreams or aspirations, but Che Eng was right—I never asked when she was still around.

I watched Che Eng finish her eggs and kaya toast and said, "She talked of you often. I remember her calling and writing you."

"Yes, she was quite homesick, lah."

"I guess she isn't anymore."

"I wouldn't know."

"Really? She hasn't kept in touch with you?"

"She did when she first came. I can tell you now. You're all grown up! Your mother came home like a typhoon, ready to pick up from the place she left off. But she had forgotten that time had passed, that life had gone on without her. She thought things, people, would have stood still for her. She had a hard time adjusting."

"In what way?"

"Well, her mother was gone, her sister was older and more bitter, and everyone had their own lives, families, businesses. We were no longer teenagers with the world before us. I don't know what your mother was expecting." Che Eng sighed and shook her head, a bit exasperated.

"I heard that she stayed with my auntie Ah Lian."

"Yes, that didn't last. They both were so cruel to each other. But Ah Lian is a special kind of person," Che Eng said acidly.

"Apparently, she passed away last year."

"Oh, I'm so sorry. I didn't know."

"I didn't know her."

"I knew your mother wouldn't last there. I offered her a place to stay after she left Ah Lian, but after a few weeks, Swee Hua didn't want to be a burden anymore. She just left without saying a word to me. Not even a goodbye. I came home one day and found her things gone."

"Nothing? No note, no phone call?"

Che Eng shook her head sadly and shrugged.

"She's really good at doing that," I snarked.

"She wasn't herself. I know in my heart she didn't do that to hurt me. And I know she didn't do it to hurt you."

"How do you know?"

"She was very unhappy. I could tell that she found leaving Canada, and then being home, difficult. Things were not easy for her. She had a hard time finding work. She was lonely. She missed you all. I tried to talk to her about what happened with Ah Loy, but she would only say she didn't want to go back."

"Did she say anything about me or my sister?"

"A little, but I could tell it was hard for her to talk about. She kept it inside."

"What did she say?"

"Only that she missed you girls. She was very private about it."

"Did you try to contact her after she left?"

"Yes, I called Ah Lian. I tried all our friends. Nobody had seen or heard from her. I even called Ah Loy."

"You called my father?"

"I thought maybe she had changed her mind and went back. He told me he knew nothing."

"She never came back."

"I see."

I could tell this was news to Che Eng. She took a sip of her coffee, ordered another one, and looked at me earnestly. "I just assumed she went back. I was surprised to never hear from her again. I know Swee Hua. She has a sensitive heart, and it can break easily. I thought I had wronged her somehow, that she had decided to cut ties with me because I pushed her too hard to make amends with Ah Lian, to talk to Ah Loy." Che Eng sighed deeply and clasped her hands together contritely." At one point, I even told her she should not have left you two young girls behind. I was only trying to help her, but she must not have liked the advice I was giving."

"That must have been hard. To be a friend to her at that time."

"I felt like it was a one-way street. She wasn't telling me anything, so I was left to ask her all these questions. It must have been too much for her to hear." Che Eng looked up at the ceiling fans, fighting tears.

"I'm sorry. I didn't mean to ..."

"Oh, but where could she be?" she burst out. "I really thought she went back to Canada."

"If she had, I wouldn't be here."

Che Eng pinned me with a searching look. "You're still looking for her."

"Yes, I was hoping you would know something."

"I'm sorry. Wo m'zai, I don't know."

"And now you're here in Ipoh. I was surprised because I had expected to meet you in Brunei."

"Yes, my mother is from here. She's ill, so I moved back for a while to take care of her."

"So you didn't live here when my mother was here?"

"Swee Hua was here? In Ipoh? I don't think so."

"Yes, according to a friend of hers. She told him herself."

"No, that can't be."

I showed Che Eng the pub napkin Alfred had written the name of the kopitiam on for me. "Apparently, she worked here. You don't think it's true?"

"This can't be correct. I can't see Swee Hua coming here and doing this."

"Well, nobody else seems to know where she's gone. It's my only hope."

Che Eng fingered the napkin before handing it back to me. She hugged me and tucked my hair behind my ears. "I hope you find Swee Hua," she said tearfully. "When you do, tell her I'm sorry, okay?"

As I walked away, Che Eng held my hand for as long as possible, as if she was not ready to let me go.

No closer to finding Mother, I ventured the next day with John and Leo to the kopitiam where she was last known to have worked. I kept checking the name Kong Heng written on the napkin against the sign above the open-air café. Satisfied that I was in the right place, I found a table while John surveyed the cuisine.

Hot woks fried blood cockles for char kuey teow, a mortar and pestle ground peanuts for tangy rojak, succulent satay smoked on the grill, popiah were rolled up on wooden cutting boards, sweet and sour asam laksa simmered in a large pot, and layered kueh lapis in a rainbow of colours beamed from a refrigerated counter.

Leo amused herself, seated on the plastic strips of a lawn chair set up as a makeshift high chair. The hot sun squeezed towards her through the bamboo shades crowning the opening of the kopitiam. She was trying to grab the dust particles floating in the air like fireflies.

My reverie was interrupted by a couple who paused as they walked by to pinch Leo's cheeks, commenting, "Those eyelashes! Only Eurasian babies have such eyes!"

Seated at the table in front of me was an older uncle wearing a white tank top and shorts, flip-flops dangling from his feet. He was smoking and talking to another uncle who was wearing neatly pressed cream-coloured pants tailored for his thin frame. His white button-up shirt was crisp, his shoes were shined, and his posture was relaxed but proper. If he were in a Chinese movie, he would have been the plantation owner. He was smoking and listening intently to the other man, who was now cleaning his teeth with a toothpick and occasionally clicking his tongue against his teeth. The sound reminded me of Father after dinner, readying himself for a smoke.

I looked around and saw women here, too, some wearing a kebaya and flip-flops. I surveyed each of them, searching for a familiar look, a recognizable smile, habitual movements, or the memorable planes of Mother's face. Although I didn't see Mother, I felt her presence. Tasting the food was like watching a classic old flick that I had seen many times before. Everything we had eaten on this trip, and especially here in Ipoh, reminded me of Mother's cooking. While sipping a soup, I realized it had been so long since I had tasted this fragrant four-spice Chinese sibut, with black, plate-like rehmannia herbs and long, thin slices of white peony root. I looked into the black abyss in my bowl, where pieces of spent hen, goji berries, and red dates bobbed, and savoured the tong Mother used to make for me when I was sad, sick, or just wanting comfort. It was as if she had placed the bowl in front of me herself.

Everyone around me in the kopitiam was Chinese. I could understand their Hokkien, and when they spoke English, I swayed rhythmically with the cadence of their accents. I felt strangely at home here, as if I had lost my memory, but my senses were alerting me to my past.

But then, I was suddenly reminded that I was a foreigner. An uncle selling drinks approached speaking Malay, and I had to tell him I didn't understand. While he gaped at me, I considered how Mother must have had to speak bahasa Melayu here and in Brunei. She had fought with Father about how English had become the lingua franca in our house, but living in this part of the world, Father would have undoubtedly fought against bahasa Melayu. Father never liked talking about the Malays, blaming them for his prior statelessness, and preferring the colonial English he was taught in school, perhaps too ardently. I looked beyond the bamboo shades to see women out on the road donning hijabs and gracefully gliding to the hawker stalls where halal food was served. I was mesmerized by one woman, who wore a long-sleeved silk blouse and a sharp watch around her wrist, her manicured fingers adorned with delicate rings, her makeup perfect and her sunglasses lending her the mysterious aura of a celebrity. The uncle in flip-flops saw me watching the women and said, "Only free-hair women here."

After finishing my soup, I went to the popiah stall. "Auntie, can I ask you something?" The woman in an apron and batik shirt motioned for a man to take over. Her hair was short and black, sprinkled with silver. Her face held many wrinkles and was dotted with moles from her ear to chin. She nodded at me kindly, and I pulled out a photo of my mother.

It had been difficult for me to select a photo to bring. The night before we were to fly out, I was sitting on the rug in my bedroom, loose photos strewn about and album pages open, panicked that I might not find anything but jarred by how much I had to search through. It was as if I had suddenly woken from a coma, still groggy as the memories of my past life flooded into my head. The photos jogged so many memories that I had forgotten or repressed.

I was about to give up when I pulled out an album from our road trip to Waterton Park. I remembered how she rubbed her ankle incessantly, always cold. Father had taken a photo of Mother alone, facing the camera, with the mountains towering in the background. She was wearing an oversized cream cardigan, her hair blowing gently to the right. Mother wasn't smiling, but the crisp air brought out the rose in her cheeks. She stood pin straight, arms by her sides. It was a beautiful portrait, and although a stranger might see it as the perfect tourist snap, I knew that behind it was Mother's unhappiness. Father had captured her perfectly in that moment.

The instant the woman from the popiah stall saw the photo she exclaimed, "Swee Hua!" But then she shook her head. She didn't speak English, so I tried Hokkien. "Lu pat kua ke ee bo? You know her?"

The woman's eyes lit up. She told me that Swee Hua had been here many years ago. But she had died a few months after.

The auntie said it so nonchalantly, like she was telling me what ingredients were in her popiah. Then she took up a cleaver and started chopping cucumber. Aghast, I quickly asked her for details.

"I don't know anything else. She was working for the cendol stall there." She pointed to a cart that displayed fruit and a transparent container of green noodles. "The uncle there may know. You go talk to him, okay?"

I was stunned by how quickly the woman dismissed me. She hadn't even asked why I was looking for her. She had forgotten about me already, crushing peanuts in her mortar and pestle. Her lineup needed tending to.

Tears welling in my eyes, I looked up at the whirling fans and saw a crow sitting in the rafters, cawing, *Oh-ah*. As I clutched the old photograph of Mother, the commotion in the kopitiam could not cover my loud sobs.

John came over to me, and all I could say was "She's dead. She's dead."

Lid

LIKE A POT OF BOILING SOUP, the pressure building within me fired up an intense heat that tossed the lid off completely. I wept uncontrollably, and I didn't care if people were watching me. John took me into his arms. I buried my face in his chest, and he led me back to our table. I sat down and hunched over, putting my elbows on my knees and my face into my hands. When I stopped shaking, I looked at John and said once again, "She's gone."

"Are you sure?"

"That's what the woman said. She knew mother's name. She sounded certain."

"Did she tell you when, or how?"

I started hyperventilating and could not stop the waves of tears on my face. John rubbed my back, letting me catch my breath. "No, she couldn't get rid of me fast enough."

"She doesn't know she was your mother."

"She could have asked!" I said loudly. Diners at the tables around us started to look over. John used his body to shield me from view.

"I'm really sorry, Lily."

"I know."

"Do you want to go talk to her again? Maybe now that the lineup has died down, she can tell you more."

"She said I should ask at that cendol stall. I guess my mother used to work there." I pointed in the opposite direction from the popiah stall, where a man was leaning against his makeshift cart, peering into his mobile phone.

"Are you ready?"

"Give me a minute."

I took a sip of my kopi ice and winced at the sweetness sitting in my mouth. The crushing heat was starting to weigh on me, and I feared that I wouldn't be able to stand up. John found a straw for Leo to chew on, and I knew I had limited time before she got bored and started to fuss. A line had formed at the cendol stall, and I waited as the uncle filled bowls with coconut milk, red beans, and pandan-infused tapioca noodles. Auntie Choo Neo tried to make cendol in Sparwood once for Father's birthday. It was the only thing I heard him say he missed from back home. She used a colander to try to reproduce the green noodles, but the consistency was off.

I still hoped there had been some kind of mix-up, that the old auntie was remembering things wrong, or we had misunderstood each other's Hokkien. When it was my turn, I ordered a cendol and pulled out the photo of Mother. "Uncle, do you know this woman?"

The man looked at the photo as he arranged the ingredients in my bowl. He nodded, looked at me, gazed down at the picture again, and then stared searchingly into my face. He said he knew her and told me to come back in an hour, when he would close his stall for the afternoon. I reluctantly took the picture back, and we locked eyes like we should know each other but didn't. The man's hair was peppered with black, and the wrinkles around his eyes drooped sadly. A cigarette was tucked behind his ear, above his sideburns. I studied him for a moment, as he was serving customers. Standing behind the counter was a lanky man, tall, and the apron he wore looked too short for him. He had a habit of scratching the back of his head as he talked, the veins in his arms pulsating with the rhythm. Limping in his flip-flops, the man appeared to have injured his right hip or knee. He looked like he'd been on a bender the night before: slow, weary, and hunched over, searching for a flat surface to lie down on.

John agreed to take Leo home for her nap, and I stayed at the kopitiam to wait for the uncle to join me. I ate my cendol, wondering why someone hadn't yet figured out a way to make it taste this way in North America. It gave me comfort knowing that I was enjoying something that could only be appreciated in this specific place and time. The last of the coconut milk sat in the bottom of the bowl diluted by ice chips. I watched as the stalls emptied their large plastic containers of rice, the clanging of metal spatulas against the woks slowed, and the soups in the large cauldrons diminished. Dishes were swept off tables and into plastic bins to be washed.

After packing supplies into his fridge and freezer, the uncle wiped his hands on his apron and lumbered over. He sat down next to me, pulled the cigarette from behind his ear, and lit it, scratching the back of his head again as he introduced himself as Peter Siew. He eyed me with a forlorn expression, and I shifted awkwardly in my seat before I told him that I was the daughter of the woman in the photo. He didn't seem surprised by this news, and I explained that it had been many years since I had seen her, and I had come from Canada looking for her. Peter said he remembered Mother because he was in love with her. I always knew that Mother was a vibrant and loving soul, irresistible to everyone. As a child, I wondered how someone like that could be so unhappy.

My Hokkien was rusty, but he understood English. So in bits and pieces, Peter told me his story of Mother. The words trickled out of his mouth, sometimes with a cigarette perched in one corner. His delivery was staccato, with many pauses to suck on his cigarette and shoot the smoke into the sky, or to rub his temple and look into the busy street where cars and scooters were honking their way out of a traffic jam. I didn't rush him.

He said that Mother came to work at the stall with his father's brother. She didn't like the work and was always searching for something else. The first time he saw her she was making cendol in the twilight during the Mid-Autumn Festival. Peter explained that he thought he saw Chang'e, the goddess of the moon. He didn't know then that she was married or had children, but she seemed like she was far away from something she loved. Peter started working at the kopitiam to be closer to her.

Over time, Peter helped Mother get a better job as a secretary for a lawyer. She spent her days managing the lawyer's appointments, transcribing dictation, writing correspondence, and filing papers. Mother found this job boring as well. Peter said she was never satisfied, always searching. One day, he went to see her at her apartment and found her drunk. She revealed that she had left her husband and children in Canada. Peter was shocked to hear she had another life. He put her to bed and watched over her that night. The next day, she acted like nothing had happened, and they never talked about her confession.

Peter was worried about Mother after that. For two weeks, he called her every day with no answer, until he got a message that the phone number was no longer available. When she didn't return his calls, he went to see her again, but she wasn't home. He went to her workplace, and they said they hadn't seen her for weeks. The lawyer was angry because she hadn't called. One day when Peter went to check her apartment, the landlord accosted him, asking where Mother had gone. He said she was now two months overdue on rent and no one had seen her. Peter asked to go inside to see if there were any clues. The apartment was clean, and everything Mother owned was still there. The landlord took Peter's number and sent him a box of Mother's things, after cleaning out the apartment to rent to others.

Six months went by before Peter heard about Swee Hua. He read in the *Star* that a woman's body had been found in the Kinta River. Police concluded she had died by suicide. No one had been able to identify her. Peter knew in his heart it was her. "Ee boh ai anee, she didn't want anything anymore," he said.

Peter was chain-smoking in deep breaths to calm himself. "I still think of her." He stared at my face. "You look so much like her."

I touched his hand and tears rolled down his thin cheeks. He went to identify the body, but it had decomposed so badly that it was impossible. He brought her hairbrush for a DNA test, and it confirmed it was Mother. She was buried at the Chinese cemetery with a stone tablet with her name on it. Peter apologized that he didn't tell me, but he had no idea how to contact us. "Swee Hua didn't have any information about you in her belongings. I'm sorry I didn't try harder."

This stung. Why didn't Mother have photos of us, mementoes? Did she really want to just forget about us? I thought about the pictures of her that I'd sifted through the night before I left Canada. The boxes I carted across the country every time I moved, preserving the few things I had left of Mother, careful not to throw anything away, hoping that one day I could return them to her. The framed photo of the two of us that I kept on my dresser. She was wearing a brown moto leather jacket, jeans, and brown leather boots. Her hair was curled and bounced off her shoulders. Father and Bea were in the background, flying a kite against the fall colours. I was standing next to her, with her arm around me. I thought about all the times I had defended Mother against Bea, Father, and Auntie Choo Neo. I was the one person who thought the best of her. Even after everything she had done to hurt me, I still cherished our memories together. How could I have so severely misjudged her, miscalculated who she was?

Peter saw my distress. "I'm sorry."

"There was no good way to tell me. I just can't believe it."

"She must have been tortured by her separation from you," Peter offered.

"She could have fixed that by coming back to Canada. Or contacting us. Or keeping memories of us with her."

"If there is one thing I know, it's that your mother did not like Canada. She did not speak of Canada often, but when she did, it was not with kindness."

"I see," I muttered.

"She did talk of you and your sister that one time. She said her daughters were the best of her, and that she wished she could have brought you home. She got angry when I tried to talk to her more about this."

Peter and I were two strangers touched by the same person, tormented by her memory. She was still casting her shadow over us, like Chang'e does from the moon. We were both sitting in the dark, enduring a slow-moving total eclipse.

文
Script

I INVITED PETER TO COME TO HAVE SOME KUEH with us at the apartment-style hotel where we were staying. In his broken English, he was friendly with John as we ate the spongy cakes and Leo fingered the rainbow-striped crumbs on her high chair tray. Peter opened the box from Mother's apartment and showed me her wallet, her identity card, her makeup, an address book that appeared almost new, and some clothes. There was nothing else.

Peter pulled out a folded sepia-tinged newspaper article from his wallet. Unfolding it, I read the headline: *Unidentified Woman Found in Kinta River Believed to Have Committed Suicide.* The very short article included an appeal to public to come forward with any information about the identity of the woman. Her death was reduced to a few words, like a public service announcement that construction was occurring, or bus routes were changing.

I lifted up some of her clothes and felt something in the pocket of a dress. Inside was a thin stack of letters held together by a pink ribbon, the kind that I had seen people in Malaysia use to tie up important papers. I was disheartened to see no English words. Peter looked at me in shock. He said he hadn't noticed the papers before and asked if I needed help reading them. I nodded.

I untied the pink ribbon and pulled out the first letter. It was a light red piece of paper and appeared to be an official document written in Malay. Peter told me it was my mother's birth certificate. He moved his finger across the page to various boxes telling me what each said, relaying Mother's name and her parents' names. He pointed at one box and told me that it said, "Bukan warganegara." Not a citizen.

"Is this a Malay birth certificate?" I asked.

"Yes. It says your mother was born in Kuching."

I realized I had seen the red paper before. It was the same birth certificate that I had found in my old mementoes box. Mother must have acquired another copy.

Peter riffled through the other folded pieces of paper and found one that looked to be a court order. I recognized the common law formatting of the decision, but it was in Malay. Peter told me it detailed Mother's adoption.

"Adoption? That doesn't make any sense."

Peter showed me that it was a court order allowing the adoption of my mother by her adoptive mother and her birth father. The names of the adoptive parents matched my po po and gong gong. Behind the court order, Peter found a letter written in Chinese addressed to my mother. He translated it out loud:

Swee Hua,

By the time you read this letter I will have left this world. I know you have a new life in Canada. Here are some documents you may need. I never wanted to tell you this, but with death summoning me, I feel compelled to share with you your true roots.

You are not my daughter. Your mother was a woman that your father sought out in hopes of having a son. After having your older sister, I was unable to have more children, and I allowed your father to search for other means. He met your mother, Eve Bacha, in Kuching one night while playing mah-jong and persuaded her to join our family. Your mother was not Chinese. She was Iban. When you were born, your father was disappointed you were not a boy and banished your mother from our house. She begged your father to allow you to stay. She told me that she could not take you home, as she would not be able to care for you. I agreed to take care of you as my own daughter.

Your father did not have the foresight or compassion to allow your mother to stay or to register your birth. This may pain you to hear, but it was as if he didn't want to admit you existed.

I tried many times to help you get a proper birth certificate and citizenship, but the Malay authorities needed your birth mother to substantiate the fact that she was your mother and was Malaysian. I tried to find your mother but could not. Having a Malaysian father was not enough to get you a birth certificate because he was not married to your mother. The law did not allow him to claim you, even after my efforts to convince your father to admit you were his daughter.

I hired a lawyer and he advised me to adopt you so that you would be able to obtain citizenship through me. He also advised your father to adopt you so as to legitimize your relationship in law. We were able to adopt you, but when they issued you a new birth certificate it still did not list you as a Malaysian citizen. We applied several times for your citizenship. For whatever reason, many attempts to try to correct your status failed. This is why we moved to Brunei. I didn't want you to know that you were different from your sister and the rest of the family.

We never returned to Malaysia. All of us believed we were Malaysian citizens, but we learned many years later we technically were not because we had forgotten to do the crucial step of registering ourselves after Malaysia became independent. We only had British Overseas Passports and old birth certificates that did not list our citizenship. It was very difficult to get Malaysian citizenship since we were no longer living there. Even after your father bought property in Malaysia and lived part of his life there, it was not good enough. We were all denied. This may be why, in later years, your aunties, father, and sister started to resent your place in Canada. They felt they moved to Brunei for you, and because of you, we were made stateless, too.

I tell you this not because you were not wanted by me, but because
you may need this knowledge one day. You are not to blame, but your
family may not want to talk to you after my departure from this world.
I did not want you to find out from the others. I tell you this so that you
may know where you come from.

I love you.

Peter said it was signed her lao bu: "mother." He put the letter
down and ran his hand through his hair several times.

I was astounded. "Did you know about her past?" I asked Peter.

He shook his head. "I didn't know those papers were in this box."
He looked at me anxiously. "Did you know about this?" he asked in
return.

"No" was all I could say.

I looked for any identifiable marks on the letter and envelope to
discern when Mother may have received this news. The envelope had
a blue and red airmail border. Her name and our address in Sparwood
were written neatly on the front. The postmark on the stamps was
dated March 1988, and the return address was from Auntie Ah Lian.
She must have sent it around the time my po po passed away. Perhaps
the birth certificate and the photo of Mother and Po Po I found had
been in this envelope as well. Staring at the date, I wondered if this
was what put Mother over the edge. She must have left to try to
recover whatever link she had to this place.

Peter riffled through the box and pulled out an empty picture
frame. Mother must have found this, too, when she returned, the
original home of the worn photo of her and Po Po in the airport, sent
to her years ago. Peter and I didn't know what more we could say to
one another. We promised to keep in touch, and then he left.

The letter left me reeling. The irony was not lost on me. Mother
always held her status as a citizen of Malaysia over Father like she was
higher class or of good breeding. She never allowed herself to relate

to Father's statelessness, how it affected his psyche, or how it drove his choices. It must've crushed her to realize that, all along, she was like him, like the swill in the Brunei River, something that officials tried to ignore and push towards the ocean. Worse, she would have considered her Chinese blood to be tainted with Indigenous blood, from her Iban mother.

Depleted, I wordlessly closed the old colonial-style shutters on our windows to shut out the daylight. I fell asleep with Leo between John and me, the last call to prayer of the day lulling us into the night.

土

Earth

PETER TOLD ME WHERE TO FIND MOTHER'S TOMBSTONE, but only after I promised I was not pregnant and would not bring Leo to the gravesite. It was like he was channelling Mother and begging me not to let the souls at the cemetery snatch my baby. Peter told me he could not come with me, as he was fearful of attending the cemetery outside of Qingming, Tomb Sweeping Festival. He warned me to leave if I felt a bad energy and gave very clear instructions. It was as if he knew that I had no idea how to properly honour my ancestors. I was grateful for his help.

On Peter's advice, I stopped at a small store to buy some oranges and incense. When we arrived, I told John to stay in the car with Leo. The driver was so nervous to be so close to the cemetery that I gave him permission to take them for a drive. I told him I would only be fifteen minutes.

It was a small cemetery that had been left partially neglected, and I had to walk among the rows to reach Mother's tombstone. It was a hot day, and my backpack was heavy. Sweat formed on my back and I quickened my pace, worried by the storm clouds overhead, pushing their way towards me.

I felt sorry that Mother was buried nowhere near family and wondered if she was lonely in the afterlife, too. The gravesite was neat and clean, thanks to Peter. I noticed the dirt around her tombstone was dry, cracks and crevices in the earth calling out for water. I replaced the incense and lit it, arranged the oranges, and knelt down to finger Mother's name engraved in Chinese. I took a photo, and then set out to leave. As I was putting my phone back in my bag, I saw out of the corner of my eye a dishevelled woman with long black hair running in a dark flowing dress. Was it E gui? Was Mother's spirit restless? Had she been waiting for me? I walked quickly back to the parking lot; Peter's advice to leave as soon as I felt something bad echoed in my head. I only started to breathe normally again once the cemetery was no longer in sight.

That night, while John and Leo were deep in slumber, I was so nauseated I couldn't sleep. Perhaps it was the series of switchbacks we drove through that afternoon when we visited the tea plantations in Cameron Highlands, winding back and forth around the mountain bends, staring at the unsightly greenhouses flanking the valley. The bubbled greenhouses of the strawberry and vegetable farms looked like pustules and abscesses, suffocating scores of migrant workers, marring the once majestic landscape. I felt like I was trapped in one of those plastic enclosures. I needed to go outside and breathe.

I stepped onto the front steps of the guest house to look at the bright full moon. The breeze from the valley where the tea plantations stood made me shiver. I pictured Mother on the edge of a bridge, taking her last breath. Was she ashamed? Afraid? Would I follow her wayward path in the dark, too?

I shuddered. Standing alone in the cool mountain air, I twisted Mother's jade bracelet around my wrist. I let fall the stream of tears held captive in my eyes all day, releasing them freely, without brushing them away. My search for Mother had been long and hard. I had wanted so badly to find her. I realized I had.

飛
Fly

ON THE PLANE RIDE ACROSS THE WORLD back home to Canada, I decided to tell Auntie Choo Neo what I had discovered. I expected her to bat away any talk of Mother, cut me off, or tell me I was foolish, but she listened without interrupting, waiting out the pauses as I tried to fight back my tears. I was grateful the overhead lights had dimmed, and everyone around me was sleeping or watching a movie.

When I was done, Auntie Choo Neo reached below her to get her bag. I was appalled. Was she simply finished listening to me and ready to move on to her magazines?

"You didn't think I knew what was going on?" Auntie finally said.

"How did you know?"

"I know you better than you think. Why go to Brunei now? You've never shown an interest before. And why upset your Father by going? I knew it must be about your mother."

"I didn't think it was that obvious."

"I also knew I couldn't stop you."

"I thought you would try. That's why I didn't say anything. You never liked Mother."

"That's not entirely true. Your mother and I had a complicated relationship. I never trusted her. I knew she was going to break your father's heart one day."

"You weren't always fair to her."

"Maybe. But in the end, I've done what no one else could have done for her. I raised her daughters."

"Of course what you did was very generous. But maybe if you had been kinder, or more compassionate ..."

"It wouldn't have changed anything, Lily. You can't blame me for this."

"I didn't mean to suggest ..."

"Never mind. I know you didn't ..." Auntie stopped talking, tears forming in her eyes.

"Oh, Auntie! I'm sorry ..." I squeezed her arm. "I know Bea and I didn't make things easy for you."

"Lily, I know it's hard growing up without a mother. Just remember that I did not want to replace her. Raising her children was not something I planned or hoped to do."

"Of course, Auntie. I never thought that you had gotten rid of her or anything like that."

"I've only tried to do what is best for you and your sister." She rummaged through her large purse and handed me a plastic sandwich bag with some papers inside.

"What's this?"

"Letters from your mother."

I stared at the bag of letters on my lap, and then turned to face Auntie Choo Neo. She couldn't look at me. It was like a bright light was shining behind me, and she was shielding herself, casting her eyes downwards to avoid the glare of the spotlight, while the heat seared the back of my head, igniting the strands of my hair into an uncontrollable flame. I had to sit, for a significant number of hours, bound by the seat belt in the airplane, next to the person who had kept Mother from me. All this time, I had thought that Mother had deliberately cut us out of her life, chosen to avoid us, ignore us, forget us. I tried to take a few breaths, reeling from the revelation my auntie had coughed up.

I asked John to switch seats with me, and for a few hours, I had fitful dreams in an unsettling sleep that brought aches to my head and neck. When I couldn't close my eyes any longer, I asked John to switch seats with me again and prodded Auntie Choo Neo to remove her headphones. I wanted to throw the aches in my head back at her.

"I can't believe you kept Mother's letters from me!" I hissed.

Auntie tried to shush me. "I have given them to you now."

"Do you think that makes it okay? How could you? They were not yours!"

Auntie couldn't look at me and her cheeks turned red. "I'm sorry, Lily. I don't know what else to say. I can't change the past."

"Do you know how many times I thought she didn't care or think about us?" I started to cry. Auntie tried to comfort me, but I pulled away.

"I thought I was doing what was best."

"You were doing what was best for you."

"Lily, I was there. I watched you and Bea suffer. I didn't want you to hold out hope. I knew she would not come back."

"How could you have known? And even if she wasn't going to come back, don't you think Bea and I had a right to whatever she sent us? It was not yours to keep."

"I know that now. All I can say is I thought I was protecting you girls."

"We didn't need protecting. We needed the truth. What if I could have reached out to her? What if I could have saved her? Does Father know about these?" I had sensed that Auntie and Father were hiding things from me all these years. Here was the proof.

"Yes, but don't blame him. I was the one who insisted we keep them from you and Bea."

Auntie couldn't say anything more. Her face was downcast, in the shadows of the overhead lights. I felt her regret pooling around me and opened the air vents above my head, trying to remove the remorse seeping from her pores.

I asked John to switch seats with me once again and pulled the letters out of the sealed bag. I sat for a few moments, staring in shock at the pile of paper on my lap. There were six letters, still in their envelopes, all sporting blue and red striped airmail borders along their edges. There was no return address, and the postmarks were from Malaysia, Thailand, Cambodia, and Indonesia. Half were addressed to me and half to Bea.

The envelopes had neat openings along the top, carved out by a letter opener. I took out the first letter like a White Rabbit candy, carefully peeling off the wrapper to avoid tearing the edible rice paper. As I unfolded the thin, delicate paper, I recognized Mother's handwriting and felt like a warm blanket was being tucked over me. I tried to read the letters slowly, to savour them like the candy I was given as a child. They were short, one-page missives that didn't tell me anything about where she was or what she had been doing. Instead, she asked Bea and me questions: How is school? What are you reading right now? Do you still play with Hilary? In the early letters, she assured us she was okay and told us she was sorry she had to leave without saying goodbye. She said she hoped we would see each other again soon. The last few letters seemed less optimistic. She wrote that she missed us, that she hoped we remembered her and missed her, too. She said she was sad we were not together. In the very last letter, Mother apologized again and said she hoped we would forgive her one day.

Inside the last envelope was more than just a letter. The plastic covering on Mother's key chain was scratched, but I could still make out the faded picture of Wayne Gretzky.

The summer Mother left us, he was constantly in the news. Auntie Choo Neo gawked at Janet Jones's wedding headdress, calling her a gold digger, like she had done before with the sultan's favourite wife. I watched Gretzky in a grey and white striped shirt on television, surrounded by a bouquet of microphones like wilted steel peacock feathers, as he announced through tears that he was leaving the Edmonton Oilers. Father sneered, "If he's stupid enough to leave Canada, he doesn't deserve his status as a Canadian!" But as Coach

Glen Sather said, "Everything changes, we all get older," Bea and I wept openly. Gretzky's announcement felt like a betrayal. But more than that, it reminded me of Mother, and how I didn't want to grow up without her. At least Gretzky said goodbye.

Years later, sitting on an airplane, staring at this hazy plastic picture of the Great One, I began to feel something different. I still remembered the sadness, but I also saw the blurred memories of us hugging after a goal, or Mother's arm around me on the couch during a game. It was like she was handing me a happy memory, reminding me there were good times to recall and cherish.

After I tucked the last letter back into its envelope, I leaned back to rest my head against the seat. I thought about my last day in Ipoh, the point on the trip when I felt the lowest. I had thought that the heat and the exertion from walking through the cemetery looking for Mother's tombstone had made my breath laboured and my chest tight. Truthfully, it was my fury at her for starting a new life and forgetting us. She had erased us from her life so effectively that Peter couldn't even find us to tell us the news of her death. She considered us strangers, unworthy of remembering.

When I first landed in Asia, I wanted so badly to find out where she was. And I did. But it wasn't enough. What I wanted most of all was to know that she thought of us, that she missed us, that she loved us still. As I collected the many stories of Mother, it was apparent that she was in turmoil, in pain, about being away from her home, but it was unclear to me whether she was also torn about her distance from us in Canada. Now, it felt like I had all the ingredients to fashion a dish—unrehearsed, improvised, and spontaneous—that would soothe me and allow me to eventually embrace forgiveness.

These letters were the last remnants of a four-spice tong. The big soup pot was stripped of the lotus root, the chicken. All that was left was a bit of broth, the flat black pieces of rehmannia, soggy clumps of angelica root, and a few strips of a white peony. Yet the brew was still pungent. When I was little, my mother would use the last of the tong to start a new batch, carrying over some of the deep flavour that had simmered in the old soup. Mother told me it was good for a tong to have memory, for that richness to fold into the new.

黄
Yellow

A FEW DAYS AFTER WE RETURNED FROM ASIA, John mentioned that Auntie Choo Neo had texted him to casually ask how Leo was adjusting to the new time zone. "Have you talked to her?" he asked, looking concerned.

I sighed. The combination of the jet lag and the emotional anticipation of sharing Mother's story with the rest of my family made me weary. I was tired of being angry. This was the woman who raised me, who witnessed my graduation, who saw me get married, and who welcomed Leo into the world as her own grandchild. It was time to let her back into my life.

I invited Auntie to visit Leo and me. When she arrived, she took my hand with regret seeping from her eyes. Her face lost colour, like she'd seen a ghost, when she noticed Mother's bracelet on my wrist. I stood my ground, defiantly wearing the jade out in the open.

Auntie Choo Neo composed herself quickly and tried a tentative smile, sliding the bracelet up my forearm tenderly. I loosened my tight fist.

Father came to visit Leo soon after our return as well. While he held her, I gently handed him the news like fresh eggs. I told him about finding Alfred and the information he had revealed about Mother. I told him about my trip back home. I told him I found Mother. It was a heavy responsibility, and I wasn't sure how Father would react. He must have wondered about Mother, despite any ill feelings he still had towards her. I hoped that hearing her story would bring him closure.

Father listened intently and offered no harsh words. He shed a few tears and embraced me, more to comfort me because it was a difficult retelling.

"I'm sorry," I said. "Are you okay?"

"Lily, I'm okay." He opened his mouth to say more, but I just said, "I know."

We sat together for some time, with Leo.

When I told Bea Alfred's story and my discovery of our mother's death, she batted the news away with an indifference that shocked me.

"This affects you, Bea. Did you know she was Iban as well as Chinese? Aren't you at all curious?"

"What part of 'I don't care' don't you understand? Listen, Lily. I get that you want to know, and that's great for you, but I don't want to be a part of anything she was a part of, okay? I'm forward-looking. I'm here for Leo. I'm going to focus on being the best aunt to her ever, okay?"

"Don't you have any compassion for Mother? What she must have felt, suffered?"

"No, I don't. She didn't have any for us. I can't believe you've forgotten how hard it was after she left."

"I haven't forgotten. I guess I'm just surprised. You've always been the one harping on about remembering where I come from and telling me to be proud of our heritage."

Bea scoffed. "That's completely different, Lily! Mom's past, her history, isn't necessarily ours. She chose to cut us off, and I've come to terms with that. I wish you would, too. Please drop it. For my sake, and Leo's."

Even after I begged Bea to read Mother's letters, she insisted she wanted nothing to do with her, holding firm in her loyalty to Father, the parent who'd stayed and done his duty. Any other approach seemed treasonous in her eyes. She didn't want to know anything, and I interpreted this as her way to avoid confronting the pain Mother's abandonment had caused her.

Bea told me not to waste time on the past because I had more important things to concentrate on. She urged me not to invite bad ghosts into my life, especially with Leo here now. But Mother continued to haunt me. I thought about how she left this world. She hadn't allowed herself to bloom and pulled the petals off the stem prematurely, painfully, denying that she needed something, someone to nurture, feed, and fertilize her. I thought about my own struggles and chose to seek comfort in a grove, where I could reach across to others. I learned to lean on my aunties, my father, my sister, my friends, and John. I would do everything I could to prevent myself from withering away on the vine like Mother.

Auntie Choo Neo, Auntie Miriam, Auntie Elizabeth, Hilary, and Bea did not disappoint. Leo's red egg and ginger party was the family gathering of the year.

In the end, I relished the planning with my family and enjoyed learning the cultural rituals. The event wasn't going to be authentic. How could it be? This was going to be my kind of red egg and ginger party. Plus, Leo was already eight months old. She was well past the age when children had their red egg ceremonies, where their name was revealed. In my childhood memories, even baby Billy's party wasn't authentic. But what was authentic? Every village or city in Asia must have its own rituals. I settled on infusing tradition into a modern celebration.

At Father and Auntie Choo Neo's home, I drew from all the branches of my Canadian family tree to put together a hybrid Asian feast. I made my favourites: char kuey teow with cockles and lap cheong, and ayam panggang sambal grilled chicken; Auntie Choo Neo made her signature satay; Father made his Hakka-style jiu gai; Auntie Elizabeth made her famous steamed fish and bok choy with abalone in oyster sauce; Auntie Miriam made some fried rice; Bea made tiger shrimp laksa and Hainanese chicken and rice; and Hilary brought Peking duck and some dim sum favourites like har gow and char siu bao. To accompany the abundance of delicacies, Hilary could not restrain herself from arranging for a local bubble tea shop to send dozens of drinks.

I put out red eggs, as well as Ukrainian Easter eggs with red batik designs. John was surprised. "Did you pull these out?"

"Yes, aren't they beautiful? I want her to know she has two cultures," I said and hugged him.

"Leo is lucky to be able to choose from two kinds of dumplings," John joked.

It was a diverse, unconventional, and, above all, delicious spread. For many of my friends, it was their first time tasting shrimp sambal and oyster sauce, or figuring out their chopsticks to pick up the har gow. This was not the typical Chinatown fare they were used to.

Auntie Carrie gave Leo a mini cheongsam, and she looked adorable adorned in the red brocade, sucking regally on her pacifier. I jokingly called Leo Tai Tai, and Hilary burst out laughing.

I was happy to see Auntie Joan sitting relaxed in Father's large recliner. It was in her restaurant that all our family gatherings took place, and she was finally not hosting, cooking, or serving. Instead, she was busy catching up with Auntie Betty, and they both kept chiding me for not bringing out the mah-jong table yet.

I hadn't seen Auntie Miriam for many years. Woo's Confectionery was still a mainstay of Sparwood. She grabbed me, hugged me tight, and handed me a red packet.

We looked up from our embrace to see Alfred arrive.

I had wanted to surprise my aunties and hadn't told them he was coming. Auntie Miriam burst into tears at the sight of him, and everyone crowded around him, embracing him and pelting him with questions.

Father, however, eyed Alfred like he was the man his wife had betrayed him with. I couldn't fault Father for this. After all, it was Alfred Mother had turned to after she left him, and it was Alfred she confided her feelings to. Despite this, Father was generous, welcoming Alfred to his home and allowing him to hold court for a while in his living room. To comfort Father, I brought him his granddaughter to carry proudly.

Alfred greeted me and handed me a red packet. He also brought me a gift: Teresa Teng's single "Ú iā hue." Alfred said, "The Hokkien title means 'rainy night flower,' or 'the torment of a flower.' It reminds me of your mother."

I played the record, and Father and Auntie Choo Neo started singing along, Auntie deftly translating the lyrics. As the record spun to an end, Father never looked happier. Holding Leo close in his arms, he brought her around to all the guests, sharing with them his granddaughter, the guest of honour.

The day after the red egg and ginger celebration I told my aunties about Mother at dim sum. They took the news with sorrow and compassion. Despite the many years that had passed, they still considered Mother their friend. Auntie Miriam cried the entire time. Like me, I think she had always hoped Mother would come back.

Auntie Joan, Auntie Betty, and Auntie Carrie asked many questions about what I saw on my journey, and I was eager to tell them because it still felt like a dream to me. Our conversation around the fragrant bamboo steamers made me feel like I was finally moving forward.

Auntie Elizabeth and Hilary said few words during dim sum. After the other aunties left to go sightseeing, or to fly back west, back to their homes, Auntie Elizabeth took my arm and walked with Hilary and me to a nearby bubble tea place. She didn't say anything, but I knew by the droop of her eyes, the tightness of her lips, and her constant physical touch, comforting me, that she was saddened by the news. Not only was Mother her friend, but Auntie Elizabeth also knew, watching me grow up alongside Hilary, what her loss meant to me.

In the months after the red egg and ginger party, Hilary checked in on me regularly and invited me to outings with Abby and her mother. I never tired of hearing Abby call me Auntie and couldn't wait for Leo to call Hilary Auntie and Abby Jie Jie. I accepted all the invitations and felt more at ease learning how to be a mother, watching my best friend and her mother, and letting them remind me that we were family.

When I told Father, Bea, and Auntie Choo Neo that Leo's middle and Chinese name would be Vóng Hua, they were perplexed. Their first question was why wasn't it in Mandarin? I was surprised by their urge to mainstream her name but insisted I wanted it to be in Hakka. It didn't escape them that part of Mother's name had crept in there, like a ghost briefly entering the room. I explained to my family that Leo's name was not just a nod to her lost po po but also an homage to our ancestors, the guest people. The yellow flower honours our Hakka heritage.

心

Heart

MAY IN OTTAWA THAT YEAR WAS GLORIOUS. The magnolias in the neighbourhood were in magnificent bloom, the tulips crowded the flower beds at the edge of the Rideau Canal, and the irises pressed their bearded faces towards the sky. The dandelions were unruly, leaving polka-dotted patterns on fields and lawns and in the cracks in the sidewalks. Everywhere, a smattering of lion faces turned into poufy balls of white spring snow.

The pollen irritated my nose, and my whole body shook with the sneezes that erupted. My allergies reminded me of Mother. When I was a child, I hoped that the end of winter, and the life sprouting from the ground, would buoy her, but she always found something wrong with spring. Coming from a land with only two seasons—rainy and dry—she must have felt it was strange to have to go through two extra transitions in the year.

Leo sat on a picnic blanket in the backyard while I hung the laundry. She was wary of the grass, something new she had never encountered before, and did not venture off the cloth. She was teething again, chewing voraciously on a plastic giraffe. I looked at the bedsheet flapping in the wind and was transported back to when I watched Mother doing the same thing. She was wearing a mustard-coloured dress with an A-line skirt that the breeze brushed along her pale legs. Her hair fell against the back panel of her dress, and her sleeveless arms reached high to secure the clothespins to the line. Although her clothes were plain and simple, Mother had a special way of carrying herself. Even when she had nowhere to go, she wore even the most modest of outfits with importance and pride. She was so elegant it was a shame no one else could see her. Bea and I were hiding behind the large sheets hung on the line. The late morning was hot, and we found some reprieve in the damp, fluttering fabric. We giggled as we poked at each other, like ghosts jerking in the wind. Mother normally would have yelled at us to stop, but that day she was distracted. She didn't hear our laughter or feel us moving around her. She looked up at the sky, as if a typhoon were upon us. I followed her gaze and saw nothing.

"It snows here even when it's warm," Mother muttered.

I looked around again and saw white dandelion pollen darting and floating among the trees, swirling in the wind. Mother rubbed her nose with the edge of her hand, moving it roughly back and forth, trying to rid herself of a stubborn itch, her skin freckled red from irritation. The fluffy seeds lightly kissed our noses and eyes, and Bea and I giggled. Mother sneezed and ran into the house to escape.

Even the most mundane, domestic task brought out Mother's disappointment, isolation, and longing. She wished she could be as free as the pollen, riding the spring gusts out of the valley somewhere more familiar and welcoming.

Sometimes I have felt the way Mother did.

Now I turn the jade bracelet around my wrist and look at Leo with affection. My daughter rubs her nose the same way Mother used to. She uses the edge of her hand and goes back and forth in a way I have never seen anyone else do. Leo sits in the grass turned towards the sun, just like the faces of the dandelions, unafraid, proud, and strong.

Author's Note

I chose to use a Chinese character, particularly a Chinese radical, to demarcate the different chapters in this story. The radicals sometimes have only a tenuous link to the story but are a poetic attempt to create a bridge between, first, all those who speak Chinese, and second, those who do not know Chinese, and the beauty of this ancient written language. The English translations of the radicals are mine, and any errors are mine alone.

部首, or Chinese radical, literally means "section header." The Chinese character may be made up of one or more radicals. For example, the word "ask" 問 uses two radicals: door 門 and mouth 口. The radical of a Chinese character is a character on its own, or a pictorial under which the character is traditionally listed in a Chinese dictionary. The radical sometimes indicates the meaning of the character. Sometimes it provides a phonetic guide. Other times it provides no meaning or phonetic information. In this way, Chinese writing is unique compared to the Romance languages. Pictorials, or graphics, are used rather than an alphabet, and often there is a meaning and poetry to the choice of the graphics. I remember learning from my Chinese teacher how to say "planet" in Mandarin when my five-year-old son was obsessing over the solar system. My teacher told me the literal and character meaning was "walking star." It seemed like a poetic way to recognize how planets were discovered by British astronomer William Herschel, who watched what he thought were shooting stars but then realized they were celestial beings orbiting the sun.

Another unique feature of the Chinese written language is that it's the true common language among people who speak all the Chinese dialects. If you are literate, you can converse with anyone, no matter which of the 200 dialects you speak. Sometimes people will use their finger to "draw" a character in their palm, or in the air, so as to dispel any misunderstanding created while conversing in different dialects. Growing up, I saw my mother do this in Chinatown. More recently, in my travels in Asia, Chinese people who realized I didn't understand them tried to communicate with me in this way. And now, when people ask me which Liew I am, I draw my last name in the air and people nod understandingly.

Finally, the written Chinese language is political. The original, or "traditional," script was replaced around the 1950s in mainland China by the simplified script (the same characters but with less detail, or fewer strokes) as the standardized written text—a tactic employed by the People's Republic of China to increase literacy rates in a largely illiterate population. Hong Kong and Taiwan, however, two Chinese-speaking countries fighting to stay outside the control of the Communist regime, kept the traditional script and still do today. My use of the traditional script in this book represents my respect for the original language, as well as the democratic aspirations of Hong Kong and Taiwan.

I tried my best to find a standardized way of writing Hokkien and Hakka Chinese words using the Latin alphabet in this book. I apologize if there are inconsistencies or errors with the translations; they are mine alone. The tragedy is that although certain Chinese dialects are becoming mainstream, some are dying, and it was difficult for me to access Hokkien/Hakka language resources.

I have played it a bit loose with the timing of some historical artifacts in the story: *Simon's Quest* was not released in North America until 1988, a year after Phillip plays the game on his own computer; the Immigration and Refugee Board of Canada wasn't established until 1989, the year after Alfred's hearing; and the Marco Polo nightclub in Chinatown closed in 1982, years before Swee Hua comes to work there.

Acknowledgments

This book was written on various Indigenous lands, in particular, the lands of the Orang Asli (Peninsular Malaysia), the Orang Ulu (Sarawak, Malaysia), Algonquin (Ottawa), and Treaty 7 (southern Alberta). All these lands have been home to me and my family in different ways, and I recognize I have been a guest in all of them. I have tried my best to respect the places in which this narrative takes place, acknowledging the Iban in Brunei and Malaysia, and the Ktunaxa in Sparwood, British Columbia. I still have much to learn and apologize if I did not acknowledge peoples or lands appropriately or at all.

This story was crafted while I was researching the legal barriers for stateless persons to obtain citizenship. Many of the themes in this book arose from narratives I heard throughout my time investigating the experiences of stateless persons and how law and legal processes have failed them. I would be remiss if I didn't acknowledge the many people I talked to about statelessness over the course of several years, including stateless persons brave enough to share their stories with me, and especially my immediate and extended family, large swaths of whom were stateless for many years. This book makes use of the material I could not include in my academic writing. And this book would not have been written if I didn't acknowledge my intergenerational trauma of being a child of a previously stateless person. There are millions of stateless persons in the world today, many of whom are children. I hope this book creates greater awareness about their plight.

Thank you to Arsenal Pulp Press and Brian Lam for believing in this manuscript. It has been a dream working with a publisher that has advocacy roots. Shirarose Wilensky, I am so grateful for your wisdom, care, and editorial prowess. Catharine Chen, thank you for your insightful contributions. I am grateful as well to Jazmin Welch,

Cynara Geissler, and Jaiden Dembo for your support in getting to publication and beyond.

I am grateful to the wide community that supported me and my work. Don Kwan for fostering community in Chinatown, Ottawa, and for reading my book, providing encouragement, and introducing me to Robert Yip. Robert, thank you for your enthusiastic support and for introducing me to fellow Asian Canadian authors Paul Yee and Wayson Choy. It was over dim sum one fateful spring day with Paul and Wayson that I learned about the Asian Canadian Writers' Workshop (ACWW) and their Jim Wong-Chu Emerging Writers Award. Thank you, Allan Cho, and everyone at the ACWW for your ongoing help with my journey. I would be remiss if I did not acknowledge the many Asian authors before me who paved the way.

To Lindsay Wong, Carrianne Leung, Jenny Heijun Wills, and Catherine Hernandez, I am in awe of your work and honoured you took the time to read mine and give generous blurbs.

Heartfelt gratitude to Janice Zawerbny for your editorial advice. To Emily Urquhart, Adrienne Kerr, thank you for reading the very first draft. Philip Huynh, Marsha Skrypuch, and Mark Bourrie, thank you for your advice on the writing business. Kenya-Jade Pinto, thank you for your encouragement and for photographing me. In grade nine, Mrs Gallant saw I had an interest in writing and encouraged me. Wherever you are, I hope this book finds you.

To my cheerleaders: my colleagues at uOttawa, the parents of F_____ Park (pandemic version 2020–2022), the PECers (Jenny Acton, Colleen McKay, Jenny Ellison, and Hayley Snell), and to Nichole Boutilier, Tara Denham, Annie Muldoon, thank you. Tracey Lindberg, thank you for your teachings and your advice on the writing world. Sarah Morales, thank you for encouraging me to embrace the narrative in all my work. Alok Gupta, Amanda Cheong, Amrita Hari, Carolyn Ramzy, Daiva Stasiulis, Eric Paulsen, Ines Kwan, Jackie Kennelly, Laila Demirdache, Laura Madokoro, Madhumita Bhattacharyya, Megan Rivers-Moore, Nadine Edirmanasinghe,

Rosanne Wong, Shane Bill, Shauna Labman, thank you for your friendship and all our conversations on food, race, migration, law, feminism, sanctuary, writing and belonging—they all informed my work.

I am so fortunate to have friends who not only read my work with kindness but also supported me through the ups and downs: Julie Delaney, Lindsay McKay, Natasha Bakht, Lynda Collins, and Ummni Khan.

Thank you to my family. To my cousins who cheer me on. To Andrew, Alysha Austin, Uncle Tahir, Jeff, Mom and Dad, warm gratitude for your support. Ophe, my best friend, I don't know what I would do without your honest opinions and amazing cover art. Maxym and Vera, thank you for reminding me to use my imagination. I hope one day you will read this and enjoy it. Finally, to Roman. I could not have done this without you. Thank you for being the equal and loving partner who allows me to thrive in my passions.

Jamie Chai Yun Liew is the recipient of the Asian Canadian Writers' Workshop Jim Wong-Chu Emerging Writers Award. Jamie is also a lawyer, law professor, and podcaster specializing in immigration, refugee, and citizenship law. Her podcast, *Migration Conversations*, features experts and migrants who have experienced immigration systems up close. With Hakka, Hainanese, and Nyonya roots in Southeast Asia, one of Jamie's pastimes is to cook and eat Southeast Asian hawker fare, including laksa and char kuey teow. She lives in Ottawa with her family. *Dandelion* is her first book.

jcyliew.com